FRAMED FOR MURDER

AN ANNA NOLAN MYSTERY

CATHY SPENCER

Comely
Press

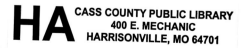

Published by Comely Press

www.comelypress.com

978-0-9917259-6-0

*To Reid, for all those nights when pillow talk
was about this book.*

1

It was dark. The road was slick from an earlier rain, and damp leaves squelched underfoot. Wendy, my three-year-old, shepherd/labrador cross, trotted ahead of me down Wistler Road. I would have worried about walking alone on a dark country road almost anywhere else, but Crane was a small town and its crime rate was practically non-existent, so I felt safe. Still, it wouldn't do to take a tumble on this moonless night, so I was being careful.

I heard Wendy snuffling and digging at something up ahead in the bush. Removing the slim flashlight that I always carried on our bedtime walks, I shone the beam in her direction, afraid that she had found something disgusting to roll in just before bed. Nothing like having to deal with a stinking, soaking-wet pet when all you wanted to do was crawl under the covers.

"What did you find, girl?" I called. The noise stopped, and I waited for her to pop out of the trees and trot back to me, but she didn't appear.

"Come here, Wendy," I called. All was still, and then I heard a piercing howl that made my hair stand on end and my breath catch in my throat. It was a primitive, uncanny sound, and it unnerved me on this lonely stretch of road.

"What's gotten into you?" I muttered. Stepping up to the trees, I peered into the dense shadows.

"Wendy?" She whined softly, and I sidled between the trees, picking my way through last year's undergrowth. She was up ahead in a small clearing.

"Come on, girl," I commanded. Instead, Wendy lowered her head and nosed at something on the ground. I trained my beam downward, and jumped. It was a man. He was lying face down, dressed in jeans and a black leather jacket, his arms lying straight beside his body. He wasn't moving.

"Hello?" I called, "are you all right, mister?" There was no response. I wanted to turn and run, but forced myself to creep closer for a better look. Taking a deep breath, I crouched down beside him. His hair was dark and wavy with silver flecks in it, but I couldn't see his face. Wendy leaned against me and nudged my neck with her wet nose. All I could hear was my own pulse roaring in my ears. I reached out to touch the man's hand, and snatched my own back again. His skin was cold, too cold. I knew that I should check to see if he was still breathing, but the thought of turning him over repulsed me. Sick with dread, I reached for his shoulder and rolled him over anyway.

I gasped and sprang back a few steps, horrified when his eyes seemed to stare straight up into mine. Wendy barked and shot past me into the trees. I took a few deep breaths and shone the light full into his face.

"Holy shit," I whispered. Sculpted cheek bones, blue eyes, generous mouth. It was Jack.

I stared down at him. My ex-husband, whom I hadn't seen for four years, was lying dead beside this country road in the middle of the Alberta Foothills, and I didn't have a clue how he had got here.

Looking past his face, I spotted a hole in the front of his jacket, right over the chest. I pulled the jacket open with hands that wouldn't stop trembling. The grey shirt beneath it had a big patch of dried blood spread across the front. I stumbled back a step, a wave of nausea overwhelming me.

Something crackled in the undergrowth behind me, and I whirled around. A brilliant light flashed in my face and blinded me. I threw up an arm to shield my eyes, but the light dropped and inched along the ground, coming to rest over Jack's body. I pointed my own light at the black shape advancing toward me. Wendy crept toward him with a menacing growl, her jowls dragged back over her teeth, but the man didn't budge an inch.

"Anna Nolan, what the hell did you do?" he asked.

2

I sighed with relief as I recognized Steve Walker, one of our local RCMP officers, until the impact of his words cut through my thoughts like a slap in the face.

"What? What are you talking about? I didn't have anything to do with this."

Steve bent to examine the body. I tried to slip past him, wanting to escape this horrible sight and let Steve deal with it, but he grabbed my arm and spun me around.

"Where do you think you're going?" he demanded. Steve was younger than me, in his late twenties, tall and good-looking with a slow grin and a low boiling point, but he was all cop as his eyes delved into mine.

"Go to hell," I said as I tried to jerk my arm out of his grip, but he held me fast. We glared at each other as Wendy slunk to my side, still growling.

"Control your dog, Anna."

"Wendy, sit," I said, looking down at her. She hesitated and sat. "Good girl," I said, patting her head automatically with my free hand before turning back to Steve. "Now what?"

"Now, you tell me what's going on here." He let me go, and I rubbed my sore arm. Steve and I sometimes ate together at The Diner with some of the other locals, and I was inclined to like him. Now, I calculated how best to handle him.

"There's not much to say. I was taking Wendy for a walk and she found him. He was dead when I got here."

Steve shone his flashlight back over the body. "I don't recognize him," he said. "Do you?"

I hesitated, wondering how much to give away, and Steve shot me a suspicious look.

"Yeah, I know him," I said, letting out a deep breath. "It's my ex-husband, Jack Nolan."

Steve inhaled sharply through his teeth. "What's he doing here?"

"Steve, I have absolutely no idea."

"What do you mean? What's he doing here in Crane?"

"I mean that I haven't seen or heard from Jack in years. I have no idea why he's here."

Steve's face was grim as he thought for a moment. "Let's go back to my cruiser," he said. "I've got to call for back-up." He indicated that I should precede him, so Wendy and I marched ahead through the trees while he trailed behind.

The brilliant red and blue lights from his cruiser sliced through the darkness at the side of the road. Steve unlocked the back door, and I waited for Wendy to hop inside before climbing in behind her. Steve shut us in and crawled into the front seat to call for back-up. When he had finished, he turned around to stare at me through the metal grill that separates the officers from their "guests."

"What are you doing here anyway?" I asked.

"We got an anonymous tip that something suspicious was happening out on Wistler Road. I drove by and heard a dog howling in the bush. When I pulled over, your dog burst out of the trees, barking like crazy. By the time I recognized her, she had turned tail and run back in. I followed her, and there you were with the body." He paused, glancing out the window at the enveloping trees before turning back to me. "Look, Anna, this is going to take a while. The forensics squad will be along in a few minutes, and I'll have to take them back to the crime scene. You're going to have to sit tight until I'm done, and then I'll take you into the station to make a statement."

I stared at him, my jaw aching from the effort of trying to stop my teeth from chattering. The impact of Jack's death, plus my horror at being implicated in it, were hitting me hard.

"All right."

He studied me. "Are you okay? You look pretty shaky."

"I guess it's colder tonight than I thought."

"Or maybe you're going into shock. Wait a minute." Popping open the trunk, he got out of the car and fetched a blanket. "Here, wrap yourself in this," he said, opening the back door and handing it to me.

"Th-thanks," I said, not trusting myself to look at him. I didn't want to admit how much finding Jack's body upset me, to him or to me. Jack and I were old history.

Steve nodded and leaned against the side of the car until another cruiser sped up, lights flashing, and pulled in behind us. Steve walked back to confer with his colleagues. A few minutes later, three officers climbed out of the vehicle and began unpacking equipment. A female officer erected orange cones and flashing lights in the middle of the road and glanced at me on her way back to the car. I stared straight ahead, refusing to make eye contact with her. Another vehicle pulled in behind them, and a man got out carrying an official-looking black bag. He joined the others, and together they donned white forensic suits. Then Steve led them back into the bush, their powerful flashlight beams bouncing off the tree trunks until they disappeared.

I collapsed against the seat, shaking all over, the memory of my ex-husband's dead face haunting me. Wendy leaned against me, and I hugged her tight for comfort. What was

Jack doing in Crane, anyway? Did he have an acting job nearby?

It was his acting career that had brought us to the Alberta Foothills in the first place. Four years ago, Jack had been filming a movie in the nearby village of Longview. Longview was small and housing had been pretty limited in those days, so we had rented a neat little cottage here in Crane. I had loved the cottage from the minute I had seen it, a one-storey bungalow with ivy clinging to weathered wood siding and a pretty rose garden out front. The location had seemed ideal on the outskirts of town with lots of privacy and access to long walks in the countryside. The shoot was scheduled for a few months, so we had enrolled our son, Ben, in the local high school just as he was ready to start grade ten. Then my Aunt Sharon died and left me the queenly inheritance of $93,000. We had been getting by on Jack's acting jobs up until then, with me picking up whatever temporary secretarial work I could find, so I was thrilled to have some financial security at last.

When the inheritance cheque arrived, Jack, Ben and I had gone out to an expensive steak house to celebrate – just the three of us, with none of the usual movie crowd around. That meal was my last happy memory of Jack. We laughed a lot, and Jack and I got pretty friendly later that night after Ben had gone to bed. When I woke up the next morning, I was feeling more optimistic about our marriage. Maybe having the money would take some of the pressure off our relationship. I made pancakes for my two men and kissed them both goodbye before walking into town to do some shopping.

But while standing in line at the bank later that morning, I overheard a movie extra telling her friend about an affair Jack was having with one of the film's stuntwomen. I shouldn't have been surprised; Jack had cheated on me religiously over the course of our seventeen-year marriage. This time was different, though. I had a nest egg, thanks to my wonderful aunt, and it would tide Ben and me over until I could find a decent job. Crane was as good a place as any to put down roots, so I made a beeline into the loan manager's office to talk about mortgages right then and there. Later, when I got home, I called the owner of our house to see if she was interested in selling. She was. A chunk of my inheritance money went into a down payment, and when Jack left town at the end of the shoot, Ben and I stayed on.

I looked up to see Steve returning through the trees. I pushed Wendy away and sat up as he climbed into the front seat and turned to face me.

"I'm going to have to take you to the station now, Anna."

"What about a lawyer?" I asked, my stomach clenched with tension.

His face hardened as he looked at me. "You have the right to have a lawyer present. Do you want one?"

I looked down at my hands. "I'm not being charged with anything, am I?"

"No, but you do have to make an official statement about how you found your ex-husband's body."

"Fine, I guess I don't need a lawyer for that. There's not much to say, since I'm not guilty of anything." He nodded and started up the cruiser. "Steve, it looked like Jack had been shot," I blurted.

"The coroner is with him right now. We'll have to wait for the report." His eyes caught mine in the rear-view mirror. Usually, Steve's eyes had a twinkle in them, but they looked plenty worried as we pulled away.

We drove to the RCMP station on the other side of Crane. Steve couldn't leave Wendy alone in the cruiser, so he led us both through the station's back door and down a concrete hallway to a small interview room. It was furnished with a scarred wooden table, a tissue box, and three plastic chairs. The overhead fluorescent lights made the room look flat and dreary. I glanced around, trying not to cringe, and chose the chair facing the door.

"I'll be back in a few minutes," Steve said, shutting me in with Wendy. I stared at the back of the door, feeling like I was wrapped in some kind of fog that prevented me from feeling or thinking straight.

"Jack is dead. Jack is dead. Somebody shot him. Jack is dead," my mind chanted over and over while Wendy sniffed around the room and finally settled at my feet. The door opened a few minutes later, and Steve re-entered carrying a glass of water and a plastic bowl. He set the glass down on the table in front of me, and the bowl on the floor for Wendy.

"Here you are, girl," he said. As Wendy rose and began lapping up the water, my eyes began to tear. I was just about to thank Steve for his unexpected kindness when the door opened and Staff Sergeant Eddy Mason sauntered into the room. He hesitated, his eyebrows rising when he saw Wendy drinking from the bowl.

"You providing room service, Walker?" he asked. Steve looked coolly back at him without saying a word. "Evening, Ms. Nolan," Eddie said, shifting his gaze to me. He shut the door and took the seat opposite me. Steve pulled a notepad from his pocket and slid into the chair at the end of the table.

I knew Eddy by sight. We bumped into each other from time to time at the Post Office, where we chatted about the weather or complained about the number of advertising flyers stuffed into our mail boxes. He was a short, rotund man with glasses perched on the end of his nose who didn't in the least resemble Santa Claus, despite the similarity in their proportions.

Eddy didn't waste any time with pleasantries. He plunged right into questions, asking me to describe the events leading up to the discovery of Jack's body. Steve took notes, keeping his face buried in his pad.

"I got home from work tonight about five fifteen. Traffic was bad – there was an accident leaving the city."

"Where is work, Ms. Nolan?"

"I work at Chinook University in Calgary. I'm the administrative assistant for the Kinesiology Department."

Eddy nodded. "How long have you worked there?"

"Four years."

"And?"

"And I had a book club meeting at the library at six, so I didn't have a lot of time to get ready. I let Wendy out and fed her, changed my clothes, and made a sandwich. I left the house about five forty-five and walked to the library."

"Who else was at the meeting?"

"There were only three of us tonight. May Weston, Erna Dombrosky, and me. One of the other ladies was sick, and Helen McDonald was away on vacation."

"Were Erna and May already there when you arrived?"

I thought for a moment. "Usually I'm last, since I'm the only one who works outside of town, but Erna came in a couple of minutes after I did."

"So then what happened?"

"The meeting broke up early because there were only the three of us. Around seven thirty. I left the library and walked home."

"Did the other two ladies leave with you, Ms. Nolan?"

"No. Erna said something about wanting to find a book, and May stayed to give her a lift home. I left on my own."

"And what happened next?"

"I walked home and read for a while."

"Did you see anyone on the walk home?"

"I don't remember seeing anyone. It was raining and I was using an umbrella. My head was down."

Eddy nodded. He seemed relaxed and in control of the situation, while my nerves were frazzled. "So, you went home and read – for how long?"

"Till nine thirty. Then it was time for Wendy's walk." Wendy stirred at the mention of her name and started to get up. "Lie down, girl," I murmured.

"It would have been dark by then. Do you always walk your dog at night? You live right on the edge of town, don't you?"

"Yes, but the dark doesn't bother me. I know the area really well and I feel safe."

"Go on. Was it still raining?"

"No, it stopped sometime after I got back from the library."

"Where did you walk?"

"Down Wistler Road headed out of town."

"Did anyone see you?"

"No, no one." I went on to explain how Wendy had found Jack's body, finishing with an abridged history of my marriage and divorce, including my lack of contact with my ex-husband over the past few years.

"When was the last time you saw Jack Nolan?" Eddy asked.

"About four years ago when we met at the lawyer's office to finalize the divorce details. Jack gave me full custody of Ben and was supposed to contact me whenever he wanted to see him."

"So, did he?"

"No."

"Never?

"No. Jack wasn't around much when Ben was growing up. He'd be away for weeks at a time on a film shoot. Other times he'd be at home, but with theatre rehearsals and evening performances, he wasn't home a lot. After we separated, he just didn't bother to see Ben."

"Yeah? Seems pretty odd, a father not bothering to see his son all those years. Must have made you pretty mad, cheating on you and being a lousy father."

I coloured. "Who said anything about cheating?" I glanced over at Steve, whose face was expressionless as he stared at the table top.

Eddy balanced his chair on its back legs. "Pretty common knowledge in a town this size. That why your marriage broke up?"

I met his eyes and looked away, flustered. It was bad enough to find Jack's body; I didn't bargain on having to explain my marriage to the police, too. "It was more complicated than that," I muttered.

"You don't say?" I didn't elaborate. "So your husband didn't visit you or Ben after the divorce. What about telephone calls or e-mails?"

I clasped my trembling hands together to steady them, and leaned my elbows on the table. "I'll tell you something, Sergeant. A year ago, I wrote to Jack care of his agent to invite him to Ben's high school graduation. Jack didn't bother to show up. That was the extent of my correspondence with my ex-husband."

Eddy grunted. "One last thing, Ms. Nolan. When you found the body, was it damp or dry?"

"Dry," I said.

He glanced at Steve, and they both stood up. "That's good enough for now. Steve will get your statement typed up and be back to have you sign it. You wait here until it's ready."

They left, leaving Wendy and me shut up in the interrogation room. I stared at my folded hands on top of the table and thought about Jack lying there all alone on the cold ground. Soon the tears started to come. Damn that man. He'd given me plenty of trouble during our marriage, but now that he was possibly murdered, and probably deservedly so, I grieved for him. I lay my head down on top of my arms and sobbed. Wendy crept over and nuzzled my leg before lying down at my feet.

After a while, the tears turned into sniffles, and I began to think. I loved mystery novels and had read plenty of them, especially Agatha Christie. In all of the mysteries I'd ever read, the police always suspected the person who found the body.

"Pull yourself together," I urged myself. "You're in a bad situation and you've got to start using your brain." I grabbed a few tissues from the box on the table and mopped my face. By the time Steve returned with the paperwork, I was in control. I noticed that he left the door open this time.

"Okay, Anna, please read your statement and sign it," he said. I did as he asked and handed it back to him.

"Okay – that's it for tonight. I'll drive you home. Just make sure you stay in town for the next few days so that you're available for questioning." Steve's bearing was stiff and he didn't make eye contact as he spoke. I wondered what he had to feel uncomfortable about. Maybe the other officers had come back from the crime scene with some damning information.

"Have you found out anything, Steve?"

"Yeah – maybe – nothing good," he replied, squatting down to pat Wendy. She licked his hand, now that the situation was non-threatening. He stood up as I got out of my chair and came around the table to lean beside him.

"Look, Anna," he said, glancing sideways, "that stuff you said about Jack not talking to you all those years – are you sure about that?"

"Positive. Once our divorce was settled, Jack disappeared."

He glared at me. "Come on, don't lie to me. We know that Jack called you earlier tonight."

My stomach somersaulted and I grabbed the edge of the table for support. "What are you talking about? Jack didn't call me," I said.

"No?" he replied, his eyes boring into mine. "The call history on his cell phone says otherwise. Did he call you at other times, too?"

"No, he didn't. I swear he didn't. What time was he supposed to have called me, anyway?"

"At seven. Was he waiting for you somewhere? Did he call because you were late for a meeting with him?"

"I don't believe it. Why would he call me?"

"You tell me," Steve said, his expression stony.

"No, I'm telling you the truth. Is this some kind of trick?" I was starting to panic and my voice grew louder. "I told you, I wasn't even home at seven. I was at the book club meeting from six to seven thirty. Talk to May and Erna. They'll tell you that I was at the library with them."

I was fighting hard not to cry. Wendy began to whine, and I squatted down to pat her while trying to control my emotions. I glanced out the door and saw a woman officer peering down the hallway at us. Steve nodded, and she disappeared.

"You believe me, don't you, Steve?" I asked, looking up at him from the floor.

"Look, we'll be checking with the other book club members tomorrow. There's no need to hold you any longer tonight." He took my hand and hauled me to my feet. "Come on,

Anna, it's late. Let's get you and your dog home." The anger had faded from his eyes.

I laid my hand on his arm. "Look, I'm sorry I shouted just now. I guess I'm pretty shook up. I just can't believe that this is all really happening."

"So, sleep on it, and maybe you'll remember something useful in the morning."

Steve drove us home and waited while I turned the key in my front door before backing down the driveway and pulling away. I went inside, dead tired and numb.

3

Before going to bed in the wee hours, I deliberated over whether or not to call Ben, but decided to spare him for the night. I didn't want to wake him up to tell him that his father was dead. There was nothing that he could do about it, and I didn't want him driving out from Calgary, where he shared a house with three other roommates, all tired and upset. He was coming home for dinner tomorrow night – make that tonight – so I decided to wait and tell him then. I did leave a message on my boss's voice mail, telling her that I was sick and wouldn't be coming into work on Friday. Dr. Magdalena Lewis had been Chair of the Kinesiology Department and my boss for the past two years, but I didn't feel comfortable telling her the real reason for my absence.

After leaving the message, I went to bed and had a lousy night's sleep plagued with nightmares. I woke up feeling exhausted. Sitting at the kitchen table looking out the deck door at my blossoming apple tree, I decided that some protein might help. I showered, dressed, and headed for The Diner, walking the six blocks to Main Street.

I reached the restaurant about half an hour before the lunch crowd, and paused to peer in the plate glass window, wanting to see how busy the place was. With a town this small, I was sure that news of Jack's death had gotten around, and I wasn't up to answering questions from curiosity-seekers. The restaurant was almost empty, so I stepped inside, walked up to the old-fashioned chrome counter, and sat on one of the five red vinyl stools. To the right of the counter, pushed up against the wall, was a huge juke-box that played hits from the fifties and sixties. Behind me, eight tables with plastic place mats and dried flower arrangements were grouped around the floor.

Frank Crow, The Diner's owner and cook, was an ardent Elvis Presley fan. Frank had visited Graceland four times and even bought one of Elvis's glittery Vegas costumes at an auction sale. The costume was mounted in a glass display case and positioned in pride of place just inside the door.

Mr. Andrews was seated at one of the tables for two with his head bent over the local newspaper, a cup of coffee at his elbow. He was a retired rancher who had never married and mostly kept to himself. I suspected that he was actually lonely because he spent most of his mornings in the restaurant, reading the paper and sipping coffee.

"Morning, Mr. Andrews," I called from the counter. He was dressed in his usual tan corduroy jacket and jeans. He grunted and nodded without lifting his eyes. Mary, the full-time waitress, was filling salt shakers at the counter, and I could see Frank working at the grill through the kitchen pass-through. "Morning Mary," I said just as Frank called, "Is that Anna?"

"Hi, Frank – yeah, it's me," I called back. Most Saturdays I ate breakfast at his restaurant, and Frank and I had become friends. He hurried out the swinging door headed straight for me.

Frank was sixtyish with long grey hair pulled into a pony tail, and a full beard and moustache. He always wore jeans, a crisp white shirt covered by a white apron, and cowboy boots when he was working. He leaned over the counter and pulled me into a bear hug. That was a surprise. His girlfriend, Judy, only let Frank hug me on my birthday and New Year's Eve.

Anything more than that, and she clipped him one alongside the head. He must have been really worried about me.

Frank let go of me and looked into my eyes. "How're you doing, honey?" he asked.

"You heard?"

"Of course. Cecilia was in this morning." Cecilia was the receptionist at the RCMP station.

Mary brought my standing beverage, a glass of apple juice, and lingered on the other side of the counter while Frank sat down beside me on one of the stools.

"That woman ought to keep police business to herself," I muttered.

"It wasn't just her – the boys were talking, too," Mary said.

I sighed. "Sometimes I just hate living in a small town."

Frank said, "Come on, Anna, you know we're all just worried about you. How're you feeling? How's Ben taking it?" Ben had bussed tables for Frank before graduating from high school, and Frank still took a fatherly interest in him.

"I haven't told Ben yet, to tell you the truth. It was pretty late when I got home from the police station last night – I mean this morning. I just crawled out of bed half an hour ago." Frank nodded as if he already knew what time I had gotten home. "Ben is coming home for dinner tonight, so I'll tell him then. I didn't want to tell him about his father over the phone."

"How upset do you think he'll be, honey?" Frank asked.

"I don't know. He wrote Jack off last June when his father didn't come to his high school graduation. I don't know how upset Ben will be when he finds out. You know, Ben and his father didn't see each other for years, but that was Jack's doing. Now they'll never have a chance to patch things up."

"Poor kid, that sure is rough," Frank said, patting my hand. "But you said that you just crawled out of bed. Are you hungry? Do you want me to fix you some breakfast?"

"That would be great. I know it doesn't sound right with my ex-husband dead and my son about to find out, but I'm so hungry that I could eat some of Henry's poutine." Henry Fellows owned Hank's Hearty Home-Cooking, The Diner's only competition in town. It was kitty-corner from Frank's restaurant and had just opened last Christmas. Henry's menu featured hot meat sandwiches and poutine. I don't think that Frank had anything to worry about.

Frank shivered and laid a hand on my shoulder. "Come on, Anna, I know things are rough, but there's no need to talk suicide."

I laughed and gave him a peck on the cheek. "Thanks, Frank. I needed a good laugh."

He winked and got up off his stool. "You just make yourself comfortable, and I'll make you some bacon and pancakes." Three strips of bacon and two big pancakes were my weekly Saturday indulgence. "Mary and I will look after you."

He went back to his kitchen while Mary considered me. She was in her early thirties, skinny as a rail and flat everywhere, which she emphasized by wearing the tightest jeans and shortest skirts known to man. The town joke was that Mary should have been a magician because she disappeared whenever she turned sideways.

"Bless his heart, I know he just cleaned off the grill to start the chicken breasts, and now he's going to make you bacon. He's a good man," she said.

I nodded in agreement. "They don't come any better. Now tell me – you know everything that's going on around here –

was my ex-husband, Jack, working on a movie somewhere nearby?"

"Don't tell me you didn't know? It started shooting outside of Longview about a month ago."

"No, I honestly didn't know anything about it. I sort of remember reading in the newspaper that there was a movie shooting in the Foothills, but I didn't realize that Jack was in it. Funny that no one mentioned it to me."

Mary nodded, popping her bubble gum. "People were just being tactful, I guess. Everybody knows what a skunk your ex was. Anyway, Viggo Mortensen is starring in it. It's a western. I think it's called *Crossed Trails*."

"Really? Who was Jack playing?"

"I don't know. Viggo's playing the sheriff, though."

I nodded, picturing Viggo Mortensen in a cowboy hat with a sheriff's badge pinned to a leather vest. "Yeah, he'd be good at that. Where are the cast and crew staying – at Creekside?" Creekside had been a working ranch until it was transformed into a motel-come-spa. The rich oil crowd didn't go near it because it was too primitive for them – guests could only access Wi-Fi in the lobby and there was no helicopter pad – but it was the only venue large enough to house a movie cast and crew around here. Jack, Ben and I had stayed there for a few days when we first arrived in Alberta, but it had been too pricey to stay there for long.

"Yeah, where else? Although I hear they've hired some of the locals to be extras so they don't have to worry about putting them up."

"Do you know which locals they hired?"

"Sorry, Anna, I don't." She looked up as Frank rang the pass-through bell. "Your food's ready."

I was forking up pancake soaked in maple syrup when I heard an engine roaring out on the street. The engine cut off abruptly and, moments later, the restaurant door was flung open.

"Morning, Mary. Morning, Mr. Andrews. Anna Nolan, what are you doing here? The whole town is talking about you. So, is it true? Did you kill that son-of-a-bitch husband of yours?"

I winced and swivelled on my stool to face Clive Wampole. Clive was a little older than my forty years, a big lump of a man who lived on a farm with his aging mother. Clive didn't own a car. He favoured a bright blue tractor as his mode of transportation, and it was as beautiful to him as a Porsche would be to other men. Because he spent so much time driving his tractor, Clive was mostly deaf, and he shouted to make up for his hearing deficiency.

"Hi Clive," I shouted. "That's ex-husband. And no, I did not kill him!" I shook my head emphatically to get my point across.

"You don't say? People are saying they wouldn't blame you if you had killed him, seeing as how he was sleeping with anything wearing a skirt out on that movie set."

I bridled a little. Jack had slept around while he was married to me, but he hadn't slept with just anyone. He did have some standards, after all – or, he used to. "Really? Who was he sleeping with?"

"What?" he bellowed.

"Who was Jack sleeping with?" I said, enunciating each word clearly.

"Well, Amy Bright, for one. I hear she's playing one of the saloon girls. I wonder if she wears one of those low-cut blouses and big, ruffled skirts that saloon girls always wear in the movies. Amy sure would look good in that."

I nodded. I knew Amy to see her. She was a little younger than me, a divorcée who ran a hair salon out of her house here in Crane. She was very attractive with big blue eyes, bright auburn hair, a curvy figure, and a friendly disposition, just the kind of woman that Jack would have gone for. Maybe that's what Jack had been doing in Crane on the night he died. Maybe Amy had had something to do with Jack's death. For the first time since discovering his body, I felt hopeful.

People were starting to come through the door for lunch and were staring at me. I pulled a couple of fives out of my wallet and waved them at Mary. "Tell Frank thanks very much for breakfast, Mary. Tell him he's a life-saver."

"Sure will. You stay out of trouble, now."

I grimaced as she guffawed at her little joke. I turned to Clive, who sat beside me studying the specials board.

"Thanks for the information, Clive," I shouted, clapping him on the shoulder to get his attention.

"Sure thing. You going now? Say, are the police going to arrest you?"

Several curious heads turned in our direction. I shook my head and yelled, "Not today, I don't think." Keeping my eyes lowered, I bolted out the door before anyone could stop me and headed for home. That was just about all the attention that I could handle for one day.

4

Friday night suppers with Ben were an institution. Even though he was enrolled in Chinook University's computer science program, our schedules were very different and we didn't get to see a lot of each other on campus. Eating dinner together once a week was our way of staying in touch. Since I was at home today, I put a pork loin in the oven. By the time Ben arrived at five thirty, I was nervously mashing the potatoes.

He came through the door with a sack of dirty laundry and kissed me on the cheek before starting a load in the washing machine. When he was ready, we sat down to eat at the kitchen table with Wendy lying at our feet. I studied my son's expression as he helped himself to a large serving of pork and some cheesy broccoli.

Ben was nineteen, and I could see traces of the man he would become in his face. He already had a man's stature, with his father's wide shoulders and slim hips, but it would take a few years for his weight to catch up with his height. He had my brown hair and brown eyes, and wore his hair shaggy with the wisp of a goatee on his chin. He had never had a problem attracting girls, but wasn't serious about anyone right now, as far as I knew.

I decided to put off telling him about Jack until after dinner, so we chatted about how his week had gone at the summer job he had with a Calgary building supply store. Ben had worked there part-time during the school year, and had been lucky enough to get full-time hours when classes were over. He put on the kettle to make a cup of tea when we finished eating, and piled our dirty dishes beside the sink. After he had fixed his tea and sat down again, I broke the news to him about his dad. Ben stared at me until I had run out of words, and then cleared his throat.

"So, he's dead, Mom?"

"Yes, honey, he's gone." There was a long pause while he absorbed these words. I could see the shock in Ben's face.

"And you found him while you were out walking Wendy? He was just lying on the ground in some bush beside Wistler Road?"

"That's right."

Ben frowned and thought some more. "You said he'd been shooting a film in Longview, but you hadn't heard from him?"

"No. Your father didn't call me or stop by the house. I would have told you about it if he had. I had no idea that he was even in this part of the country."

"And the police haven't told you how he died yet?"

"No, it takes some time to get the test results. But it looked as if he was shot in the chest. I'm pretty sure that it was murder." I watched Ben, waiting for his reaction to that ugly and frightening word. He scowled and got up from the table.

"I've got to put my load in the dryer."

"Ben?" I called after him as he rushed from the room. The washer and dryer were in the basement, and I heard his feet pounding down the stairs. I decided to give him a few minutes to himself, and loaded the dishes into the dishwasher. I was cleaning the sink when I heard his step behind me.

"Mom?"

I turned, and he wound his arms around me and lowered his head to my shoulder. "Are you okay, honey?" I asked, and he started to cry, quiet tears at first that grew into wrenching sobs.

"He never, he never . . . ."

"What, honey?" I asked, stroking his back.

It all came out in a gush. "I wrote him a letter last Christmas. Sent it to his agent. It was a really angry letter about him not showing up for my graduation. The agent said he gave it to him. And Dad never wrote back. He didn't call. He just didn't give a damn about me!"

"Oh, Ben, I'm so sorry," I said, tightening my arms around him, tears spilling down my own cheeks. He clung to me. "He loved you. I know he did. He would have made a better friend for you than a father, now that you're older. He was a funny guy, passionate, a real charmer, but he was such a lousy father."

"I hated him," Ben said in a wild voice muffled by my shoulder.

"What?" I asked, pulling away so that I could see his face.

Ben straightened and wiped his face with his sleeve. Then he looked me in the eye. For a moment, I saw an expression so full of anger and hatred that it frightened me. I gasped. He stared back at me, his expression changing into one of concern.

"Mom, are you okay?" he asked, taking my hand. "I'm sorry, I haven't been thinking about you in all of this. You found his body – that must have been a big shock. How're you feeling?" As he put an arm around my shoulders and led me back to my chair, I wondered if I had imagined that horrible look. Maybe I was still in shock from Jack's death.

"Would you like me to stay tonight?" he asked, crouching down beside me at the table.

"Thanks, but don't you have to work tomorrow?"

"Yeah, but that's no big deal. I can get up in time to drive in."

"I don't want to impose," I said, not sure that I wanted him to stay. To tell the truth, he frightened me a little. I needed some time alone to think.

Ben stood up, patted my shoulder, and stepped back toward the sink. "No problem. I'll finish cleaning up, and then we'll take Wendy for a walk." Wendy's tail thumped on the floor and we both turned to look at her. "Damn," he said, turning back to the sink, "this is so totally bizarre. Are the police saying it's murder?"

I watched his back from my chair. "No, they're waiting for the coroner's report before they say anything."

Ben was silent as he wiped down the counter. "Could it have been suicide?" he asked with a shrug.

"I don't see how. Not unless he walked there – there was no car around. And why would he choose to kill himself in the middle of nowhere?"

Ben let out the dish water and dried his hands. "I guess not, then," he said, putting down the towel and turning to me. His face was calm. "Ready for our walk?"

"Sure. Thanks for finishing up."

Later that night, I had a nightmare. In my dream, I was back in the bush crouched over Jack's body. I looked up and saw Ben emerging from the trees with a gun in his hand, his face contorted with rage. There was blood dripping from his hands, and he wiped a long streak of it across Jack's face. Jack's body started to spasm and blood gurgled from his mouth. I ran away into the trees, and woke with my heart racing. As I lay in bed gasping, I could hear Ben's soft snores drifting down the hallway.

Ben's confession that he had hated his father, coupled with that dreadful expression on his face, must have really disturbed me. I knew that Ben had resented his father growing up, and I didn't blame him in the least for that. But hatred? That was a powerful emotion. I had never hated Jack and, heaven knows, he had broken my heart often enough to give me cause. But I had made my peace with our marriage and with the trouble his cheating had caused me, and now I mostly felt indifferent when I thought about Jack.

I sat up to rearrange my pillows into a more comfortable position and lay down again, but it was no use – I was too restless to get back to sleep. Unwanted thoughts careened around my head like the ball in a pinball machine. I turned on my bedside lamp and picked up a framed picture of Ben and me from my side table. It had been taken at the beach when he was eight years old. In the picture, I was sitting on a towel smiling up at the camera as Ben crept up behind me with a plastic pail full of water and a big, mischievous grin lighting up his face. He was missing a front tooth, and his goofy expression always made me smile. I mentally compared that face with the angry young man I had seen today, and shook my head. If it hadn't been for that stupid dream, the thought of Ben shooting Jack would never have crossed my mind. There, I had admitted it. I was afraid that Ben had shot Jack.

The idea was ludicrous. Where would Ben get a gun from, anyway? He was just nineteen – still a kid. He was my son. He couldn't have done such a terrible thing. And there was absolutely no proof that he had done anything, nothing but an ugly suspicion brought on by a bad dream. No, I was just going to have to bury that thought deep within my subconscious and never let it torture me again.

In the end, I had to get up and go look at Ben asleep in his bed, his face so young and vulnerable, before I could go back to sleep.

5

Saturday morning the telephone woke me up. I raised my head to squint at the clock-radio beside my bed. It was eight o'clock.

"Hello?" I mumbled into the receiver.

"Anna Nolan?"

"Yeah, who's this?"

"Mrs. Nolan, my name is Larry Hubert. I'm a reporter with the *Calgary Record*. I want to do a background story on your ex-husband, Jack Nolan – a look at his personal life, his family and friends – that sort of thing. Can I ask you some questions?"

"No comment," I said, banging down the phone. I had no desire to be quoted as the "grieving ex-wife" in the newspaper. What a hell of a way to be woken up. I got out of bed and shuffled down the hallway to see if Ben was still there. The bed had been made and he was already gone.

I decided to lay low that day and avoid people, so I drove to a grocery store that I occasionally used at the south end of Calgary to buy my weekly supplies. While waiting in line at the check-out, I picked up the Saturday paper and saw the headline, "Actor Murdered During Local Film Shoot," sprawled across the front page. Beside the article was a picture of Jack taken about ten years ago, probably at a film premiere, judging by the tuxedo and the winning smile he always saved for the press. Scanning the article and following the story to page two, I saw my name mentioned as his "former wife." It said that Jack's body had been discovered out on Wistler Road by a "passerby," and that the investigation was ongoing. Thank heaven the police hadn't disclosed me as the passerby to the reporters. Happily, Ben's name was omitted from the article altogether.

I tossed the newspaper into my cart and checked out of the store as quickly as I could before heading back to Crane. As upset as I was, I couldn't help but notice that it was a beautiful day, warm and windy with a Chinook cloud stretched low and grey across the snow-etched mountains. I itched to get outside for a long ramble, but spent the afternoon industriously cleaning the house. Poor Wendy didn't get a walk until after nightfall when I figured there'd be nobody out on the streets to recognize me. We had broken from our routine; I avoided the walk into the countryside now. I just didn't have the stomach for it anymore.

As we returned to the house after our walk, I saw a strange car parked in my driveway and a man I didn't recognize sitting on my front porch bench. I slowed down, reining Wendy in beside me. I sure hoped it wasn't that newspaper reporter who had called this morning. We advanced toward the house cautiously until I could make out Steve Walker in my porch lamp. Relieved, I waved and strode up the front walk to my house.

"Evening, Steve. I didn't recognize you at first," I called. He was out of uniform in a pair of jeans and a light blue shirt. Wendy wiggled up to him, and he bent down to pat her while I plopped onto the bench beside him. He lifted his head and I could see that his expression was grim. My stomach sank. "What can I do for you?" I asked warily.

"We got the coroner's preliminary report back today," he said. "I thought I'd come by to tell you about it rather than asking you to the station. Nice night – want to talk out here?"

"Sure," I replied. "I appreciate you coming by the house. What did you find out?"

"Mr. Nolan died from a single 45-calibre bullet through the heart. And he didn't die where you found him – his body was moved, although there wasn't enough evidence to show where he had been murdered. The coroner estimates the time of death between six and nine. I called May Weston and Erna Dombrosky, and they both swore that you were sitting in the library with them from six to seven thirty."

"That's great news. Now you can count me out. I came straight home after the meeting, Steve. I wouldn't have had time to kill Jack and move his body." But, peering into Steve's face, I could see that he still looked worried.

"Maybe. You could have killed him if you had done it right after the meeting. You had an hour and a half."

"Less than that, unless I killed him at my house, which I didn't do. It was a quarter to eight by the time I got back from the library. I left my car at home and walked over to the library, remember? So I would have had a little over an hour, tops. Hardly enough time to have met with Jack, killed him, and moved his body."

Steve sighed. "It sure would have helped if someone had come to the door while you were home and could vouch for you being here." I shook my head and looked away. "Well, it wouldn't hurt if you volunteered to let the forensics squad go over your house, just to rule it out as the murder scene. And your car, since Mr. Nolan's body was moved."

I raised my eyebrows but swallowed back my response, which was to tell him to get a search warrant. How could the police seriously suspect that I had killed Jack? What about a motive and an adequate amount of time to have murdered him? But I reconsidered, deciding that I'd gain more from the police by co-operating.

"Sure, that's no problem. They can do it anytime – tomorrow, if you like. I know from the mystery novels I've read that it's almost impossible to destroy traces of blood from porous surfaces."

Steve rolled his eyes. "Mystery novels. Things don't get solved as neatly as they do in books, you know."

I rolled my eyes right back. "I know that. I live in the real world. I even know that crimes don't always get solved." Steve nodded.

"What about motives?" I said. "Have you thought about who had the strongest motive for killing Jack?" His eyes darted to me and flicked away again. "No – me? You're kidding. What reason could I possibly have had for wanting to kill Jack after all these years?"

"It was no secret how you felt about your ex-husband. I remember overhearing Erna Dombrosky tell you last fall that she'd seen Mr. Nolan on TV. You made it pretty clear then that your ex was a jerk and that you were glad to be rid of him."

"Yes, I remember that conversation, but so what? Lots of people think their exes are jerks."

"Okay, but let's look at it from a police perspective." Steve stood up and began to pace around my little eight-foot wide porch. "Jack Nolan was found dead out on Wistler Road and you're the only known connection he had to Crane. What was he doing in Crane that night? Was he trying to see you again – or maybe Ben? Did he think that Ben was still living with you? You keep saying that you hadn't talked to him since your divorce."

The last thing I wanted was for Ben to get dragged into the investigation. I almost asked Steve if he had checked on Amy Bright's whereabouts that night, but I didn't want him to think that I was trying to deflect suspicion from Ben and me by accusing Amy. Instead, I leaned back on the bench and crossed my legs, trying to look nonchalant. "I think you're on a bit of a fishing expedition there, officer," I said.

Steve gave me a hard look. "Here's another possibility. Maybe you arranged for someone else to kill him."

I snorted and straightened up. "You mean, like a hit man?"

Steve stopped pacing and sat back on the bench beside me. "Don't laugh. It's a genuine possibility. You have friends."

"Yeah, I can just see seventy-nine-year-old Erna Dombrosky going after my no-good ex-husband with a .45 because he cheated on me four years ago."

"Or, you could have paid someone to do it. Look, Anna, I'm trying to warn you here. Don't think that you're not under serious suspicion just because we haven't arrested you yet." I stiffened. "Number one: you had a motive for killing Mr. Nolan. He cheated on you for years, and you wanted revenge. Number two: he called you that evening, even though you swore he hadn't spoken to you in four years. Number three: there's at least an hour and a quarter of your time unaccounted for that night. No," he said as I started to protest, "being home by yourself doesn't count. And number four: I found you standing over his body."

Okay, I was getting riled. I'd been helpful up until then, but he was talking crazy about hit men and arresting me. I swivelled around until our knees were touching.

"Look, I already explained how I found Jack's body," I said. "Yes, that creep cheated on me repeatedly during our marriage, so I divorced him. But I fell out of love with Jack years before our marriage ended, and I was glad to be free of him. I didn't want anything more to do with him, and I never saw him again or spoke to him after the divorce. I didn't kill him, and I certainly didn't ask anyone to kill him for me.

That's it. That's all I know." I jabbed him in the chest to emphasize my point.

Steve grabbed my wrist. "Anna," he said in a threatening tone. That was enough for Wendy, who had climbed to her feet during my speech. She barked and grabbed Steve's arm between her teeth. "Shit!" he yelled.

"Wendy, bad girl! Let go!" I shouted, whacking her on the shoulder. She released Steve, ducked her head, and crawled under the bench. I'd had her since she was a puppy, and she had never attacked anyone in her life.

"Steve, I'm so sorry," I said, springing to my feet as he jumped up. Lights snapped on next door, and I saw Betty Hiller, my neighbour, peering out from her front door. "It's okay, Betty," I called, waving before turning back to Steve. He was examining his shirt sleeve. As I looked over his shoulder, I could see a couple of small punctures in the fabric.

"It's all right. I don't think she even broke the skin," he said, sparing me a glance. Then he turned to my dog and said, "Gee, Wendy, I thought we were friends." He squatted down beside her and held out his hand. She glanced at me with big eyes, the whites showing around the irises, before looking back at him.

"It's okay, Wendy," I said in a reassuring voice. She came out from under the bench to sniff at Steve's hand.

"Good girl," he said, scratching behind her ear. Her tail waved and she relaxed.

"Steve, I'm really sorry. I'll pay to replace your shirt," I said.

"Never mind. We were both getting a little excited. I'll let it go this time, but just make sure that she never attacks anyone again. There could be some serious repercussions if she did. Unofficially, though, I'm glad that she defended you," he said with a small smile.

"Yeah, too bad she wasn't around when I was married to Jack."

"He didn't . . ." The smile faded and he put a hand on my shoulder.

"No, he never touched me," I hastened to assure him. "I never had that kind of trouble with Jack." I didn't want to give Steve any false ideas about Jack being a wife-beater.

"Good, because I'd hate to hear of anyone mistreating you." He stared into my eyes for a moment, long enough to make me feel uncomfortable, before removing his hand and standing up. "I'm going to go now, while everyone's still friendly. But what I said before still stands. Stick around town so that you're available for questioning. And if you can think of anything that might help the investigation, give me a call."

"Will do, and thanks, Steve. I'm glad that you're not upset about Wendy."

He paused to look down at her. "Nah, I love dogs, and she's a peach. Bye girl. Bye Anna." He nodded and left the porch while I took Wendy inside the house. She had a big, long drink, and then I gave her a jerky treat. Talk about mixed messages, but she had just defended me, and I was grateful.

"I think you've got the right idea, girl," I said, headed for bed with her following me down the hallway. "Men are just trouble."

6

The following morning was Sunday. Sunday mornings I always attended mass at St. Bernadette's Catholic Church, and today was no exception. I waited to hear the church bells ring before I dashed out my door, however, not wanting to arrive early enough to chat with my fellow parishioners. When I got there, Father Winfield was waiting at the back with his three altar servers. I nodded to him and slipped into the first available empty pew just as the hymn began and the procession started up the aisle. My neighbour, Betty Hiller, hurried in behind them and sat down at the end of my row. During the offertory collection, Betty slid across the pew to sit beside me.

"Hi Anna, how're you doing? Jeff and I were so upset to hear about your husband's death," she whispered. "You have our sympathies." Jeff, Betty's husband, was a plumber and a volunteer firefighter who could be called out on an emergency at any time, so he slept late on Sunday mornings as often as Betty let him. She volunteered with the church babysitting service, and had probably been waiting in the nursery until just after the hymn began to see if anyone required her help.

"I'm okay. Thanks for asking. How are you and Jeff?" I whispered back, trying to keep the conversation short. Betty could talk your ear off, and I had had to dissuade her from visiting too often when we first became neighbours.

"We're both fine. So – did you hear what happened to Henry Fellows' restaurant this morning?"

That wasn't the question I had expected to hear. "No, did something happen?"

"I'll say." Her short blond curls were trembling with excitement. "Somebody plowed his car right into Henry's restaurant this morning. Henry was inside getting breakfast ready when it happened. He wasn't hurt very badly, but he could have been. The car drove right through the wall and demolished half his kitchen before taking off again. Henry went into shock, so the EMS took him to the hospital. But the really disturbing news was what he told one of the ambulance attendants after it happened. He said that Frank was driving the car that did it – that Frank had tried to kill him!"

I stared at her for a moment with my mouth open. "You have got to be kidding. That is the most ludicrous thing I've ever heard. Why would Frank want to kill Henry Fellows?" I asked.

"Henry claimed that Frank was afraid of the competition from his new restaurant, so he drove into Henry's kitchen, trying to make it look like a hit-and-run accident. You ought to see it. There's an enormous hole in the wall facing the side street, and part of the roof collapsed. I saw it on the way to church this morning."

"What about Frank? Has anybody seen him?" I asked.

"No, he and Judy supposedly left for Lethbridge last night to visit Judy's mother."

The congregation stood up as Father Winfield began the communion prayers, and Betty and I had to cut our conversation short. The remainder of the service was a blur, I'm ashamed to say, because I couldn't stop thinking about the bizarre news. I very much wanted to see the damage for myself, so as the last notes of the recessional hymn died away, I nodded to Betty, bid Father a brief good morning, and rushed out into the street. St. Bernadette's was six blocks away from the restaurant, so it took all of five minutes for me to jog over.

As I hurried down Main Street toward Hank's Hearty Home-Cooking, I could see a police cruiser and a fire truck parked out front on the street. The building was encircled by yellow tape, and orange plastic cones blocked off traffic to the side street where the kitchen was located. I darted around the corner and paused to stare at the damage. Betty had been right; there was a huge hole in the side of the restaurant, and the roof over the damaged section had collapsed. Shingles, insulation, broken bits of siding, and plastic were scattered across the sidewalk and along the boulevard where the grass was all torn up. A couple of guys from the fire department were starting to nail heavy green plastic over the hole. I walked right up to the yellow tape to have a look inside the kitchen while it was still visible. The place was a disaster. There were broken cupboards, boxes and cans, flour, pots, and utensils strewn all across the floor. The fridge was tipped over, and dishes of food and cartons of eggs and milk had spilled out, adding to the mess. I shook my head, wondering who could have done such a crazy thing. While I was looking, Steve Walker and our local insurance agent, Harold Gibbs, emerged from the alley behind the restaurant. Steve was gesturing towards the fat black tire tracks cut into the boulevard's soft earth while Gibbs nodded and made notes on a clip board.

I followed them and overheard Steve saying, "Judging by the tire tracks, it looks like a full-sized truck went through the wall. It had to be heavy enough to break through the siding and the wall studs clear on through into the kitchen. There weren't any skid marks on the street to indicate that the driver applied his brakes prior to hitting the building, so the damage was intentional."

"Right," said Gibbs.

"He – or she – came down the side street and made a right-hand turn into the building. Had the perpetrator wanted to do some real damage, he could have hit the front of the building from Main Street and gone through the plate glass window, the seating area, and into the kitchen. Good thing he didn't – the damage would have been much worse if he had hit the gas line."

"Yup," said Gibbs.

Steve looked up and saw me standing behind the insurance agent. He nodded. "Hi Anna," he said.

"Hi Steve. Pretty bizarre, eh?" I said, gesturing at the building.

"Yeah, haven't seen anything like it before. Who'd drive into a building on purpose?"

"So, you don't think that it might have been an accident? Maybe a drunk driver did it," I suggested.

Steve pointed at the tire tracks on the boulevard. "Nah – even a drunk would have tried to stop when the truck came up over the curb. There's no sign of it. The driver drove off the road and into the building without decreasing speed. This was definitely done on purpose. Whoever it was, it's going to be impossible to hide the damage to his vehicle. We'll catch him for sure."

I took a step closer to the two men and lowered my voice. "Steve, I heard some nutty talk about Henry blaming Frank for the accident."

Steve looked down at his boot and knocked some mud off the heel. "Between you, me, and Mr. Gibbs here, yeah, Mr. Fellows was saying something about that to the EMS guys, but he was pretty upset and going into shock when he said it.

I don't know if he actually saw anything – Mr. Fellows was knocked down from behind."

"Are you trying to track Frank down?"

"Yeah, they called him this morning at Judy's mother's house in Lethbridge and suggested that he and Judy return sooner rather than later. They're on their way now."

Mr. Gibbs, a stocky, middle-aged man with a fringe of rust-coloured hair around his pink dome, spoke up. "Hey, Anna, I've been hearing some pretty interesting talk about you this week, too. Two crimes in Crane in one week – it's practically a crime wave." He gave me a big wink. "Steve, I hope you can protect the rest of us from these dangerous criminal types."

I blushed, and Steve took Gibbs by the arm. "See you around, Anna," he said, leading the insurance agent away. I decided to avoid conversation with the knot of gawkers chatting on the sidewalk, and went home. When I got there, the forensics squad was waiting for me. It felt as if the whole world had gone crazy.

7

It was weird going back to work on Monday morning as if everything were fine and my whole life hadn't been turned upside down by Jack's murder, but I had a living to earn, so I went. To make matters worse, it was raining and misty and visibility was poor, so I drove into Calgary with extra caution. There were herds of deer that wintered in the fields alongside the roads, attracted by the hay the ranchers left out for their horses and cattle, and they could jump in front of your car in a matter of seconds. Still, I managed to make it safely into the city and parked in the university lot. Hurrying through the rain into the main building and down the hallway, I passed a couple of early bird students waiting for their instructors. I arrived at the Kinesiology Department office, unlocked the door, flicked on the lights, and hung my coat on the back of the door. Re-opening it, I looked across the hall and saw that my boss hadn't arrived yet. Grateful for some early morning peace, I sank into my chair and turned on the computer. Seconds later, Dr. Bryan Carmichael materialized on my door step. Bryan, a muscular young man with a shaved head and a silver ear stud, was dressed casually in a t-shirt and sweat pants. The dress code was pretty relaxed for Kinesiology instructors because their teaching involved physical demonstrations and lab work.

"Hi Anna, how's it going? Did you have a good weekend?" he asked. Obviously, he hadn't read the *Record's* report of Jack's death.

"Not bad," I said. "You?"

"Pretty good. I've got my spring course outline ready for printing. Do you have any Printing Services forms?"

"Sure – they're right over there on top of the cabinet," I said, pointing to the credenza that held all the forms.

"Oops, I always forget where you keep those things. My bad." He grinned. "I'll just grab a few and get out of your hair."

"Okay Bryan," I said, entering my computer password.

After he left, the mail cart rumbled down the hallway and stopped outside my door. Alice Cobb, the Chinook University mail person for the past twenty-seven years, walked into my office with a bundle of mail in her arms. She was a compact, wiry woman who always wore her long grey hair plaited in a single braid down her back.

"Morning Anna," she said, dumping her load into my inbox and removing the outgoing mail. "How was your drive in this morning?"

I looked up and smiled. I liked Alice; she had taken me under her wing when I had arrived four years ago, explaining how things worked and where to find the kinesiology labs. "Pretty dismal with the rain. How was yours?"

"The same," Alice said. Like me, she preferred living in a small town and commuting to work. "Say, I saw a picture of Jack Nolan in Saturday's paper. He was your ex-husband, right?"

"That's right."

"Sorry for your loss, but gee, he was a good-looking guy. Thick hair, nice eyes, great body. Yum! I wouldn't have been too quick to kick him out of bed." Alice talked big, but she'd been with the same guy for thirty-five years. I'd never met her Mike, but I'd heard so much about him over the years that he almost seemed like a close friend. She sat down on the edge of my desk and fiddled with her braid.

"I don't know about that, Alice. You were probably a lot savvier when you got married than I was. Maybe you wouldn't have let him into your bed in the first place."

"Oh. You mean pretty boy, but not a lot of substance, eh?" she said, winking at me.

"That about sums him up," I replied with a smile. Alice had a way of getting to the point that I appreciated. Unfortunately, our conversation was interrupted by the sound of high heels tapping down the hallway. Alice jumped up and said, "Catch you later," before hurrying out the door.

"Bye," I called after her.

Magdalena stuck her perfectly-coiffed head into my office and said, "Good morning, Anna."

"Morning Magdalena."

"I have a meeting with the Dean at nine. Have you got that budget report ready?"

I scooped up a binder from the top of my desk and held it out to her. Magdalena walked the rest of the way into my office, as beautifully turned out as always in a brown tweed suit with a lavender scarf tucked into the neckline of her cream-coloured blouse. The strap of her tailored leather briefcase was slung over one shoulder, and her pointy-toed, chocolate-brown stiletto pumps didn't look as if they had just tramped through a muddy parking lot. I felt inferior in a navy and white-striped cotton sweater over navy slacks with sensible black flats. Her blond hair was swept up into a neat French twist, while I held back my long, brunette hair with gold barrettes.

"Thank you," she said, taking the report. "I hope that you're feeling better. Did you have a nice weekend?" As she studied me, I wondered if she had seen Saturday's newspaper report of Jack's death. Silly me – of course she had. Magdalena always kept up with the news.

"I'm much better, thank you," I answered, ignoring the question about my weekend and not volunteering any information about the murder. If she wanted to know about Jack, she was going to have to come right out and ask me.

"Good. The meeting should run about two hours. Please ask Bryan to drop by my office at 11:10."

"Certainly, Magdalena."

"Thank you." She nodded, turned on her heel, and strode away. I exhaled and relaxed. Magdalena and I had worked together for two years now, but I would certainly not classify our relationship as "close." She knew about Ben – I had introduced him to her at the start of the fall term – but I'd never discussed my marriage with her. It might have been a foolhardy wish, but I hoped to avoid that topic now, especially since Jack had been murdered. I suspected that my boss would have blamed me for allowing my life to become messy. Magdalena liked to run a tidy ship, and she wanted all of her crew members to be ship-shape.

I managed to avoid her in a day heavy with meetings and sped off home as soon as the work day was over, thrilled that I hadn't been forced to discuss Jack's death with anyone but Alice. When I got home, Wendy greeted me with her usual ecstatic tail-thumping and rear end-wiggling routine, and I let her out into the back yard. Kicking off my shoes and heading toward the bedroom to change out of my work clothes, I heard the doorbell ring. I glanced at my watch and saw that it was 5:05. Who would be calling on me at this time of day?

The man standing at my front door was a complete stranger. I considered myself of average female height at 5'5", but I had to crane my head upwards to see his face. He must have been 6'4", and lean. He wore a tailored black suit, grey shirt, and a silver and blue-striped silk tie. He was young – maybe thirty – and clean-shaven with close-cropped, blond hair.

"Anna Nolan?" he asked, and I nodded. I wondered who he could be. He was too expensively dressed to be a door-to-door evangelist.

He held some ID up before my eyes. "I'm Sergeant Charles Tremaine of the RCMP. I've been asked to lead the investigation into your ex-husband's death. There are a few questions I'd like to ask. May I come in?"

I stared at the picture on his ID and raised my gaze to his face. His cool grey eyes looked back at me. "Where's Steve Walker?" I asked. "I thought that he was the officer conducting the investigation?"

"Constable Walker has been assigned to another case. I work with a national criminal unit that investigates homicides throughout western Canada." He paused, and waited for me to respond. In the ensuing silence, I realized that Wendy was barking at the deck door. She must have heard the doorbell ring and got excited. She didn't like it when people came into the house while she was stranded outside.

"Yes, of course, come in. Please take a seat in the living room. I just have to let my dog back in."

Sergeant Tremaine followed me into the house and stayed in the living room while I opened the kitchen slider for Wendy. She went bounding past me headed straight for the living room. Not wanting the officer in charge of my ex-husband's murder investigation to be molested by my dog, I rushed into the living room, just in time to see her sniffing Tremaine's outstretched hand. He squatted down to scratch behind her ear, and she sat at his feet.

"I see you've made a friend," I said. He rose and pushed his hands into his trouser pockets. "Her name is Wendy," I said, attempting to be pleasant.

"Hello Wendy," he said solemnly before looking back at me.

"Please, have a seat," I repeated. He extended a hand toward the couch and waited for me to sit before taking an armchair. He might be stiff, but he had good manners. "I can tell that you're not from around here," I said, making nervous conversation. Tremaine spoke with a rather posh British accent.

"No," he replied. "Mrs. Nolan, I understand from Constable Walker that it had been a number of years since you last spoke with your ex-husband."

"Four. Why was Steve Walker assigned to another investigation?"

"Constable Walker was re-assigned because your friendship constituted a conflict of interest. Why do you insist that you hadn't spoken with Mr. Nolan for four years when his cell phone showed that he called you on the night of his murder?"

"I don't know why Jack called me that night, but as you must know, I was at a book club meeting when he called. I didn't speak to Jack, and since he was already dead when I found him, I have no idea what he wanted. If Steve was removed from the case, why wasn't Eddy Mason from the local station assigned in his place?"

Tremaine considered me for a moment, and I followed his glance down to my stockinged feet. I felt at a disadvantage beside this elegant man. "Mrs. Nolan," he said, but I interrupted him before he could continue.

"Please don't call me 'Mrs. Nolan,' Sergeant. I kept the 'Nolan' because I've always hated my maiden name, but 'Mrs.

Nolan' makes it sound as if I'm still married to Jack. Please, just call me Anna."

"What was your maiden name?" he asked.

"Butcher," I said, colouring. The name sounded obscene given the circumstances.

"I see," he said, unfazed. "Anna, this is a small town. All the officers in the detachment know you. Some of them eat at The Diner with you. Staff Sergeant Mason is concerned about bias, particularly with the victim being an actor in a high-profile film. There's been national press coverage of his death. It was prudent to bring in someone from a major criminal unit with no ties to the investigation's chief suspect. I normally work homicide investigations, so that's why I was chosen."

My mind froze at the words "chief suspect." I couldn't believe it. I knew that I was a suspect, but "chief" made it sound so hopeless. I slumped back onto the couch. "I'm the chief suspect?" I squeaked. His gaze was beginning to unnerve me, so I looked away.

"Are you aware that you are the sole beneficiary of a $300,000 life insurance policy on Jack Nolan's life?"

"Whaat?" I said. "Jack had a $300,000 life insurance policy?"

"That's right. I've discussed your financial situation with your bank manager. I know that $300,000 would pay off your mortgage and the balance on your credit card with money to spare."

"It's not such a big balance," I said. "Wait a minute – are you allowed to talk to my bank manager?"

"This is a homicide investigation."

"Please, wait just a minute. Let me think." Information was coming at me too fast and I was getting confused. "I remember that Jack and I took out life insurance policies when Ben was born so that we could take care of him if anything happened to either one of us. Jack must have kept his up all these years."

"Why would he do that? And why would Mr. Nolan retain you as his beneficiary after your divorce? Why not change it over to your son, for instance?"

"I don't know. Maybe he felt he owed me. Jack never did pay me any child support."

"Why didn't you tell Steve Walker about the insurance policy?"

"Because I forgot about it. Jack took it out a long time ago. How was I to know that he kept up the payments?" I got up from the couch to pace around the room. Tremaine rose from his chair, and Wendy stood up, too.

He raised one hand. "Look, I just arrived yesterday. I've read the constable's preliminary notes and your statement. The test results from the crime scene haven't come back yet. I have a lot of people to question, particularly the people on the film set in Longview. I will be investigating you, including interviewing people who know you. Is there anything you want to tell me about Mr. Nolan's death before I do that, anything you haven't mentioned already?"

I shook my head, frowning.

He removed a card from his jacket pocket. "I'll be in touch. Please don't go anywhere so that you're available for questioning. If you do remember anything pertinent to the case, please ring me at the number on this card." I took it from him wordlessly, panic driving coherent speech from my mind.

He looked at me for a long moment. "That's all for now. I'll let myself out, Anna. Good night." He reached down to pat Wendy's head and left the room. I heard the front door open and close behind him.

Sinking back down on the couch, I felt as if I had been released from the hypnotic gaze of a cobra. "Oh crap," I said, "what am I going to do now?"

Wendy pushed her head into my lap and stared at me with her big, brown eyes. I thought that it was empathy until I realized it was supper time.

"Sorry, I forgot to feed you," I said. "Let's go get your food." Her head bounced up and her tail started thumping. Life was so simple for dogs.

As she gobbled down her meal, I decided to buy my supper at The Diner. I sure didn't feel like cooking after that last bombshell, and there wouldn't be many people there on a Monday night. I changed into jeans and a long-sleeved shirt, and walked over to the restaurant.

When I got in the door, I looked around the place in surprise; I couldn't believe how crowded the restaurant was. And, wonder of wonders, Frank was sitting at one of the tables surrounded by a bunch of his regulars. I had never seen him at a table before. Mary bustled by with four plates of food balanced in her hands. I heard the bell ring on the kitchen pass-through and glanced over. Judy was working in the kitchen and it wasn't even a Saturday. Mary breezed by again, and then turned back to me.

"You better order tonight's special and go find a seat at Frank's table while there's still room, Anna. Half the town's here."

I followed her to the counter, where she was gathering up dirty dishes. "What's going on?"

"Everyone wants to hear what Frank has to say about Henry's accident. Tonight's special is beef stew and biscuits with a side salad. Frank's got two big pots of stew simmering on the stove, so all Judy has to do is dish it up."

"Sounds great – I'll have that, please. And bring me a glass of the usual, would you?"

"You got it," she called over her shoulder as she picked up the next orders and headed to one of the tables.

I threaded my way through the crowd to Frank's table, where he beckoned for me to join them. Erna Dombrosky, my friend from the book club, sat beside him, her bright, intelligent eyes observing everything. Steve sat at the end of the table in his police uniform – he must have just come off shift – and nodded at me as I sat down. I gave him a significant look that meant, "We'll talk later." I wanted to find out whatever he knew about Sergeant Tremaine. My neighbours Jeff and Betty were there, as was Mr. Andrews, slowly turning the pages of the *Foothills Gazette* and ignoring everyone. Just as I sat down, he pointed a knotty finger at a picture and said, "Where'd they get that picture of you, Frank? You look pretty shifty."

Frank half-rose to get a better look at the paper over Betty's shoulder. "Ha, that's a picture of me making the financial report at the Rotary Club's annual meeting. You're just not used to seeing me with my reading glasses."

Betty peered at the picture, her pretty, plump face dimpling. "I think it's the suit and tie. Makes you look like a lawyer." Everyone laughed, and Frank grinned good-naturedly.

"Hey, Anna, how's it going?" he asked, turning to me as he sat back down. "You're not the only celebrity in town now. I bet the guys at the station are happy to have something more exciting to do than passing out speeding tickets for a change." This was directed at Steve, who tilted back in his chair with a cup of coffee.

"If you're nice to me, Frank, I'll see that you and Anna get adjoining cells when they arrest the two of you."

"Hey!" I protested, just as Mary set my juice and plate of food down. She handed me a napkin with cutlery rolled up inside. "Thanks, Mary. That smells awfully good," I said. My rumbling stomach made me realize how hungry I was.

"Let me know what you think of it, Anna – I added cumin to the recipe," Frank requested.

I took a bite of the fragrant beef and potato, and chewed. "Mmm, it's delicious. I think I like this better than your burgundy wine stew. The pearl onions are a nice touch, too."

Frank smiled. "Thanks."

Betty leaned forward in her chair, brandishing a knife as she buttered her biscuit. "Anna, Steve was just telling us about Henry Fellows."

"Yeah, what's the news, Steve?" Jeff asked. He was blond, like his wife, and stocky.

"He was released from the Foothills Hospital at noon today," Steve reported. "One of the guys went over to his house this afternoon to ask him some questions. He said that Henry has a few bruises and a limp, but seemed fine, otherwise."

"What about this nonsense that Frank drove into his restaurant?" I asked.

"Well, Henry's not pressing any charges. That's about all I can say for now."

Erna piped up, "Did anyone point out that Frank doesn't own a pick-up truck, Steve? How could Frank have done that kind of damage to Henry's wall with his Corolla? Which doesn't have a scratch on it, from what I saw on my way in just now."

Frank looked at Erna with mock alarm in his eyes. "Erna, are you checking up on me?"

Erna laughed and patted his arm with her small hand. She was a tiny bird of a woman, a retired high school teacher.

"Of course not, but your car is always parked out front of the restaurant, and anyone can see that it hasn't been in an accident. Unless you stole a truck to do the damage, and then abandoned it."

"Hmm," Steve said, "that's a good theory, Mrs. Dombrosky."

"Now, Erna, don't go giving the police any bright ideas," Frank said.

Erna winked. "Maybe the police should put me on their payroll. I don't miss much, and it would surely help stretch my pension."

"Don't even think about it, Steve. That woman knows too much," Frank replied. Everyone laughed. Erna had lived in Crane all her life and was said to know where the skeletons were buried.

During a lull in the conversation, I asked, "So, has anyone met Sergeant Tremaine yet?" Steve regarded me steadily while heads swivelled in my direction.

"Who's that?" Betty asked.

"He's a special RCMP investigator who's leading my ex-husband's case. He came over to my house half an hour ago to ask me some questions."

"Yeah, he dropped by the restaurant after lunch today to have a cup of coffee," Frank said. "He asked some questions about the people here in town. He's not your typical officer, is he, Steve? He seemed a little – reserved." Everyone turned to look at the young constable, who shrugged.

"He's one of the bright boys with the criminal unit who gets loaned out from time to time. His last assignment was a big homicide case in Vancouver. You remember those two teenage boys they found in the dumpster?"

Betty screwed up her face. "Oh, that was a nasty one. He was involved with that?" Steve nodded.

"So, what's he doing in Crane?" Frank asked.

"It's standard procedure to send someone from one of these special investigative units when there's a homicide in a small community, especially when the victim isn't local. Guess they think it's a good learning opportunity for us small-town cops. I haven't had a chance to talk to him yet myself. What did you make of him, Anna?"

"Oh, he's pretty impressive. I wonder how he ended up in Canada. He sounds like a Brit."

"Yeah, he's originally from England. Got a university education over there before doing his police training here. That's all I know about him."

"It doesn't look as though he dresses on a cop's salary," I added.

"No, it sure doesn't," Steve agreed.

"Anyway, if he talks to any of you about me, please put in a good word. It looks like he thinks I'm the prime suspect." I laughed shakily while everyone stared at me. "That's right. Sergeant Tremaine just told me that I am the beneficiary of a $300,000 life insurance policy on Jack's life. It's probably the same one Jack took out when Ben was born, and he kept me as the beneficiary all these years. I didn't even know about it until the sergeant told me today. It gives me a nice, shiny motive for wanting to kill Jack, as if finding his body wasn't enough to make me look guilty."

The news was greeted with silence. My friends either looked at each other or at the table top, anywhere but at me. All but Mr. Andrews, who continued to flip through the newspaper pages and ignore us. I noticed that he had worked his way up to the Classifieds. Erna reached over to pat my arm.

"Don't you worry, dear. Everyone knows that you're innocent. You just go home and have a stiff drink and a good night's sleep. Things will look better in the morning." She smiled, and I smiled back at her.

"That's good advice, Erna. Has anyone else got advice for me?"

Steve looked straight into my eyes from across the table. "Just don't lie to him, Anna. From what I've heard, he's pretty smart. Always tell him the truth, no matter how bad you think it makes you look."

I gulped, nodded, and ate my dinner. Once I got home, I remembered Erna's advice about having a stiff drink. I wasn't much of a drinker and was saving an unopened bottle of wine for company, so I had to settle for an extra chocolaty hot chocolate before going to bed.

8

Yesterday morning, I had been worried about my ex-husband's murder. Today, I was worried about being the chief suspect in his murder investigation. As I drove into Calgary, I thought how precarious was the life I had worked so hard to build for myself after the divorce. I had everything that I needed: a house, a job I could count on, a few good friends, a dog to keep me company, and the book club. Ben was doing just fine, too. But if the unthinkable happened and I was convicted of Jack's murder, I would be put in prison for a good long time and Ben would be labelled the son of a killer. Even if I wasn't convicted, some of the people in Crane might always believe that I had killed Jack. They might even treat it as a joke, as Clive had done at The Diner. That would be unbearable, people winking at me and gossiping behind my back. And what if the people at the university found out? Would I have to give up my job and start over again somewhere else?

My earlier life had been totally different. I had arrived in Toronto at the age of eighteen to pursue a career in acting. I had left behind my parents and everyone else I'd known in the small lakeside community I'd grown up in, determined to make a success of myself no matter what people had thought. "Anna is so shy. Anna is such a loner. How could she possibly go on the stage?" everyone, even my parents, had asked.

I'd enrolled in a college acting class where Jack happened to be the teacher. Ten years older than I was, and with an established stage career, he had been magnificent. Handsome, charismatic, self-assured, he'd swaggered about the stage impressing the hell out of us students. I was totally besotted, and couldn't believe my luck when Jack started flirting with me. To this day, I never knew what attracted him to me. We got together after the course ended and, well, sparks flew, the earth shook, and all of those other clichés. I was deliriously happy; not only did this gorgeous man love me, but he introduced me to important directors and actors that I had previously only admired from my seat in the audience.

We married less than six months after we started dating, me in a tea-length white dress with flowers in my hair, and Jack in a suit without a tie. My parents warned me against marrying so quickly and to a man with such an unstable career, but I dismissed their concerns as petty. After all, my father had never approved of my frivolous acting ambitions, and my mother didn't even have a job, so what did they know about life? I was going to follow my dreams.

The first year of married life had been bliss. Jack and I both got acting jobs, and we'd meet up at a bar or a restaurant after our shows and stay out all night with our friends. I adored my husband, I felt privileged to be working as an actress, and I had the freedom to do whatever I pleased. My spirits were flying, but I fell back to earth the second year of our marriage when I discovered that Jack was cheating on me. When I confronted him about the affair, Jack actually got down on his knees, tears streaming down his face, and swore that it would never happen again. I was devastated, but I had seen for myself that women were attracted to Jack like bees were to pollen. He was a passionate man exposed to a lot of temptation, and he had made a big mistake. Was I going to break up our marriage over a single mistake? I admit that I went crazy for about a month after I found out, but we eventually patched things up and got on with it, albeit a little less joyfully than before.

When Ben came along, however, it became apparent that we couldn't sustain our carefree lifestyle. Someone was going to have to provide stability for our child, and it made sense that that somebody should be me, at least until I could restart my acting career. That's what I told myself, anyway.

For the first fifteen years of his life, Ben and I followed Jack across the country while he pursued acting opportunities and I tried to make a string of apartments feel like home to our small family. Unfortunately, Jack also had access to a steady stream of pretty young actresses. After a series of humiliations, I finally realized that my husband's cheating wasn't going to stop. I had a choice to make, and I decided that a bruised ego was of little consequence compared to the hardship and disgrace of raising my son on welfare. So, I decided to ignore Jack's dalliances as long as he didn't rub my nose in them. Fortunately my husband was a consummate liar, and his stories didn't become insultingly transparent until the latter part of our marriage.

Well, that segment of my life was over and done with, and I had done pretty well for myself since leaving Jack. Now my new, precious little life was threatened, and I felt both frightened and angry. It just wasn't fair. How could a dead ex-husband jeopardize everything? I felt powerless to do anything to help myself. The real world wasn't anything like it was in Agatha Christie's books where Miss Marple could solve murders simply by observing human nature, or Poirot by using his little grey cells. I fumed about it as I parked my car and stomped into the university.

My work day began with a two-hour computer training session, the result of a recent software upgrade, and I wasn't back at my desk until eleven. I was just going through my e-mail when I heard Magdalena's door open across the hallway and a familiar voice said, "Thank you for taking the time to see me, Dr. Lewis." I looked up and saw Tremaine standing in her doorway, shaking Magdalena's hand.

"My pleasure, Sergeant Tremaine," she said. Her eyes met mine across the hallway. "Let me know if there's anything I can do to help with the investigation. We all want this to be over as quickly as possible for Anna." Following the direction of her eyes, Tremaine turned to look at me while Magdalena closed her door. I beckoned for him to come into my office, and waited to shut the door behind him before turning to confront him.

"What are you doing here?" I asked, practically spitting, I was so mad. It had never occurred to me that Tremaine would question my boss. I didn't want her finding out the sordid details of my personal life from the police.

"Anna, I told you that I would be questioning your associates," he replied, leaning against my desk, perfectly calm.

"Yes, but what's she got to do with this case?" I asked.

"Often it's the people at work who know you best."

"Magdalena doesn't know anything about Jack. I've never spoken to her about my marriage."

"I apologize if you're upset by this intrusion into your professional life, but this is a homicide investigation."

"Yes, you keep saying that."

Just then, the door burst open and Ben stormed in. He stopped dead when he spotted Tremaine and stared at him with open hostility. "What are you doing here, Tremaine?" he demanded.

I turned to the sergeant. "You know Ben? You've already spoken to him?"

"Oh yeah, Mom. He came to the house at seven thirty this morning and woke up me and my roommates. We all had to troop down to the kitchen to answer a bunch of questions. It took so long, I was almost late for work. When I got there, my boss asked me to make a delivery, but I detoured here first to tell you about it."

We both glared at Tremaine. If he felt nervous being trapped between an irate mother and her hostile son, he showed no sign of it.

"Thank you again for your time this morning, Ben," he said. "I thought that you'd prefer answering my questions at home rather than coming down to the station. Now, if you'll both excuse me, I have other business to attend to." He waited for Ben to stand aside before strolling out the door. Ben watched him leave before turning back to me.

"He's a cool bastard, I'll give him that. Now, what's all this about an insurance policy?"

I explained about the two insurance policies Jack and I had bought when he was born, and how his father had held onto his and left me as the beneficiary. Ben frowned and said, "Gee, that doesn't sound so good. You'd better be careful around this guy. He was asking some pretty loaded questions this morning, you know? He even asked me where I was on the night Dad was killed, and asked the guys to confirm the time I got home."

I felt a knot of anxiety inside my chest. "I'm sorry," I said. "I should have called you last night to warn you about Tremaine. It just didn't occur to me that he would show up at your house this morning. That was stupid of me – of course, he'll begin by questioning everyone who was connected with your father. Don't worry, I'm sure that he doesn't seriously suspect you." In my heart, I prayed that he didn't, anyway.

"Especially since I was out with Tracy that night. We saw a movie, got some pizza, and were home by midnight."

"Tracy? Who's Tracy?" I asked, a silly grin plastered across my face. Whoever she was, I blessed her for giving my son an alibi for the night Jack was murdered.

"Never mind Tracy – she's a girl I just started seeing. I'm worried about you, Mom. The way Tremaine was talking, I think he really suspects you." Ben came close and hugged me to his chest. I was surprised; usually he gave me a peck on the cheek or a pat on the back. I hugged him back, and then loosened my grip to look up into his face.

"Hey, honey, don't look so worried," I said. "The insurance policy was a big shock to me, too, but it doesn't prove anything. The police can't ignore the evidence just because I happen to have a motive for killing your father. For one thing, the timing doesn't work. I was at the book club for a good chunk of the three hours the coroner set as the time of death. And another thing – the police said your father's body was moved. Well, the forensics cop practically had his nose to the upholstery of my car yesterday, and I know he didn't find any evidence of a body.

Ben's eyes bugged out. "The police looked at your car?"

"And the house, too. It was all voluntary. Don't worry about it. Letting the police check out the house and the car will help to clear my name. They won't find any evidence against me because there isn't any." Ben shook his head, not looking very convinced.

"And another thing – when they find the murder weapon, the police will be able to trace it back to the murderer, right? So everything will work out fine, you'll see. It's just scary right now because Sergeant Tremaine suspects everyone at this stage, but he has to. It's his job. Give him some time. I'm sure that he'll find the right person in the end.

Ben frowned. "I sure hope so. And I'm sorry about all of this. Dad's still making trouble for you, even after he's dead. He probably got killed by some woman he dumped or by somebody's jealous husband. I bet he had it coming to him, whoever it was."

I sighed. I hated to hear Ben talk that way about his father, even if he were right. But, knowing Jack, a rejected lover or a jealous husband was the most likely killer.

I got Ben calmed down and out of my office only to have Magdalena pop in. "Anna, may I see you in my office, please?" she asked. I got up from my desk and followed her in, my stomach tightening. This was not a good day for my stress levels.

"Please have a seat," she said, indicating the chair before her desk. I sat down while she closed the door and took her place behind the desk. "Sergeant Tremaine told me about the murder investigation."

"I see," I said, swallowing nervously.

"Yes. I suppose that you were too overwhelmed to speak to me about it just yet?" I couldn't miss the sarcasm in her voice.

"I had hoped that the investigation would be confined to Crane and wouldn't interfere with work," I replied. "I'm sure you understand how much I'd like to keep this investigation private, Magdalena. Jack's murder had nothing to do with me, really."

"Except that whoever killed him wanted you to find his body." I stared at her, flabbergasted by her words. She studied me for a moment. "I assume by your expression that the thought hadn't occurred to you?"

"N-no, it hadn't. But that isn't necessarily true, is it?"

"Think about it," my boss said, leaning forward on her elbows. "Sergeant Tremaine said that you usually follow the same route when you walk your dog at night. He also said that your ex-husband's body had been moved after he was killed. Therefore, whoever killed him moved the body to a place where you and your dog would be sure to find it." She relaxed back into her chair. "I wonder why? It poses some interesting questions, doesn't it?"

I shook my head, feeling like an idiot. She was probably right about the murderer leaving the body where I would find it, but I hadn't made the connection before. I would have to think about that some more when I was alone. "I don't know what to tell you, except that I'm sorry Tremaine sprung it all on you," I said.

She shrugged. "Of course, if it affects you, I want to hear about it. By the way, the sergeant asked me some questions about you. Would you like to know what they were?"

"Yes, please." I had really wanted to know what the two of them had said about me, but I couldn't think of a way to ask Magdalena.

"Let's see," she said, staring off into space while she collected her thoughts. "He began by asking about your work habits. I told him that you were reliable. Then he asked if I had overheard any telephone conversations or observed anything to indicate that you were in contact with your ex-husband. I told him no. Finally, he asked if I was acquainted with your son. I told him that I had met him once, but very briefly. That was the gist of it."

"That's all? That's not much," I said, delighted with my boss's discretion. Tremaine wouldn't find anything damning in that tidy little exchange.

She considered me. "I'm sure that this investigation must be quite stressful for you. Do you require any time off work?"

"Thank you for asking, but no, not at this point. Of course, they're sure to call me as a witness when there's a trial."

"Very likely. Well, please keep me informed of any disruptions to your work schedule."

"Yes, I'll do that, Magdalena, and thank you again, very much."

"You're welcome." She pulled a file from her desk tray, and I gathered that I was dismissed. As I stood, Magdalena looked up at me. "Sergeant Tremaine seems very astute and cautious. I'm sure that he will exhaust all possible avenues of investigation before coming to a conclusion."

What was this? Was she trying to reassure me? "Yes, he seems to know what he's doing," I responded.

She nodded before returning her attention to the file. I left her office feeling a little better; at least Magdalena seemed to be on my side. Perhaps there was an upside to this horrible mess after all.

9

I stewed about the case on the drive home that night. Magdalena's deduction that the murderer had left Jack's body where Wendy and I would find it suddenly made the murder a whole lot more personal. Someone was trying to frame me. Worse, someone was trying to frame me who knew my habits. That meant that the killer was either someone I knew or someone who had been watching me. My heart rate quickened and I tightened my grip on the steering wheel as I wrestled with that idea.

The murderer also had to be someone who benefitted from Jack's death, or someone who hated him enough to kill him. I couldn't think how anyone other than me benefitted from his death; Jack didn't have much of anything. As to hating him, that was a definite possibility. His whole life had revolved around acting and women. Jack had been a womanizer, and "cherchez la femme" definitely seemed to apply to his murder. But I had been out of touch with him for four years. What I needed to know was what Jack had been up to and who he had been doing it with since our separation.

Clive had talked about Jack sleeping with some of the women on the movie set, particularly Amy Bright. I didn't know the movie people, but I did know Amy well enough to say hello to her. Maybe I should follow Miss Marple's example and talk to a few likely people about Jack. I could get some inside information from the movie folk that they wouldn't want to share with the police. If I passed it on to Tremaine, he might be impressed by how cooperative I was being, plus I might find something that would help him solve the case. It was better than hiding out in my house, waiting to see if Tremaine was either going to find Jack's killer or tighten a noose around my neck. I could begin by going over to Amy's house on the pretext of wanting a manicure. She would know that I was married to Jack, and I could steer the conversation around to his murder. Yes – I had a plan! It felt good to be able to do something to forward the investigation.

When I got home, I ate supper and took Wendy out for a walk. I wanted it to look as if I just happened to be passing by Amy's house when I remembered that I needed a manicure. I wouldn't be able to get much information out of her if she was suspicious of me.

Amy's house was on a side street five blocks away from mine, on the boundary between the old part of town and the new subdivision. It was a cute little two-storey with white siding and a neat front lawn enclosed by a white picket fence. A driveway ran up the left side of the house with a detached garage set in behind. There was a wood sign advertising Amy's hairdressing business on the front lawn with an arrow pointing to the side entrance reserved for customers. Not knowing if she were busy with a client, I decided to try the front door first. I rang the doorbell a couple of times and waited, but Amy didn't appear. The curtains were drawn and it didn't look as if anyone was home, but there was a strong odour of wood smoke about the house. Surely she wouldn't have lit a fire and left it? She had to be around somewhere. I stepped off the porch and craned my neck upward to see the chimney, but there was no smoke coming from it.

"Come on, Wendy. Let's try the side door," I said.

We didn't get a response there, either, so we wandered up the driveway. A high wooden fence separated the driveway from the backyard with a gate leading between them. I spotted smoke wafting over the gate. It smelled like wood smoke. What was she up to? People didn't barbecue with wood. I hesitated, not wanting to trespass, but timidity wasn't going to help me. I unlatched the gate and pushed my way in, pulling Wendy in behind me and closing the gate. I looked around. There was a deck running along the back of the house with a fire pit sunk into the grass before it. A fire was burning in the pit and Amy was standing beside it, her back to me, with a poker dangling from her hand. I noticed a small pile of clothes lying on the grass beside her.

I walked up behind her and said, "Hi, Amy, what are you doing?"

She whirled around in surprise, swinging the poker toward me in defence. Wendy growled and leapt at the poker, knocking Amy to the ground.

"Get her off me, get her off!" Amy screamed as she wrestled for the poker. Wendy clenched it in her teeth and growled, shaking her head.

"Wendy, off!" I commanded, hauling on her leash. She growled even louder and Amy screamed again before letting go of the poker.

A man's face suddenly appeared over the fence. "What's going on in there?" he called. "Hey, Amy, do you want me to call the police?"

"No!" Amy and I both shouted. Startled, we exchanged a look. Amy looked frantic. "No," she mouthed at me, her eyes begging me to comply.

"It's okay," I called. "My dog thought the poker was a stick. When Amy didn't throw it, my dog grabbed it and Amy tripped and fell. Wendy, lie down!" I grabbed the poker from her mouth and shoved Wendy onto the grass. She whined, flattening herself onto her belly while I helped Amy up.

"Gee, lady, you should have better control of your dog. A dog that big could really hurt someone," the man said.

"I'm okay," Amy called, brushing herself off. "Thanks for checking, Jim. That was very kind of you."

The man shook his head and disappeared while Amy and I gazed at each other. My hair had toppled out of its knot and was hanging in my face, while Amy's shirt had half-pulled out of her shorts.

"You're Anna Nolan," she said in a soft, girlish voice. "I recognize you. You used to be Jack's wife."

"That's right. I was just stopping by to see if you could give me a manicure. I hope you can forgive this misunderstanding with my dog. I don't know what's got into her lately." I said this over my shoulder as I strolled over to have a look at the fire pit. When Amy saw what I was doing, she hurried after me. Bending to examine the pile of clothes, I spotted a man's white shirt lying on top.

"What's this?" I asked.

She flushed and bit her bottom lip. "Uh, they're just some old things I don't wear anymore," she said.

"Really?" I said. "Most people donate their clothes to charity when they don't want them anymore."

"I guess I'm just too lazy to bother doing that," she said, twisting her fingers together.

"Why didn't you just throw them in the garbage, then? Why go to all the trouble of burning them? Unless you've got something to hide?"

Amy laughed nervously. "Don't be ridiculous. I have nothing to hide."

I bent down to pick up the shirt, revealing a pair of men's white briefs underneath.

"Hey!" Amy shrieked, snatching the underwear off the pile, only to expose a pair of men's black dress socks.

"Amy Bright, either you're a cross-dresser or you're the worst liar in the world," I said. "Who do these clothes really belong to? Or, should I say, who did they used to belong to? You were seeing Jack, weren't you?" Amy gasped, and I pressed my advantage home. "These were Jack's clothes, weren't they? What are you doing with them, and why are you burning them?"

Amy's eyes darted around the yard as if she were afraid that someone was spying on us from the shadows. Stepping a little closer, she said, "Please, Anna, don't tell anybody," in a low, urgent voice. "Yes, these are Jack's things. The last time he came over, he asked me to do some laundry for him so that he wouldn't have to go to the laundromat. I told him that I didn't mind."

"When was that?"

Her voice got even quieter, as if she were a small child confessing to a transgression. "Last Thursday, the day he died. He followed me home after we were finished shooting and stayed for the afternoon. I barbecued him a steak for supper. Only, no one knows that Jack was here, and I was afraid to say so in case I got in trouble. That English police sergeant was over here today, asking about Jack. Please don't tell him about the clothes – he might get the wrong idea." Amy looked at me beseechingly, her big, blue eyes looking scared.

"Look," I said, "maybe we should sit down and talk about this. Sergeant Tremaine has been asking me about Jack, too."

Amy smiled. "Oh, I'd like that. I've been so nervous since Jack died, I didn't know what to do. It would be nice to talk to someone about it."

I gestured toward the deck. "Shall we?"

"Okay," she said, leading me to a table and some chairs. I was excited, feeling in charge of the situation for a change. Finally, someone was more afraid than I. Pulling out a deck chair, I sat down while Amy perched on a bench beside me.

"How long did you know Jack?" I asked.

"Not long, just a few weeks. We met on the movie set. He was really nice to me. We used to talk about acting while we were waiting to shoot our scenes. He even took me to a party for the actors and the director at an expensive restaurant once. I mean the actors with big parts, not us extras. After that, Jack came over a couple of times for drinks. He said my house was real homey, and that he missed having a woman waiting for him when he got home. Jack was lonely, you know."

"Yeah, poor Jack," I said. She nodded, not noticing my sarcastic tone. "How long was he with you on Thursday?"

She closed her eyes to remember. "Let me see. He came to the house around three o'clock after he was done for the day. He parked his car in my garage so that no one would see it in the driveway. Jack said that we should keep our friendship secret because the director didn't like the actors dating each other. 'That kind of thing can cause trouble on the set,' he told me."

More likely, he didn't want to be spotted around town in case word got back to me, but I kept that thought to myself.

"We had a couple of beers, and one thing led to another – you know. Later on, we had supper, and he left around 6:20 to take care of some business. I know that it was 6:20 because I had a 6:30 hair appointment and I was watching the time. And that was the last time I ever saw him." A tear slid down Amy's cheek, and she wiped it away with the back of her hand.

"Did he say where he was going?" I prompted.

"No, he didn't tell me. To be truthful, I was a tiny bit jealous. I heard Jack tell a guy once that he had some 'business' to take care of when he meant that he was coming to see me. I thought it was pretty cute at the time, referring to me as business. So, when he told me last Thursday that he had some business to see to, I thought that he was leaving me to see another woman."

"Was Jack seeing anyone else from the movie?"

"I don't know. I'm not there all that much. They only need me for a few scenes now and then. But Jack was good-looking and funny, and he flirted with the actresses and the female crew members all the time, so he might have been seeing someone else and not told me."

"Would that have hurt your feelings?"

She shrugged and smiled. "Not so much. Jack and I both knew that we were just having some fun together. I did ask him once if he was serious about someone, though. He wore this diamond and ruby ring all the time, you know, and I wondered if a girlfriend had given it to him. He told me that it was from an old flame, but she had died, so he wore it in memory of her. That's why he was so lonely – he couldn't get over her, even though she died years ago." Amy sighed. "Jack was so romantic."

I just about gagged when I heard about the ring. I had given it to him the night before we were married. It had been my grandfather's ring, a handsome, square-cut diamond with a fat ruby set on each side. Pretty valuable, but my father wouldn't wear it because he thought it was too gaudy. He gave it to me to give to Jack, however, saying that it would suit an actor just fine. Jack had loved that ring and wore it all the time. Closing my eyes, I tried to picture his body lying on the ground on the night of the murder. I couldn't remember seeing the ring, and I was sure that it would have caught my eye if he had been wearing it.

"Amy, did Jack wear the ring over to your house last Thursday?" I asked.

Her forehead creased as she thought. "I'm pretty sure that he did. He always wore it when he wasn't filming."

"Any chance he left it behind with you?"

"Oh, no, I'm sure that he didn't. He hardly ever took it off."

I thought for a moment. I just couldn't believe that this simple-minded woman had killed Jack, but whoever had done so must have taken the ring. Now we had both the ring and the missing gun to incriminate the murderer, if he – or she – still had them in his or her possession.

"Amy, I think that we can help each other out," I said. Her eyes widened and she looked hopeful. "Inspector Tremaine suspects me of killing Jack because Jack left me some insurance money, but I didn't do it, and I want to find out who did. You know the people over at the movie set – are they still filming, by the way?"

"Yes. They flew someone in yesterday to replace Jack. They'll have to reshoot the scenes that he was in."

"Okay, I want you to find out all the gossip you can about Jack. Talk to the crew, talk to the other extras, and try to find out if Jack was seeing someone else. I know that your feelings could get hurt, Amy, but Sergeant Tremaine suspects both of us, so if we find out who really killed Jack, we'll be off the hook.

Amy nodded her head eagerly. "That's a really good idea. But what should I do with the rest of Jack's clothes?"

I paused. The clothes were pretty important evidence. I didn't want to rat Amy out to the police, but I was afraid to hold back something as crucial as Jack's whereabouts on the day of his murder.

"Look, I think that it would be a good idea if you told Sergeant Tremaine about last Thursday," I said. She looked frightened and shook her head no. "Now, wait a minute, Amy. Just hear me out. Tremaine has to find out where Jack was the day he died, right? He's not going to rest until he's got Jack's whole day figured out. He's bound to find out that Jack was here sooner or later, and if you hold out on him, it's going to make you look guilty. You don't want that, do you?"

Amy shook her head, looking worried. "You're probably right, I should tell him, but the sergeant's so scary. I'm afraid to talk to him. Please, can you be here when I tell him?"

She stared imploringly into my face, and I did a mental eye roll. I'd never seen anyone look so helpless before. What the hell, I'd help Amy if she told Tremaine the truth. The closer the sergeant got to finding the killer, the better off I'd be.

"Sure, I can do that for you," I said. "I know that he'll appreciate your help, and it'll look better if you volunteer the information."

"You're right. Can we call him right now and get it over with?"

And that's how I ended up having a three-way conversation with the last woman to ever sleep with my ex-husband, and the cop investigating his death. Actually, the conversation between Tremaine and Amy was pretty amazing to watch. When she had been alone with me, Amy had radiated a helpless, child-like quality. With Tremaine, that quality somehow amplified itself into full-blown, pheromone-rattling sex appeal. Amy was like a real-life Jessica Rabbit. When Tremaine arrived, she somehow managed to squeeze him onto the bench beside her. She was so close to him that he had to keep his elbows down while taking notes to avoid jabbing her in the ribs. It was amusing to watch him trying to maintain a professional demeanour with Amy being so openly seductive.

"I guess I got confused as to which day you were talking about when you dropped by before, Sergeant Tremaine," she was saying. "But then Anna came over for a manicure, and we started talking about Jack. I told her that Jack was here with me on the afternoon he died. She thought that it was really important to tell you. Jack was a sweet, dear man, and I would do anything to help you catch the person who killed him." She stared up into his eyes like he was the woodsman come to save her from the big, bad wolf. Tremaine glanced down into her upturned face; at that angle, it would have been impossible for him to miss the magnificent cleavage so amply displayed by her low-cut t-shirt.

"Very admirable, Ms. Bright," he said, a little smile playing at his lips.

"Please call me Amy, Sergeant."

"Of course. Now you mentioned that you have some of Mr. Nolan's clothing?"

"Yes, sir, I put it in a bag for you." She turned and picked up a plastic grocery bag containing the clothes that had escaped the fire. "Here it is."

"Ms. Nolan," Tremaine said, turning to me, "Ms. Bright claims that your ex-husband was wearing a diamond and ruby ring when he left here last Thursday. Are you certain that Mr. Nolan was not wearing that ring when you discovered his body?" He waited for my answer, the smile completely gone from his face now.

"Yes, I'm sure that he wasn't wearing the ring."

"And from Ms. Bright's description, you believe that it was the same ring you gave Mr. Nolan on the night before your wedding?"

"Yes, Sergeant."

"Very interesting. Ladies, thank you for your help. I'll take the clothing with me and have it checked by forensics, although I doubt we'll find anything since Ms. Bright laundered the clothes. By the way, would you mind dropping by the station tomorrow, Ms. Bright, to provide us with your fingerprints? It would help the investigation."

"I'd be happy to do that for you," she said, practically crawling into his lap.

"Thank you," he said, scrambling to his feet and tucking the notebook into his jacket. Amy got up, too, and leaned in toward him.

"Ms. Nolan, are you leaving now?"

I glanced at my watch. It was going on nine. "Yes, it's getting late."

"Let me give you and Wendy a lift home."

"That's not necessary. It's only a five-block walk."

"But it's getting dark. I wouldn't feel comfortable letting you walk home alone in the dark."

"It's very kind of you to be concerned, but Wendy and I could use the walk."

"Let me walk you home then. I'd be glad of the exercise, too."

"Poor guy," I thought, "maybe he's afraid that he won't be able to get away from Amy if I leave him alone with her." I accepted his offer and rose to my feet. Tremaine turned back to Amy and extended his hand to her.

"Thank you again for the information, Ms. Bright. I'll look forward to seeing you at the station tomorrow. Shall we say at 9 a.m.?"

"I will if you promise to call me Amy," she said, holding onto his hand.

"Amy it is, then," he said with a smile. "See you tomorrow."

"Night-night, Sergeant," she said, beaming. Obviously, she was over her fear of Tremaine. I could feel the heat she was generating from where I was standing. How on earth was she doing that? I shrugged. It was none of my business what went on between the two of them.

"Coming?" Tremaine asked, glancing at me. I smiled, and Wendy and I followed him across the lawn to the gate. I turned to wave goodbye to Amy, and she gave me a "thumbs-up" gesture. I nodded before following Tremaine down the driveway and out onto the sidewalk.

The evening air had cooled and I wanted to zip up my jacket. "Would you mind taking Wendy for a moment?" I asked. He nodded and I handed him the leash. When I straightened up from fastening my jacket, he began walking away before I could take the leash back. Wendy trotted contentedly beside him while I hurried to keep pace with his long legs.

"How long have you known Ms. Bright, Anna?" he asked.

"Amy was already living here when I moved into town. We speak to each other on occasion."

"And why did you visit her tonight?"

"To be frank, there was talk around town that she had been seeing Jack. I wanted to find out if it was true, and how well Amy knew him." I thought that my honesty would disarm him, but he didn't even blink.

"Why?"

"If I'm going to walk with you, you're going to have to slow down," I said, starting to puff a little.

"Sorry," he said, shortening his pace, "I do that to people. So, why did you want to find out how well Ms. Bright knew your husband?"

I decided to try for a more even footing with Tremaine by appealing to his human side. "Come on, Sergeant. If it had been your ex-wife who was murdered and you were the prime suspect, wouldn't you want to find out everything you could?"

He stopped and turned to face me, his expression sober. "Anna, let me remind you that this is an official police investigation. Prying into the case could land you in serious trouble. Please, stay out of it. Have a little faith in my abilities. I'll find out who did it. The Mounties always get their man – or woman. Haven't you heard that?"

"That sounds promising. Do you have any other suspects?" I asked, staring into his eyes. He blinked first. I shook my head and took Wendy's leash from him, setting off again.

"I'm following various lines of inquiry," he said.

"Amy Bright being one of them? You don't seriously think Amy did it, do you?"

"I don't know."

I ignored his reticence. "I had my first real conversation with her today, and I don't believe that Amy is a murderer. She's too nice, for one thing, and besides, I don't think she has the brains to do it. If Amy had killed Jack, the police would have found her standing over his body with a smoking gun."

"Instead of finding you," he replied with a blank face.

"Ah, but with no murder weapon, and I had an alibi, or most of one," I countered.

Tremaine said, "It doesn't take much of a brain to shoot a man and dump his body beside the road, Anna. It could have been sheer coincidence that you and your dog found Mr. Nolan."

"What's Amy's motive?" I asked. He didn't answer, and I glanced sideways at him. Tremaine's expression was contemplative as he strode along beside me, his shoulders hunched and his hands in his pockets.

"Are you cold?" I asked.

He shrugged. "The temperature changes quickly here in the Foothills."

"With the amount of heat Amy was generating, I'd have thought you'd have stayed warm for a long time to come."

He grinned at me. It transformed his face, making him look younger and a whole lot more approachable.

"You noticed that, did you?"

"Are you kidding? How old are you, by the way?" The words were out of my mouth before I thought better of them. Holy smokes, would he think that I was flirting with him?

"Old enough to know better," he said. I snorted, relaxing a little. "Thirty-one. And you're forty."

I nodded. "Forty with a grown son."

"Ben," he said, his face turning serious again. He looked away, and suddenly I felt afraid.

"Ben has an alibi," I said.

"A partial alibi. He and his girlfriend met at the theatre at seven fifteen. He doesn't have an alibi from six to seven. Remember, the coroner set the time of death between six and nine."

I swallowed because my mouth had suddenly gone bone dry. "Ben didn't tell me that he only has a partial alibi. Where does he say he was between six and seven?"

"Running errands. He said that he stopped at the chemist's for some toothpaste and dropped off a book at the library. Tossed the book down the return chute and threw out the chemist's receipt, so he doesn't have any proof. He said that he'll try to find the clerk who waited on him at the store – when he has the time."

My breath came more quickly. "Maybe if I talked to him, he'd be a little more cooperative."

"I don't think that's necessary. After he made that comment, I impressed upon him the importance of coming up with a complete alibi."

"I'm sure he will. I'm sorry if the two of you got off on the wrong foot." It was obvious that Tremaine's questions had alienated Ben, and that my son wasn't going out of his way to be helpful. That kind of attitude would hurt Ben in the end.

"I hope so," Tremaine said. "He certainly didn't hide the fact that he didn't like his father very much."

We had reached the end of my driveway. I turned to face him, forcing Wendy to sit at my feet.

"He didn't do it, Tremaine," I said. He didn't respond, and his eyes were guarded. I took hold of the end of his sleeve and gave it a little shake. "He didn't do it, Tremaine," I repeated. "I'll prove it."

I saw a flicker of concern in his eyes. "No, Anna," he said. "No playing amateur detective. I don't want the murderer to see you as any kind of a threat. Remember your son and stay out of this – please." His hand twitched, and he shoved it into his pocket.

My mouth stretched into a tight little smile. "You said that I'm your prime suspect, remember? What murderer are you talking about?"

He frowned. "I can't discount anyone at this stage, including you and your son. That doesn't mean that I'm not concerned about your safety."

"Of course. You're just doing your job. No problem. You don't have to worry about us. But, it's chilly and I'm going inside now. See you around, Tremaine."

I pulled Wendy to her feet, and we went inside the house and shut the door. I snapped the leash off her collar and thought about Ben as I headed into my bedroom. Why hadn't he told me about the big hole in his alibi? I looked out the window and saw Tremaine still standing in the driveway. Our eyes met, and he turned and walked away.

I had changed out of my clothes when there was a knock at the door. I threw a robe over my pyjamas and hurried to answer it.

"Steve, what are you doing here?" I asked, surprised to see him. He was in uniform, and I looked past him to see his cruiser in the driveway. "What's wrong?"

"I heard that Tremaine got called out to meet with you and Amy Bright tonight. I came over to see if everything went okay. Are you all right?" I looked into his worried eyes and saw something that I hadn't seen in years.

"Uh, yes, I'm fine. Thanks. Why don't we sit out on the porch?" I didn't want him inside my house. I liked Steve, but he was still a kid and I didn't have time for any of his delusions.

"Sure, if it's not too cold for you," he said, taking a seat on the bench. Remaining on my feet, I leaned against the wall and folded my arms over my chest.

"Nope. I'm surprised that you didn't pass Tremaine on the way over, by the way. He left here on foot about five minutes ago."

"I came in from out of town," he replied. My porch light wasn't on and his face was in shadow. "So, what's going on with Amy Bright?"

"I just found out tonight that she was with Jack on the afternoon he was killed."

"Huh," was his only comment.

"Yes, but I don't think she had anything to do with his death. Do you know her?"

"I know who she is, but I've never spoken to her. She has that hairdresser business – right?"

"Yeah. She seems like a nice person."

"What did Tremaine have to say?"

"I think he's a little more sceptical than I am." I thought about our conversation concerning Ben's partial alibi. "He's a little more sceptical than everybody, in fact."

"He should be. He has to be."

"Uh huh," I said, taking a seat beside him. I crossed my arms again and my shoulder nudged up against his. It was a small bench. We sat together quietly in the dark, staring out across the lawn. The open front door let out a pool of warm light, and I could hear Wendy snuffling at the screen.

"I shouldn't be here," Steve said. "I shouldn't be talking to you about the investigation."

"I didn't think so," I said. "It's kind of you to worry about me, Steve, but I don't want you to get into trouble with Tremaine. I don't want any of my friends to get into trouble over this investigation, and especially not with Tremaine."

"What do you mean?"

"Well, he's sharp, isn't he? And intimidating. I don't think anything gets past those eyes of his. He's not like you boys."

Steve's eyes were suddenly cool as he turned to look at me. "He's a notch above the local police, you mean?"

"More experienced, I would say." Suddenly, I felt flustered. "Well, he can hardly help it, can he? He gets sent out on those big homicide cases."

"Not like us local hicks."

"Come on, Steve, I didn't say that."

"He's only three years older than me, you know."

"What?"

Steve jumped to his feet. "I've got to get going. I'm sure there's something important I should be doing, like handing out speeding tickets or arresting someone for drunk and disorderly. See you around. Good luck with Tremaine."

"Steve, don't be like that!" I called after him as he climbed into his cruiser and reversed down my driveway. I watched his tail lights disappear as he sped away toward town.

What had gotten into him? It wasn't like Steve to be so touchy. I shook my head and shrugged. He'd get over it in time, I guessed. And there was an upside to our little spat. Now I didn't have to worry about letting him down easy.

10

At work the next day, I was back to worrying about Ben and his alibi. Had he really been running errands between six and seven, or was he hiding something from Tremaine? My hand went to the telephone two or three times, but it was a dumb idea to call Ben. He was at work and he couldn't talk freely in front of his co-workers. Besides, if I asked him flat out about his alibi, he might think I had some crazy ideas about his involvement with his father's death. Which I had, heaven help me, but he didn't need to know that. In the end, I decided to let it ride and wait for Ben and Tremaine to hash out the alibi between them.

On the ride home, I wondered if Amy would be calling today with news about Jack and his fellow actors. The trouble was, I didn't know what her shooting schedule was or if she could come up with an excuse to hang around the set and ask questions if she wasn't needed, so I had no idea when I might be hearing from her again. There was no message waiting on my voice mail when I got home. Frustrated, I took Wendy for a hike after supper. It tired me out, but didn't do anything to improve my state of mind. It was still bright when we got home, so I left Wendy inside the house and walked to the Post Office to pick up my mail. The usual stuff was waiting in my box: one bill and three grocery store fliers.

Leaving the Post Office, I walked over to Hank's Hearty Home-Cooking to see if anything had happened at that crime scene. Nothing had changed except for the removal of the orange traffic cones. I assumed that the police weren't letting Henry begin the clean-up until they had gleaned every scrap of evidence that they could find. Some of the green plastic covering the damage had torn loose in the wind and was flapping against the grey siding. It was a depressing sight, giving the impression that the investigation had been abandoned.

Henry's accusation against Frank was just plain crazy. Had Henry claimed that Frank had been driving the truck that ran into his restaurant just because the two men had never got along? The only two things they had in common was their membership in the Crane town council and their ownership of restaurants. Frank was laid-back, a survivor of the "flower-power" generation, while Henry was priggish and nervous. I knew that Henry drove Frank crazy on the town council with his resistance to change and overly-cautious attitude. For example, Frank was all for promoting Crane with Alberta Tourism to bring more business into our sleepy little town, but Henry was afraid of attracting the "wrong kind of folks." It took Frank forever to pass anything new through council with all of Henry's questions and foot-dragging, even when it was something as innocuous as a municipal garden contest. There was definitely some animosity between the two men, but Frank would never have driven a truck through Henry's restaurant. Wondering if my friend, May, whose store was right across the street from Henry's, had heard anything, I wandered over to May's Groceries and More for a chat.

May was alone that night. Her son, Gerry, had helped out in the store during the day and on alternate weekends ever since May's husband had died of an unexpected heart attack six years earlier. May lived in a snug apartment over the store while her son and his family owned a two-storey a couple of blocks away. My friend was a huge Calgary Flames hockey fan and had erected a sign with the team's trademark red "C" on the store's roof. Every time the Flames won, May lit up the sign for a whole week. That bright red light cut through blowing snow like a beacon on blustery evenings, and let me know that home and safety were not far away when I was driving back from the city.

The store interior had an old-fashioned appearance thanks to the painted green plank flooring and the original green wooden shelves that May's husband had built twenty-eight years ago. Three wide windows across the front of the building provided lots of daylight, while banks of fluorescent lights illuminated the store at night. A garish red and blue lottery machine glowed beside the cash register next to the front door. May was sitting on a stool behind the register, her slippered feet propped up on a shelf, engrossed in our next book club selection. We were working our way through the mystery classics, and this month's selection was Dorothy Sayers's *Gaudy Night*. I was a big fan of Sayers, so I didn't mind reading the book again. As a matter of fact, I had a soft-cover collection of her novels in my living room bookcase, right next to the Agatha Christies.

"Hi, May, how's it going?" I asked, crossing the narrow space between the door and the cash register. I took a moment to study her candy bar selection, and decided that a dollar-sized bar wasn't going to be big enough for tonight. Tonight I needed the $2.50-sized bar with caramel and almonds.

May looked up, her blunt-cut, grey hair swinging away from her square, rosy face. She had given up smoking six weeks ago and always had something in her mouth these days. Tonight's treat was a lime sucker.

"Hi doll, what are you doing wandering around? It's pretty chilly out there." Her button brown eyes crinkled up at the corners as she smiled at me.

"I just couldn't settle down. Too much on my mind. How's business?"

"Can't complain. Having a movie crew over in Longview sure helps bring in the tourists. DVD rentals on Viggo Mortensen's movies are way up, too."

"Oh yeah? Have you got a copy of *Hidalgo*? I've always liked that movie."

"I'll check. Chocolate and Viggo Mortensen – sounds like a great evening to me." She climbed down off her stool and hunted through the DVD collection stacked on the shelves behind the counter. Fortunately, she was tall and could reach all of them. I couldn't have reached without a stool.

"So, what have you heard lately about Henry's hit-and-run?" I asked.

"The wheels of justice grind slowly," she replied as she ran a finger over the movie case titles. She grabbed the correct DVD and turned back to me. "Frank said that the police traced all of the vehicles that he and Judy ever owned, but didn't come up with anything. Now they're combing through all the driveways and garages in town, looking for a green pick-up truck. See, the police found some green paint scraped onto one of the studs at the crime scene, so they're thinking the vehicle that did it was green."

"Makes sense," I said with a nod.

"Yeah. Erna rushed right over as soon as she heard, and we wracked our brains over who owns a green pick-up, but we couldn't come up with anyone. I have a theory, though."

"What's that?"

"I think that the hit-and-run driver isn't local."

"Really? How come?"

"Well, how do we know that it wasn't someone from Calgary, say? Henry might have blamed Frank to shift suspicion from some unsavoury part of his life that we don't know about – yet."

"Like what?"

"Like maybe Henry is involved with illicit drugs and owes money to a gang. Maybe some thug tried to rub him out."

I smiled. I couldn't think of anyone less likely to be tied up with the drug scene than Henry. "That's pretty imaginative."

"Well, who knows? Or maybe it was a woman. You know how they say 'cherchez la femme' whenever there's a murder, or an attempted murder, in this case."

"Gee, May, there's got to be a better way to kill a man than driving a truck through his restaurant."

"Yeah, but that's what we're supposed to think. Of course, anyone who did that had to be a psychopath. A psycho is probably the only kind of woman who'd be attracted to Henry in the first place."

I laughed. "Poor Henry. First this happens, and now he's got you speculating about his love life."

May tapped her nose. "Between Erna and me, we'll figure it out. It's only a matter of time."

"Maybe you two should open your own private detective business. You could run it out of the store."

"Well, if I ever retire, I may just do that." I handed May a $10 bill and she handed me back my change.

"Thanks for the news, May. I feel a lot better now."

"That's good. A little juicy gossip always cheers me up. Enjoy your evening."

"You, too," I said before heading out the door for home.

11

I didn't hear anything from Amy until the following night. I was putting a load of laundry into the dryer around nine thirty when the doorbell rang. Wendy padded down the hallway to meet me at the front of the house so that we could check out our visitor together. I turned on the outside light and opened the door to find a woman standing there wearing big, black sunglasses, a head scarf, and a trench coat.

"Can I help you?" I asked, wondering who would be wearing sunglasses at night.

"Anna, it's me – Amy," she giggled, whipping the glasses off.

"Wow. I didn't recognize you. What are you doing in that get-up? Come on in," I said. "Can I take your coat?"

"No thanks. I'm cold, and I'm not wearing much underneath."

I didn't want to hear any more about that, so I didn't respond as I led her into the living room. I indicated the couch and turned on a lamp while she sat down. She took off the head scarf and released her golden auburn hair.

"I like your living room, Anna. It's very soothing," Amy said, getting comfortable. My decorating taste ran to a minimalist style with stream-lined furniture and very little clutter. A couple of large, pewter-framed pictures of poppies gave the room a splash of colour. "The grey and white on your walls is real pretty. I have a lot of chintzes and prints in my place because I like my house to feel cozy, but I like the cool tones in this room, too."

"Thanks." Curiosity getting the better of me, I asked, "Amy, why are you dressed like a 1950's movie star?"

"I'm in disguise. I left my car at home and walked over so that no one would recognize it outside your house. I figure that we can't be too careful with a murder investigation."

"I guess you're right," I said, sitting down on my white faux-leather recliner. "So, did you hear any gossip about Jack on the set?"

"I sure did. I was talking to the make-up lady – her name is Patty – and she was very helpful. She said that Jack had been very attentive to the movie's leading lady, Karen Quill. She said that Karen was bawling her eyes out in make-up the day after Jack died, and had to take a pill and go lie down in her trailer."

The name tweaked a dim memory. "Karen Quill – she's a Canadian actress, right?"

"I think so."

"What does she look like?"

"She's real pretty, about 5'3", late twenties, blond hair with ash streaks. Her eyes are a gorgeous violet colour, but I think she wears coloured contacts."

The description solidified my memory. "Yes, I remember Karen. She and Jack did a play together in Ottawa about seven years ago. I had my suspicions about them even then."

"Wow, do you think she and Jack had a history of – you know?"

"Yes I do. Did the make-up lady have anything else to say about Karen?"

"Uh huh. She told me that Karen's husband is one of our cameramen – Connie Primo."

"Connie?" I asked, confused. "Are they a lesbian couple?"

"No, that's 'Connie,' short for 'Constantine.' He's Greek. Anyway, Connie and Karen have been married about four years, and he's the jealous type. Seems to have a real temper, too. Patty said she's heard Connie yelling at Karen in her trailer."

"Interesting," I responded. "Did your make-up lady say Jack was seeing anyone else?"

"She did mention a stuntwoman – Jessie Wick – but she said that Jack and Jessie were an item years ago on another movie he did in Longview. She didn't think there was anything going on between them now."

I cringed. Jessie Wick – I hadn't forgotten that name. Four years ago, Jack and I had separated because he was having an affair with Jessie. I had never met her and hadn't wanted to know anything about her, at the time.

"Are you okay, Anna? You look kind of pale all of a sudden," Amy said.

I looked at her and shrugged; that was water under the bridge. "I'm okay. Their affair happened while I was still with Jack, that's all. It's not anything I didn't know about."

"I'm sorry," Amy said, getting up to put an arm around my shoulders.

"Don't worry about it. You did really well getting that information about Jack. Did Patty mention anyone else?"

"No, that's it. Of course, you already know about Jack and me. So, what do you think?"

I thought that Amy was pretty clueless to remind me about her and Jack, but out loud I said, "I think that Karen sounds like our best bet. Maybe we could go talk with Karen – find out what her relationship was like with Jack and if her husband knew about it." Amy nodded. "So, where can we find Karen? Is she staying at the Creekside Motel and Spa?"

"No, she and Connie rented a house on some acreage outside of Longview. I'm sorry, I don't know the address."

"Never mind. Where does the movie crowd hang out these days when they're not working?"

"A lot of them like the Silver Spur. We could try going there tomorrow night. It's always popular on Fridays."

The Silver Spur was a Longview bar decorated to look like an old-time Western saloon. The storefront had a facade of timber logs and a railed wooden porch complete with hitching post, no doubt for folks who rode their horses into town and wanted to drop by for a drink. The inside was furnished with rustic tables and chairs, a massive wooden chandelier with electric candles, and a bar with a brass foot rail. The back room had a couple of pool tables and some electronic gambling machines, a concession to modern times. May and Erna had taken me there for a drink a couple of years back. It wasn't my cup of tea, but it was good for the tourist trade.

"The Spur, eh? Why don't I pick you up around eight thirty tomorrow night and we'll drive over to the Spur to see if Karen is there. Are you free?" I asked.

"Sure. I don't make appointments for Friday nights. What do you think we should wear?"

"Oh, I guess I'll dust off my Stetson and chaps."

"Really? You have chaps?"

"No, Amy, I'm just kidding. I'll probably wear jeans and boots. We'll want to blend in with the Friday night crowd."

"Okay, I'll wear the same thing. This is so exciting. I'm really looking forward to it. We'll be just like the women cops on that old TV show, *Cagney and Lacey*."

"You bet," I said, smiling at her enthusiasm. I led her to the door and smiled again as she carefully looked from side to side before donning her sunglasses.

"See you tomorrow," she said over her shoulder before slipping out into the night.

"Bye Amy," I responded, shaking my head as I shut the door behind her.

12

I was sitting at my desk the next morning when the telephone rang.

"Kinesiology Department, Anna Nolan," I chirped.

"Hi Anna. It's Charles Tremaine."

I hadn't expected to hear his voice and was silent for a moment. "Are you there?" he asked.

"Yes. Hi Sergeant," I said, fearful of what he had to say.

"I have a message for you from the coroner's office. They said they're ready to release your ex-husband's body to you."

"Oh," was all I could say. I had given some thought to funeral arrangements after I had discovered Jack's body, but it had been driven right out of my mind by everything that had happened since then. Jack's father was gone and his mother was back in Ontario in a seniors' assisted-living facility. Aside from her, Jack had no close family other than Ben and me.

"Normally a funeral parlour would take care of this for you. Have you contacted anyone?"

"Actually, Sergeant, I haven't. I know that I should have taken care of this already, but I guess I dropped the ball."

"Don't worry about it. I talked with some of the constables before I called you, and they recommended Fergusons in southern Calgary. Do you know them?"

"Yes, I've been to one of their services. They're fine. Sorry, let me give them a call and I'll take care of it."

Tremaine had their phone number ready and gave it to me. "Will you be holding a church service?" he asked.

"Yes, I'd like to have a funeral at St. Bernadette's in Crane, but I haven't spoken to Father Winfield yet. Jack has a mother whose health isn't very good. I thought about having Jack cremated and flying his ashes back to Ontario so that she can bury him in the family plot."

"Sounds like a good plan. It's kind of you. Not everyone in your shoes would bother to do it."

"There's no one else to do it, but thank you. I'll make a call and take care of it. Thanks for your help, Tremaine. I appreciate it."

"You're welcome, Anna. Bye."

"Bye." I hung up the phone and mused about the sergeant for a moment. He had been very considerate on the phone just now. Was there a nice guy underneath that cool exterior, or was he after something? I tucked that thought away while I looked up Jack's mother in my address book. Carlene had always been kind to me, and I still sent her birthday and Christmas cards every year. I had broken the news of Jack's death to her on the phone a few days ago, and it had been a heart-wrenching experience. She had cried and said that she couldn't understand why anyone would murder her son and then dump his body alongside the road, of all places, and I was unable to comfort her with a reasonable explanation. She was calmer when I phoned her today, and grateful that I was sending her son's ashes home. I felt very sad saying goodbye to this poor woman who had lost both husband and son in the course of her lifetime.

I made two more calls: first to Ferguson's to arrange for the cremation, and then to Father Winfield about the mass. I hadn't talked to him about Jack's death yet, although I assumed that he knew about it. He told me that he could perform the funeral the following Tuesday.

"The sermon will be a bit sparse. I met your ex-husband when you and your family first moved to Crane, but I didn't see much of him after that."

"No, he wasn't much of a church-goer. I don't expect you to say very much about him under the circumstances."

"Don't worry, Anna. I have a stock sermon for this kind of situation. Ben will be coming, I assume?"

"I sure hope so. He was pretty upset with his father before Jack died, so I'm not sure he'll want to attend the funeral."

"That's unfortunate, and hard on you. I hope to have a chance to talk with Ben after mass, if he comes. Will anyone else be attending, do you think?"

"Well, Father, there really isn't anyone else. I don't want to invite the people from the movie set. They didn't work with Jack for very long, and I don't want them to come out of a sense of obligation. Jack's mother isn't well enough to travel, and he has no other family. The people here in Crane didn't really know Jack, either. It might be just you and me, Father, unless Ben decides to come. I'm sorry to ask you to do this just for me, but I want to have a mass said for Jack. It wouldn't be right to cremate him without praying over him. I hope you understand."

"I understand and I totally agree with you. Remember the parable of the shepherd who leaves his flock to go in search of a single lamb? Each of us is important in God's eyes."

"Thanks for understanding. I'll have Ferguson's contact you about Jack's ashes, and I'll see you on Tuesday at ten."

Ben came for supper that Friday night, as usual. I had stopped at an Indian restaurant for take-out curry before leaving Calgary, so it took me a little longer to get home. Ben was already playing with Wendy in the backyard when I came in the door.

"Hi honey, how are you?" I called, opening the sliding door onto the deck. Ben tossed a rubber ball to Wendy and turned to look at me. He seemed relaxed and in a good mood.

"I'm starving. What's for supper?"

"Indian tonight, plus I've got some peanut-butter cup ice cream in the freezer for dessert."

"Great, my favourite. We'll be right in. Come on, Wendy."

"You feed her and I'll set the table."

We both avoided the subject of the murder while we ate dinner, and I didn't mention the funeral until after dessert. Ben stared down at the table as I gave him the details, not saying a word until I was through.

"I know where this is going, Mom."

"Where, honey?"

"You're going to ask me to come to the funeral."

"I'd appreciate it if you thought you could." Ben didn't say anything, and I sighed. "I know how you feel about your father, Ben, and how his murder must complicate things."

"You'd be wrong about that. Just because he got himself killed doesn't make him a better father."

"No, it doesn't. And I know that it was really hard all those years that he wasn't there for you. I'm not going to give you a sermon on how much he really loved you, but I'm hoping that one day you'll begin to remember the good times you had with your dad. Like the time he took you camping, or your sixth birthday party when he got your TV hero, Captain Eddy, to stop by. How about if I play the guilt card and ask you to come so that it won't be just Father Winfield and me at the funeral? He wants to talk to you, by the way."

Ben sighed. "Oh great. Pastoral counselling."

"Yes. Anyway, give it some thought, and I guess if I see you at the funeral, I'll see you."

"I'll think about it, but I'm not promising anything."

"Fair enough. So, did you see your new girlfriend this week?" He rolled his eyes, and we went back to chatting about less controversial subjects.

13

Ben left at eight fifteen for a date with his girlfriend back in Calgary. I picked up Amy a few minutes later and we drove to Longview, arriving at the Spur by a quarter to nine. All of the parking spots were taken in front of the bar, so we were forced to park a little way down the street.

Amy and I strode down the sidewalk beneath a purple-tinged sky, the clamour of people having a good time spilling out of the bar up ahead. We climbed the two steps onto the split-rail porch and pushed through the swinging doors, pausing to take a look around. The place was packed and all of the tables were full. There were small brass lamps sitting on the wooden tables, and the flickering light cast a warm, honey glow over the scene.

Amy grabbed my arm. "There she is, sitting by herself at that table for two," she said, nodding toward the actress. "Come on, I'll introduce you."

We had discussed the best way to approach Karen on the drive over, and decided that we should play upon our common bond with Jack. He had been gone for a week, now, and if Karen was feeling sentimental, she might enjoy an opportunity to reminisce about him with us.

Amy halted beside Karen's table and beamed down at her. "Hi Karen, remember me? I'm Amy Bright, one of the extras on the movie. I was in the bank robbery scene they shot yesterday."

Karen, her silky blond hair skimming her shoulders, squinted up at Amy. "Oh, right – I remember you. You were 'frightened mother with little boy' who got shoved out of the way by the gunman. How's it going, Amy?"

"Just great, thanks. This is a friend of mine, Anna Nolan. Her name might sound familiar to you. She's Jack Nolan's widow. She was feeling kind of blue tonight, what with Jack gone such a short time and all, so I invited her out for a drink. The tables are pretty full – do you mind if we join you?"

Karen eyed my face for a moment. We had met at a cast party years ago, but I doubted that she remembered me. She had taken good care of herself, I noticed, although there was a certain hardness around her eyes that hadn't been there before. She was an attractive woman, and I wondered why she was sitting alone.

"Sure, pull up a chair. My husband, Connie, is out back shooting pool with some of the guys. I've been saving a seat for him, but it doesn't look as if he'll be back anytime soon."

I nodded my thanks, borrowed a chair from the table behind me, and sat down with Karen and Amy.

"So, you're Jack Nolan's widow?" Karen asked.

"Not exactly. Jack and I divorced four years ago."

"That's what I thought. Jack told me that he was divorced."

I studied her, wondering what she meant by that comment, and in the ensuing silence a waiter hustled over to our table. He was young, maybe a little older than Ben, and wore the bar uniform: a white shirt with garters to hold back his sleeves, black pants, and a full-length white apron. His hair was parted straight down the middle and slicked back. The waiters' costumes were less revealing than the waitresses', who wore low-cut, off the shoulder gingham blouses, flouncy short skirts, and frilly aprons.

"Welcome to the Silver Spur. What can I get you, little ladies?" he asked.

Amy studied him with delight, as if she were just about ready to gobble him up. Apparently young men were fair game to her. "Well, look at you," she said to our waiter. "Don't you look handsome in your uniform. Doesn't he look adorable, Anna?"

I smiled at the young man, who was entranced by Amy's cleavage and didn't bother to look my way. "Very handsome," I answered.

"I hear that you have a special ladies drink at the Spur – what's it called again?" Amy asked.

"It's called a 'Lady Killer,' ma'am," he replied with a grin.

"That sounds like fun. I'll have one of those, please. What are you going to have, Anna?"

"I'll have a white wine spritzer and maybe some chicken wings, if you've got them."

The waiter dragged his eyes away from Amy to look at me. "Sure do. We have mild, medium, hot, and 'Somebody grab a bucket of water – my mouth is on fire!' zesty," he drawled. "What will you have, little lady?"

I smiled, appreciating his effort to stay in character. "We'll have two pounds of the medium wings for the table. Thanks."

The waiter left, and Amy began chatting about the movie. Karen wasn't paying much attention to us, her chin cradled in her hand and her eyes gazing about the room. I decided that it was time to engage our leading lady in conversation.

"Karen, you look very familiar to me," I said with a phony frown. "I'm sure that Jack introduced us at a cast party for *A Christmas Carol* a few years back. Didn't you play the Ghost of Christmas Past in that?"

Karen's eyes swivelled back to me. "That's right. Boy, that seems like ages ago. I wasn't even married then."

"I remember how good Jack thought you were in the part. He said that you had a lovely, ephemeral quality that added a supernatural element to your characterization." I thought that flattery was the best way to win Karen over, but I didn't want to lay it on too thick.

"Did he really?" Karen said, her eyes lighting up.

"Oh yes. He said that when you were on stage, the audience couldn't take their eyes off you, and that it was an uphill battle to get their attention during your scenes together."

"Did he say that? How kind of Jack – he always was so supportive of his fellow actors," Karen said with a gracious smile, lapping up the compliments.

The waiter returned with our drinks. Amy's Lady Killer was some sort of tri-coloured, layered affair with cream floating on top. "Ooh, that looks yummy," she squealed.

"It sure does. Karen, let me buy you a drink. Would you like one of those?" I asked.

Karen snickered. "No thanks, that thing looks like it has about a thousand calories in it."

"Oh, come on, you don't have to worry about your figure. I bet you work out all the time. You're so toned," I replied.

Karen glanced down at herself. She had on a t-shirt that proclaimed "Actresses do it onstage." "Thanks, I have a portable gym I take everywhere."

Amy sipped her drink while the waiter clicked his pen and waited. "Wow, this is so delicious," she said.

"It sure looks good. I'll have one if you have one, Karen," I said.

"Well, why not? Just one won't hurt, I guess. Let's live a little!"

"That's the spirit! Two Lady Killers, my good man," I said with a flourish.

"Coming right up, little ladies."

An hour later I was still nursing my drink while Karen and Amy had moved on to vodka cocktails. Karen's eyes had become glassy, while Amy couldn't stop giggling. We were acting as if we were the best of friends, just three women letting down our hair and enjoying a night out on the town.

"Have a chicken wing," I said, pushing the plate toward Karen.

"Thanks," she said, helping herself to her fifth and biting hungrily into the meat. Diet forgotten, she tossed the well-chewed bone over her shoulder and reached for another. The bone bounced off the shoulder of a middle-aged man sitting at the table behind us, who started and turned around to stare at Karen.

"Sorry," I mouthed at him. The man shrugged good-naturedly and turned back to his friends. "Girls, I have something I want to say about Jack," I said. Karen and Amy blearily tried to focus on me. "Don't get me wrong – Jack and I had our problems – but I really miss him. He was one hell of a man." I lowered my voice and leaned in closer, drawing them in. "Actually, I think that he was just a little too much man for me, to be completely honest. You know what I mean." I wiggled my eyebrows. "It was probably best that we parted, but I'll always love him."

"You're right," Karen said. She put her face so close to mine that I could smell the seasoning from her chicken wings on her breath. "He was a real 'man's man,' you know, but he sure knew how to take care of the ladies." She winked and leaned back in her chair. "Not like the little wiener I married. Ha, 'wiener!' That's the perfect word to describe him." She nudged my arm and wiggled her eyebrows at Amy, who giggled some more.

"I don't think I've met your husband, Karen. Have you met him, Amy?"

"Uh huh, he was shooting our scene yesterday."

"Yeah, that's right," Karen agreed. "He's always with the second-string crew, shooting the crowd scenes with the extras. Connie's problem is that he's a big gorilla. He hasn't got an artistic bone in his body. He can't handle the scenes with the tender emotional parts – you understand? Passion? Romance? He's no good with them. Just like in real life, come to think of it. The ape thinks he owns me. If I'm not ready for him on a second's notice, he gets angry. What a shithead."

"But Jack wasn't like that," I prompted, trying to drag her back to the subject.

"Jack? Hell no, that man was smooth – and sexy. He could get me revved up in no time and keep things simmering all afternoon. And sometimes into the evening, too." She winked at me. I smiled back. Oh yeah, I just loved hearing all about her sex life with my ex-husband.

"I guess that you had to play it pretty close to the vest, spending time with Jack while your husband was working on the film?" I asked.

Karen nodded and tapped the side of her nose. It took her two tries to find it. "You know it, Anna. People around here have big mouths." She looked at Amy and said "shhh," laying her finger over her lips. Amy tried to wink back, but was having trouble closing only one eye.

"Because I guess that Connie would have been pretty jealous if he had found out about you and Jack," I prompted.

"Course he would have. He thinks he's some sort of a he-man because he's European and has some hair on his chest.

Ha! Hasn't got much left on top of his head. He's got a lousy temper, too. He tried to shove me around when we first got married, but I got even with him. I wouldn't let him bully me, no sir."

"What'd you do?" asked Amy, her eyes bright with curiosity.

Karen crooked her finger, motioning for us to come closer. We bent our heads together over the table. "I got him drunk one night and shaved his privates. He wouldn't use a men's room for weeks after that until the hair grew back in." She grinned and nodded while Amy shrieked with laughter.

"What's all this? Having fun, ladies?" a voice growled from behind us. I looked over my shoulder and saw a squat, dark, balding man with small eyes leering down at us. Amy pointed at him and laughed even harder. He shrugged, grabbed a chair from another table, and joined us.

"Who're your new friends, Karen?" he asked.

"This is Amy. She's one of the extras on the movie," Karen said, pointing to her.

"Sure, I've seen you around. Good to see you again, Amy."

"And this other lady's Anna Nolan, Jack Nolan's ex-wife."

Connie turned to look at me, the smile disappearing from his face. "Jack's ex-wife, huh? You've got my condolences, lady."

"Thank you."

"I don't mean because somebody offed him. I mean for ever having married the jerk in the first place."

I frowned at his rudeness. "Not a fan of Jack's, Connie?"

"Don't be such an asshole, Con," said his wife. "She's grieving over him."

"Watch your ugly mouth, Karen. I told you about calling me that."

"Okay, dick-head."

He leaned forward and grabbed Karen's wrist. She gave it a sharp twist and broke free, leaning back out of his reach. "Stop being so grabby. You're just showing off in front of my friends."

"Ah, shut up. You've had too many. We should be going. I have an early start tomorrow."

"Well, I'm not called until tomorrow night, and I don't feel like going just yet. It's only . . . ." She stopped to squint at her watch.

"It's 10:35," I said helpfully.

"Mind your own business," Connie said, leaning too close to me. He scowled, making his face even more unattractive, and blew beery breath in my face. I flinched and pushed my chair back an inch. He smiled, thinking that he had intimidated me.

"Oh, get lost, Connie. You're such a downer. You're no fun anymore. Just leave me and my friends alone," Karen said.

"Why, so you can have some more fun, you moron? You want the producers to hear that you were drunk in the Spur again? I told you it's time to go, so get your fat ass out of that chair and get moving."

"Fat ass!" she shrieked. She grabbed her cocktail and threw the dregs into his face.

Connie roared and jumped out of his chair. He lurched toward Karen, who leapt back out of his way, knocking over her chair.

"All right folks, that's enough. Everybody calm down, now," said an authoritative voice from behind us. I looked up to see Steve Walker standing next to our table, a pool cue held nonchalantly in his hand. He must have been playing pool in the back room all the time we had been there. I felt relieved; I didn't fancy getting into a barroom brawl. He was ignoring me, however. I hoped things weren't going to be awkward between us.

Connie glared at Steve as the young constable laid a hand upon his shoulder. "Come on, Connie, let's not have any trouble here. Who's the lady?"

Grimacing, Connie muttered, "That's my wife, Karen. I wasn't looking for any trouble. I was just trying to get her to come home with me."

Karen took a step toward the table. "What's the matter, Con, you scared of this guy?" Steve was out of uniform in his white shirt and jeans, so she had no idea that he was a cop.

"This is Constable Steve Walker, Karen. He's with the RCMP," I said.

"You mean Constable McDreamy, don't you?" she replied, leering at Steve. Connie frowned.

"Nice meeting you, Karen," Steve said. "It might be a good idea if you and Connie went home to discuss your differences in private, don't you think? A lady like you doesn't want to air her disagreements in public." He gave her a winning smile.

Karen sniffed and looked around the room, noticing the other customers staring at us for the first time. Some of them must have been fellow cast and crew members.

"You're quite right," she said, her manner changing. Now she was the grand lady. "I don't know what's got into my husband. Let's go, Con."

"That's what I've been telling you," he grumbled, trying to take her arm. She wouldn't have anything to do with him, however, and brushed him aside as she bent to retrieve her purse from the floor. Straightening unsteadily, she smiled at Amy and me.

"Ladies, thank you for a wonderful evening. I hope to see you again soon," she said before following her husband to the cashier with as much dignity as she could muster. Steve winked at me, and I flashed him a quick smile, but I didn't have time to worry about him now.

"Come on, Amy, this is our chance," I said, jumping up from my chair.

"Our chance for what?" she asked in confusion.

I whispered in her ear, "Our chance to follow them home and find out where they live. Come on, I don't want to lose them."

Amy looked worried as I pulled her to her feet. Connie had settled his tab and he and Karen were headed out the door by the time we waded through the tables to the cashier. I paid our bill and rushed Amy out onto the street after them. Karen and Connie were still bickering as they crossed the road and unlocked the doors to their late-model Jeep.

"Come on, run," I said, dragging Amy to my car.

I unlocked the passenger door, shoved her in, and had the car started and u-turned by the time Connie pulled away from the curb. I idled for a few seconds before pulling in behind them, not wanting to follow too closely. We drove down the main street and picked up speed as it became the highway, then slowed to turn right down a secondary road. We were the only two cars on the road, and I was worried that Connie might notice my headlights. Hopefully, he and Karen were too busy arguing to pay any attention to us. We continued on for about five minutes until they turned right again down a gravel road. Connie was driving too fast and fishtailed, spewing gravel behind him. He corrected the car and proceeded a little more cautiously while Amy and I slowed to follow them. They came upon a private driveway barely visible through the trees and turned in. I slowed and waited a few moments before turning in behind them. They had already disappeared around a bend when I pulled over and parked at the bottom of the driveway.

"Now what?" Amy whispered. The driveway was bordered by deep bush on both sides, blocking our view of the house. I cut the lights and turned off the engine.

"We've come this far. I want to see what they're doing. Let's leave the car here and hike up to the house."

"Do you think that's a good idea?" she asked, frowning at me. "What if they see us? How're we going to explain our being here?"

"Don't worry. It's dark and they'll have the lights on inside the house. They won't see us. I want to know what happens when they argue in private."

"You mean, does Connie hit her?"

"Right," I said, peering out the windshield.

"That's not very nice," she said.

I shrugged. "He'll hit her or not hit her whether we're here or not. Look at it this way. If he does start hitting her, we can call 911 and take off before the police arrive."

"Well, I guess that would be okay. But it's so dark. We could trip over some branches or something and really hurt ourselves. Besides, I'm not feeling very well. I'm awfully tired. I think I had a bit too much to drink." She leaned her head back against the head rest and shut her eyes.

I looked at Amy and decided that she might be more hindrance than help. "Don't worry about it, I'll go by myself," I said. "Why don't you stay in the car and have a little nap?"

"Huh?" she said, opening her eyes.

"Hold on, I've got a blanket in the trunk. I'll get it so you won't get cold." I reached for the door handle.

Amy looked around through the car windows. "I don't know. I might get scared out here all by myself."

I opened the car door and got out. "There's nothing to be afraid of. Just lock the doors and you'll be perfectly safe. Who would be walking around at this time of night, anyway?"

I popped open the trunk, grabbed the blanket I kept for emergencies, and eased the trunk shut. Climbing back into my seat, I spread the blanket over Amy, who watched me with worried eyes. I opened the glove box and retrieved my flashlight.

"Go to sleep. I'll be back before you know it." She sighed and closed her eyes, snuggling down into the blanket like a good little girl. I locked the car doors behind me and pocketed the remote control. Turning on the flashlight, I followed the beam along the twisting driveway, the trees blocking out most of the moonlight. I crept along as quietly as I could, but it was a gravel driveway and I could hear the stone crunching beneath my feet. Something scurried in the damp leaves beside me, and I jumped. I shone my flashlight into the trees, but didn't see anything.

"Must be mice or some other night life," I told myself. "Certainly nothing big enough to worry about. Whatever it is, it's probably afraid of me."

I continued up the drive, wishing that the house wasn't stuck so far back in the bush. How much further was it? Last year's brittle leaves still clung to the trees and rustled in the wind. The ground smelled damp and mouldy, and the evening chill was beginning to penetrate my clothes. I wished that I had worn a jacket. Just as I was beginning to doubt the sanity of my plan, the driveway widened out into a parking area in front of the house. The Jeep was parked there beside some sort of muscle car, sleek and low to the ground.

"Looks like Connie and Karen like their toys," I said to myself.

Lights were spilling out of the downstairs windows. Bending over and creeping between the parked cars, I could see Connie and Karen standing in the middle of the living room, Connie gesturing wildly about something while Karen held her hands over her ears. He shouted and grabbed her by the arms. Karen shoved him in the chest, and Connie tripped backward over a coffee table. He got up from the floor and rushed at her. Karen darted behind the sofa and ran around the end toward the fireplace. She grabbed the fireplace shovel and stalked back toward him, the shovel raised menacingly over her head. Connie backed away, shouting at her. He must have said something really ugly because she started chasing him around the room, swinging the shovel and trying to clobber him with it.

"Gee," I mumbled to myself, "I hope she doesn't kill him, but I sure wish that I could hear what they're saying."

"Yes, that would be convenient," a voice said right behind my left ear.

I nearly jumped out of my skin, grabbing at my chest and whirling around with the flashlight in my hand. I ended up shining it into Tremaine's face.

"You idiot, you nearly gave me a heart attack," I gasped, lowering the light. Suddenly remembering the couple in the house, I turned back and crouched down between the cars again. I peered towards the windows, but couldn't see Connie or Karen.

"Where'd they go?" I muttered.

Tremaine, who wasn't bothering to hide himself, pointed over my head. "Right there on the rug in front of the fireplace."

"What?"

I looked in that direction and saw Connie lying on top of Karen. She wasn't struggling; on the contrary, her arms and legs were clamped around him. As I watched, Connie rose up on one elbow and began fumbling with his pants, yanking them down around his knees and exposing his bare backside.

"Ew, I think I burnt my eyes!" I squawked, before clamping my hand over my mouth. I didn't want them to hear me.

"That's what you get for spying on people," Tremaine said, still behind me. "You can get up now. I don't think there's much chance of them looking out the window at the moment."

I straightened and turned to face Tremaine. His expression was severe, his arms folded over his chest. He uncrossed them and took a step toward me. At that moment, I was more afraid of him than I was of Karen and Connie.

"I have to get back to Amy," I muttered, ducking my head and trying to push past him. Instead, he grabbed my shoulder and spun me around.

"You don't have to worry about Amy. She was sound asleep when I walked past your car a few minutes ago."

"So, what are you doing here?" I asked.

"Shouldn't I be asking you that question?" he snapped. "Come along – show's over – let's get you back to your car." He turned on his own flashlight and gestured for me to precede him. Once we were past the cars, he paced down the driveway beside me, looking grim.

"How did you know I was here?" I risked asking with a sidelong glance.

"Steve Walker called after you followed Karen and Connie out of the Silver Spur 'as if your pants were on fire,' as he so colourfully put it. He was afraid that you and Amy might be up to something, so he asked me to check on the Primos. I'd already interviewed them at home, so I knew where they lived. What did you expect to gain by following them here, Anna?"

I glanced at him, thinking fast. "If you must know, I was afraid that Connie might hurt Karen once he got her home. He was acting very aggressively at the bar, and they were both drunk. I followed them to check up on her."

"I see. And what were you going to do if he started beating her?"

"Call 911."

I tripped over a stone and Tremaine grabbed my elbow to steady me. I was too busy keeping up with him and trying to gauge his reaction to my lies to watch where I was going.

"And what were you and Amy doing talking to the Primos in the first place?"

"Oh, the Spur is an old haunt of mine. Amy and I hit it off the other night, so she invited me out for a drink. We bumped into Karen at the bar, and Amy introduced us. The tables were really crowded, so we joined her."

"That's odd. Constable Walker is a regular at the Spur and he said he's never seen you there before."

"Uh, that must be because he's always in the back playing pool." Suddenly, Tremaine swung me around and started pulling me back toward the house. "What are you doing?" I sputtered, stumbling after him.

"I'm taking you back to the Primos to see if they want to press trespassing charges."

"Hey, wait a minute," I protested, ineffectively digging my heels into the gravel. "Let's not be rash."

Tremaine dragged me along beside him. "Anna, you just told me a pack of lies. If you won't tell me the truth, the least I can do is keep you out of harm's way by putting you in jail for a day or two. Maybe that's what you need to realize how serious this situation is."

I stopped and wrenched my elbow from his grasp. "All right, all right, here's the truth," I said. "Amy heard that

Karen Quill and Jack were sleeping together, and I wanted to find out if Connie was the type to kill Jack if he found out that his wife was cheating on him." I glanced at Tremaine for his reaction. There was a steely look in his eyes that made me look away again.

"Don't you think that I already know about Jack and Karen's affair?"

My mouth gaped open. "How did you hear about it? Not from Karen, I bet."

"Anna, I am the police. I question people, and they tell me things. If I don't believe them, I keep digging until I discover the truth. That's what I'm paid to do. Why do you continue to involve yourself in this investigation when I've warned you to stay away?"

I was afraid of Tremaine at that moment, and when I'm afraid, I have a tendency to mask my feelings with aggression. I guess it's the old "fight or flight" instinct, and I'm not as fast as I used to be.

"Okay, hot shot, just because you're the police doesn't mean that I can't talk to people and look around myself, especially when it's my head that's in the noose."

"Hot shot?" he said, his lips twitching.

Okay, now he was laughing at me, which really made me mad. "Look, you told me that I'm the prime suspect in this case. Has that changed?"

He paused for a moment, his eyes becoming cautious. "No."

"Then just leave me alone. I promise if I find out anything important, I'll let you know right away. Come on, Tremaine, I could be useful to you."

Tremaine took a step closer until we stood toe-to-toe. "Anna, I want you to listen to me very carefully because I'm not going to say this again. You cannot be of any use to me in this investigation. As a matter of fact, you're a liability. I've questioned the Primos, who have been cooperative up until now, and I'm corroborating their alibi. What I don't need is your ham-fisted interference spooking them and ruining their cooperation. Now, I do not want to see or hear of you trying to interview suspects, spy on people, or anything else that you can come up with, do you hear? I swear that if I find you doing anything illegal, I'll haul you away to prison before you know what happened. Have I made myself perfectly clear?" He grabbed me by the shoulders and gave me a shake to emphasize his point.

I'm not proud of my reaction that night – okay, secretly I am. I swung back my foot and kicked him as hard as I could in the shin. As he hopped around on one leg, cursing, I shouted, "Don't you ever touch me again! How dare you threaten me! What kind of a cop are you, anyway? Haven't you ever heard of police brutality? I swear I'll make a complaint to the top RCMP guy if you ever touch me again. Just leave me alone!"

My voice cracked on the last bit and I ran back to the car. Tremaine had parked in front of me, blocking the driveway leading up to the house. I aimed the remote at my car, flung the door open, and jumped in, slamming it shut behind me. Amy woke with a start. I turned the engine over, jammed the stick shift into reverse, and spun the car around. Tears I couldn't stop began to spill out of my eyes as I turned onto the side road and headed, much too quickly, back to town.

"Anna, what's wrong?" Amy asked, huddling on her side of the car. "Are you okay? Did you get caught?"

"Nothing's wrong and I didn't get caught – by the Primos, anyway. I just bumped into Tremaine. The nerve of the man. He makes me so mad! Just give me a minute to calm down." I reached the main road and began taking deep, relaxing breaths. Amy stopped watching me to stare out of her window. By the time we were a few miles outside of Crane, I had stopped shaking and started thinking. Something Karen had said at the bar had caught my attention.

Amy glanced at me. "Do you feel better now?"

"Yes, thanks. Sorry if I scared you," I muttered.

"Was Sergeant Tremaine mad at you for spying on the Primos?"

"Yes, but never mind him. I've been thinking of a plan, and I'm not going to let that bully stop me. We made a good start tonight, Amy, but we didn't get enough information out of Karen. I want to know what she and Connie were doing on the night Jack was killed. Now, Connie said he's working tomorrow, so he won't be home. Karen said she isn't called until tomorrow night – right? So why not try a two-pronged attack? Why not drive back to their house in the morning, too early for Karen to have gone anywhere, but late enough for Connie to have left for work. You can ask her to go shopping with you – how about the Saturday market? While she's getting ready to go, you slip me into the house. Then you can pump Karen for information while you're out shopping." I glanced at her. "What do you think?"

Amy frowned and bit her lip. "I guess I could try, but what will you be doing in the house while Karen and I are gone?"

"I'll be looking for the gun that killed Jack." Amy gasped. "Come on, how can it fail? No one will be home. I'll have lots of time to look around. Believe me, I'm a pro when it comes to searching a house, thanks to Jack and his cheating. If I find a gun, the police can check it out to see if it's the murder weapon. And we know that whoever shot Jack took the ring, so if I find either the ring or the gun, we'll have conclusive evidence."

Amy shook her head. "I think we ought to leave this to the police."

"Come on, Amy, please help me," I pleaded. "I can't do it on my own. I'll be frank with you – I don't think that Tremaine suspects you of murdering Jack, but he sure suspects me. He just told me so. Please?"

Amy sighed. "Okay, I'll try," she said in a resigned voice.

"Thanks, you're the best," I gushed. Under my breath, I muttered, "Charles Tremaine, I am so going to prove you wrong!"

14

Amy picked me up on Saturday morning, and we were at the Primos' house by ten. "Okay, park where we parked last night – right there before that bend in the driveway," I instructed after we turned into their lane. "I'll get out and sneak up to the house through the bush. Give me ten minutes, and then pull up and park. I'll be hiding in the trees just to the left of the house. I'll wave when I'm ready, and you get out of the car and ring the doorbell. If everything seems okay once you're inside, open the door for me and I'll hide until you and Karen leave. How's that – am I forgetting anything?"

"It sounds fine, but I'm awfully nervous. What if Karen doesn't want to go shopping with me?" Amy asked.

"Well, if it doesn't work out, don't worry about it. We'll think of something else. And don't be nervous. Just concentrate on having fun with Karen. If you can get her to tell you where she and Connie were on the night of Jack's murder, all the better – right?"

"Okay, I'll try. I promise I won't let you down."

"Thanks Amy, I knew I could count on you. I'm going to get out now." I peered through the car windows first to make sure that no one was around. "Good luck."

"Good luck," I heard her whisper as I shut the door behind me and scurried into the bush beside the driveway. The ground was wet; the sun couldn't penetrate through the thick trees, and the snow had only recently melted here. I was dressed in dark sweat pants and a brown jacket, hoping to blend in with the trees and fallen leaves. I had to negotiate my way through the bush where no path existed, watching the ground closely to make sure I didn't trip over a root or a twig. My pants kept snagging on the undergrowth, making my progress slower than I had anticipated. I glanced at my watch a couple of times, hoping that Amy wasn't getting impatient.

Truthfully, I was pretty nervous myself. If I had told Amy that I was uncomfortable sneaking into the Primos' house and going through their things, she would have backed out and refused to help me. I'm a fairly conservative, law-abiding citizen, after all. Maybe the law didn't consider it a "break and enter" when someone opened the door for you, but I was pretty sure that Tremaine would consider that a technicality and make good his threat to haul me off to jail if I was caught inside the Primos' house.

I forced my way through to the trees beside the house and checked my watch again. Twelve minutes had passed, and there was no sign of Amy. Where was she? Damn, we should have synchronized our watches before we had split up.

I heard a car approaching and peeked out from behind a tree to check. Yes, it was Amy. She parked the car in the driveway and sat inside, waiting for my signal. I waved at her, but she didn't move. Maybe she hadn't seen me? I waved more vigorously, but still she just sat there. What was she waiting for? If Karen had heard the car drive up, she was going to wonder why someone hadn't come to the door by now.

Never mind, Amy was getting out of the car. But instead of walking up to the house like she was supposed to, she leaned against the car and started scanning the trees. I stepped out from behind my cover and waved both arms over my head. This time she spotted me. Amy nodded, shoved back her shoulders, and marched up to the front door like she was going to her own execution. She looked so serious that I had to smile. She rang the bell, and then looked over her shoulder back at me. I pointed vigorously toward the door before ducking back behind my tree. Amy turned just in time to see Karen, dressed in jeans and a lilac shirt, open the door. Amy smiled and began talking while Karen listened and nodded from time to time. Amy finished her speech, and I held my breath, wondering if Karen would fall for it. Karen smiled and opened the door wide to let Amy inside, the door squeaking loudly as she did.

I jumped up and down with excitement. My plan had worked! Amy was in! After a minute, the door squealed opened again and Amy stepped out onto the porch. She crouched over the door mat and appeared to be studying it. Had she dropped something? Finally she straightened and walked back inside, leaving the door ajar. Wow, Amy was slicker than I had thought. Even I had been fooled into thinking that she had lost something on the door mat, and I had been expecting some sort of a trick to leave the door open.

Now it was my turn to go inside the house. I left the security of the trees and sprinted for the front porch. Climbing the stairs as noiselessly as I could, I tiptoed to the front door, flattened myself against the wall, and peeked inside. I could hear Karen's voice coming from upstairs. Amy was waiting in the hallway. When she spotted me, her arms spiralled like a windmill, beckoning for me to come inside. I snuck through the door and closed it carefully; fortunately, it didn't squeak this time. Amy made stabbing motions at a room across the hall and I hurried into it. It was an office with a large wooden desk in the middle of the room and a chair tucked in behind it. Amy watched from the doorway as

I crawled under the desk and pulled the chair in as close as I could. The desk had a solid front, so I couldn't see out, but no one could see in. I heard Karen coming down the stairs.

"Found my purse, Amy," she called. "Tell me, does this market have any cowboy art? My sister asked me to find her a picture with horses in it while I was in Alberta."

"Oh, sure, it's got all kinds of horse pictures, with and without cowboys. I can't believe you've never been to the market yet. It's really popular. We should get a group together from the movie set and go. I know that they'd have a blast," Amy said.

"Whoa, wait a minute. Let's just wait until I've seen it before you go making any plans."

Their voices trailed off and I heard the front door close behind them. A few minutes later, their car started up and drove away. I finally had the house to myself.

I crawled out from under the desk and gazed around the room, looking for a likely hiding place for a gun. Studying the office walls, I peeked behind two framed pictures of hunting dogs for a safe, but no such luck – not that I would have been able to open a safe if I had found one.

The desk drawers contained nothing but a package of printer paper and a couple of pens. The desk top held a computer and a printer, but nothing else. There was no desk calendar marked "meeting with Jack Nolan" on the day my ex-husband had died.

I stopped to think. If I were renting a house, where would I hide something small? The woman of the house might think of hiding a gun or a ring in a canister of flour or maybe wrapped in foil in the freezer, but Connie wouldn't do that for fear of Karen finding it. Of course, you wouldn't have to hide a gun if you had always owned one. You could store it in a display case or inside an end table drawer.

I took a tour of the first floor. It consisted of a living/dining room, kitchen, office, a closet with a stacked washer and dryer, and a powder room. There was a side table in the dining room, but it contained only table linens, candles, matches, and a deck of cards. Checking the closet by the front door, I remembered to look inside the coat pockets, but didn't find anything. Next I tried the powder room. People were always taping things to the inside of the toilet tank in the movies, but still there was nothing.

I had been in the house for about twenty minutes by now, and I was beginning to feel uneasy. Even though I knew it would be at least an hour before Karen and Amy could possibly come back, I had the creepy feeling that I was being watched through the downstairs windows. Making a lightning-fast inspection of the rest of the first floor, I hurried upstairs. It was a three-bedroom home, two of the bedrooms sharing a bathroom, and a master with an ensuite. I made my way carefully through the extra bedrooms, searching the bureaus, beds, and closets, but I came up empty. I investigated the main bathroom before turning my attention to the master.

This was the most likely spot for Connie to hide something since it was so close to hand. Starting with the ensuite linen closet, I shook out all the towels and linens, but found nothing. The drawer in the bathroom cabinet was jammed full of Karen's make-up things and hair brushes. Underneath the sink, I found a man's toiletry bag. Crossing my fingers, I unzipped the bag. There was nothing in it but an electric razor and a travel soap container. The soap container rattled when I shook it, and I opened it eagerly, only to discover a shard of soap. Putting everything back the way I'd found it, I checked the medicine cabinet before moving on to the bedroom.

The room had a large, double-doored closet with mirrors. I slid the left door open and discovered Karen's side of the closet. Looking at all the clothes and shoes jammed inside, I decided that Connie wouldn't risk hiding anything amongst Karen's things. I slid the other door open and immediately spotted a zippered bag lying on the top shelf. Standing on tiptoe, I pulled the bag down and laid it on the bed. Unzipping it, I discovered a hand gun and box of ammunition. Bingo! Maybe this was the murder weapon. I stared at the gun with a great big grin on my face, but my excitement soon fizzled. I didn't know anything about guns. Did this gun fire the right-sized bullet? Wait, what about the ammunition box? I knelt down beside the bed to have a better look at the box without actually touching it. ".45 ACP," it said. All right! I didn't know what "ACP" meant, but at least it was the right calibre bullet. And what were a cameraman and an actress doing with a gun, anyway? I jumped up and did a little happy dance. Connie was a possible suspect and he was in possession of a gun. Tremaine was still busy checking out Karen and Connie's alibi, while I had already found a gun. I had beaten old stone face at his own game.

In the middle of my excitement, I heard a noise in the driveway. It sounded like a car door slamming. How could that be? I checked my watch and saw that Karen and Amy shouldn't be back for another fifteen minutes, at least. I ran across the room to the front windows and poked my head around the curtain. Connie was getting out of the car! Holy smokes, what was he doing home? I stared at him as he limped toward the house. His clothes were all muddy. He must have had an accident and come home to clean up. Damn it, that meant that he would come upstairs to his bedroom. Not only that, but Karen's car was still parked in the driveway, so he would expect her to be at home. If she didn't turn up, he would look for her.

I ran back to the bed as the front door opened and closed. I had to get the gun bag back into the closet before he came upstairs. I hesitated, wondering what to do about the gun.

"Karen, I'm home," Connie shouted from downstairs. "I took a fall on the set and cut my leg. It's bleeding – again. I need some clean clothes." I could hear him moving around downstairs, looking for Karen. I opened the box of ammunition, snatched one of the bullets, and shoved it into my pocket. Maybe the police could tell if it was the murder weapon by testing the bullet?

"Karen, are you upstairs?" he yelled. I froze for a moment, listening. Hell, he was already climbing the stairs. But what if the police had to have the gun the bullet was fired from to determine if it was the murder weapon? I didn't know for sure, but the cops on TV had the gun tested, didn't they? I could hear Connie at the top of the stairs. There was no more time. I grabbed the gun and shoved it inside my pocket, retrieving the bullet, and stuffing it down my bra. I didn't want it falling out of my pocket and lying on top of the carpet where Connie could see it. I could hear him nosing around the other bedrooms, looking for Karen. Zippering the bag shut as quietly as I could, I ran on tiptoe to the closet, stuffed it back on its shelf, and eased the door closed. Connie was coming down the hallway toward the master. Looking around frantically for a place to hide, I bolted across the carpet, flopped onto the floor beside the bed, and wiggled underneath it just as he came into the room.

"Are you in here?" he called. I lay still, holding my breath, my heart thudding in my chest. "Where is she?" he muttered, flipping on the overhead light and limping over to the closet. I turned my head sideways to watch his feet. His sneakers were all muddy, and he kicked them off without bothering to untie them. I heard cursing. His belt buckle jingled, and I watched as his pants hit the carpet. They were filthy and torn. He stepped out of them and left them in a heap on the floor. Groaning, he hobbled into the bathroom. The lights flicked on, and the linen closet bi-fold opened and closed. A few seconds later, he was running water in the sink. The water stopped, and I heard a sharp intake of breath. The medicine cabinet door squeaked open, and I heard him digging around inside. His injuries probably weren't too serious or the movie people would have sent him to the hospital. I decided I'd better stay put in case he came out again in a minute.

I had been so distracted by Connie that it took me a few moments to realize that someone was moving around downstairs. "Connie, are you home? What are you doing home so early?" Karen shouted. Oh great, just what I needed. Now they were both home. I heard someone talking to Karen downstairs and recognized Amy's voice, too.

Connie came limping out of the bathroom. "Karen? I'm in the bedroom. Where you been?" he yelled.

Someone ran up the stairs and into the bedroom, dropping plastic bags and a wrapped package on the floor just inside the door. Karen said, "Amy dropped by and we went to the Farmer's Market. What have you done to your leg?"

There was a pause, and Connie said, "Uh, hi Amy."

"Oh for pity's sake, get in the bathroom, Con," Karen said. "Do you think Amy wants to see you in your underwear? You're dripping on the carpet, too. What a mess." She strode across the floor and herded him into the bathroom.

"What was that – it looks like you bought a picture?" Connie said.

"Yeah, I bought it for my sister," Karen replied. I could hear a number of tissues being yanked from a box. "Here, dry your leg."

I wiggled to the edge of the bed and stuck my head out to see what was happening. Amy was standing beside the closet, facing the bathroom.

"Amy!" I said in a sharp whisper. She started and looked around the room. "Down here," I said. She looked down and spotted me on the floor. Her eyes grew huge.

"Anna!" she squeaked before clapping her hand over her mouth. Connie and Karen were still clattering around in the bathroom.

"How much was it?" Connie asked.

"Was what?" Karen asked.

"The picture – how much money did you spend?"

"About a thousand," Karen replied, sounding distracted. "What did you do, fall off a cliff? You're really banged up."

"A thousand bucks! For your sister? Why can't she buy her own damn picture?"

"Because she wanted a Western picture for her family room, and they don't have so many of them in Montreal."

Amy hurried over to the bed and bent toward me. "What are you doing down there?" she whispered. "You've got to get out of here right now!"

I didn't say anything, just whipped the gun out of my pocket with a big smile and waved it in her face. A second later, I wondered if it were loaded.

"Anna!" she squeaked. We both heard the sound of heels clicking across the bathroom tile, and I jammed the gun into my pocket and dodged back under the bed as Amy whirled around.

"You still here?" Karen said. "Sorry, I forgot about you. You better go. I gotta help my clumsy husband get cleaned up and back to work, and then I've got some lines to learn."

"Okay, Karen," Amy said in an odd, strangled voice.

Karen paused. "You look kind of funny. Something wrong?"

"No, no, everything's fine," Amy said.

"What's the matter, you don't like the sight of blood or something? Or is it Connie in his underwear that's making you feel queasy? Not a pretty sight, I know," she said with a cackle. Boy, that woman had an annoying laugh.

"No, it's not Connie. You're right. I don't like the sight of blood."

"Well, thanks for taking me to the market today. It was fun."

"You're welcome. Maybe we can go again sometime."

"Sure. Call me. Maybe we'll go out for a drink together. Bring Anna Nolan, if you like." I heard a snort from the bathroom. "Shut up, Connie," Karen yelled.

Amy said, "Sure, I'd like that. And I'm so glad we found that painting for your sister. I'm sure she'll like it, since she likes horses so much. The foal in the picture is so cute, and the background is really impressive. The cliff, I mean. With the mother horse standing on the cliff, you can almost feel the wind blowing through her hair – I mean her mane." Amy sounded crazy, and I prayed that she'd get out of the bedroom before she gave me away.

"Karen, come on. I need you in here," Connie yelled.

"Keep your pants on. I'm just saying goodbye to Amy," Karen replied. I took the opportunity to stick my head out from under the bed and jerk it at Amy. Amy waved her hands in the air and grimaced before Karen turned back to her again.

"Sorry, Amy, don't have any more time to stand around and chat. See you later."

"Bye," Amy said. She paused, and then left the room. I heard her walk down the stairs as Karen went back into the bathroom.

"She gone now?" Connie asked.

"Yeah, you can come out," Karen replied. They came out together, Connie favouring his right leg. Karen said, "You'd better get dressed and go back to work. You said they may need you this afternoon." I watched Connie's feet approach the bed until he stopped and turned his heels to face me. I braced myself as he sat down heavily, the box spring sagging toward my face.

"Help me, Mommy," he said in a pathetic little boy's voice.

Karen sighed. "Sheesh, you're such a baby." She opened the closet door and I heard the clang of a wire hanger. "Here, put this shirt on," she said. She must have tossed it to him because I heard her burrowing in the closet again. She walked back to the bed and said, "Here's some pants."

After a moment, I heard a slap. "We don't have time for that, Con, you've got to get back to work," Karen snapped. I held my breath. I didn't know what I'd do if Connie and Karen started fooling around on top of the bed.

"You never have time," Connie complained.

"Oh shut up, you pig. We just did it last night."

"Yeah," Connie said in a husky voice, "and you seemed to like it." I heard a smack, and Karen squealed.

"You *were* kinda manly last night, all grabby and take charge," Karen said, kicking off her shoes. She sank down on the bed and the box spring brushed against my forehead, forcing me to turn my face sideways. Karen giggled and the bed creaked as their weight shifted. "Who's my little cuddle bear?" she said in a girlish voice, then shrieked and giggled some more.

The doorbell rang. Hallelujah, I was saved! Karen and Connie lay still on top of the bed. "Don't answer it," Connie said.

They waited. The doorbell rang again. "I'm going to look out the windows and see who it is," Karen whispered, the bed lifting and clearing my face. I heard her pad across the floor to the window. "It's Amy," she said after a moment.

"Shit, what's she doing back here?" Connie said.

"She just looked up and saw me," Karen said. "I've got to go down and see what she wants." Connie groaned as Karen put on her shoes and walked out of the room. "Get dressed," she ordered from the hallway.

Connie cursed as he rolled around the bed, putting on his clothes. A minute later, Karen called from downstairs, "Con, Amy's got car trouble. Come down and have a look."

I silently cheered Amy's inventiveness as Connie got off the bed, shoved his feet into a pair of slippers, and left the room. A couple of minutes later, I heard them talking downstairs. Amy's voice became high-pitched and insistent, Connie said something in a rumbling voice, the front door opened and shut, and everything was still.

I wiggled out from under the bed, checking that the gun was still in my pocket, and ran down the hallway to the top of the stairs. Bending in half, I peered through the glass panels on either side of the front door. The hood of Amy's car was raised and Connie was leaning into the engine. I heard him shout something, and then the car's engine roared into life. I sprinted down the stairs and ran for the front closet, all the while listening to Amy speaking very loudly over the engine noise. I pulled open the closet door, jumped inside, and slammed it shut just as the front door opened again.

"Stupid bitch. There was nothing wrong with her engine," Connie muttered as he and Karen stepped inside. A horn tooted, and the car drove away.

"She's nice. Just not too bright," Karen said.

The door closed and everything was quiet in the hallway. After a minute, Connie said, "What say we go back upstairs, eh, pussy cat?" Karen giggled. The two of them headed back down the hallway and climbed the stairs to the second floor. I heard their footsteps overhead, and then nothing. Easing the closet door open, I listened for a moment before slipping out. I tiptoed to the front door and paused. Sometimes the door made a terrible squeak. Maybe I wouldn't set it off if I didn't open the door very far?

I managed to open the door about a foot without any sound at all. Pressing my lips together, I inserted a shoulder into the space and tried to slip through. All went well until I got to my hips. I started inching the door open, squeezing my butt muscles together in hope of making it more compact. I was almost through, just a tiny bit more to go, when the damn door went "squeeeak." I froze, holding my breath, waiting to hear if anyone noticed. All went well for about three seconds until Connie yelled, "Hey, who's down there?"

That was enough for me. I threw the door open and bolted for the trees alongside the house. I knew that Karen and Connie had an excellent view of the front parking area from their bedroom windows, and I didn't want them to see me running down the driveway. Once in the trees, I skidded on some damp leaves, grabbed hold of a branch to steady myself, and kept on running. My pant leg caught on a twig and I had to rip a hole in it to free myself, but I didn't care. I was in full flight mode. I saw the bend in the driveway up ahead and burst out of the trees, running through the gravel. My breath was rasping in my throat and I had a stitch in my side. I spotted Amy's car parked at the bottom of the drive, Amy standing beside it with the driver's door open. She jumped up and down when she saw me, and ran the rest of the way to meet me and give me a big hug.

"I just about had a stroke when I saw you under that bed, Anna Nolan," she cried, giving me a shake. Without waiting for a response, Amy grabbed my arm and pushed me into the car before darting around to the driver's side and jumping in herself. She started up the engine, spun the car around, the tires spewing gravel, and skidded out onto the street without bothering to check for traffic. Fortunately, there weren't any oncoming vehicles, but I was slammed against the passenger door because I hadn't had time to fasten my seat belt.

"Take it easy. Try not to kill us," I complained, clicking the restraint into place. Glancing at her, I was just in time to see a fat tear slide down her cheek.

"Amy, I am so sorry," I said, feeling terrible. Her bottom lip started quivering. "Please don't be upset," I said. "It's all over now, and no one got caught. You were so fantastic, coming up with an excuse to get Connie and Karen out of the house. I hid in the front hall closet until they went back upstairs, and then I snuck out. We did it! And, guess what? I think I may have found the murder weapon." I took the gun out of my pocket to show it to her again.

"Put that away," Amy shrieked. "I hate guns."

"Okay, no problem. I'm sorry," I apologized again, shoving it back into my pocket. Only then did it occur to me that I had been handling the gun with my bare hands. Groaning, I sank back into my seat, wanting to kick myself for being so stupid. I had panicked when I heard Connie coming down the hallway, and had picked up the gun without thinking.

"What's the matter?" Amy asked.

"Nothing. I just did something incredibly stupid," I said, glancing out the window.

"Oh no," she whispered, turning to look at me with frightened eyes.

"No, nothing that bad. It's just that I realized I've been holding the gun with my bare hands."

Amy turned her attention back to the road. "So, now you've got your fingerprints on the gun."

"Yeah," I muttered, "and maybe wiped Connie's off, too. How could I have been so stupid? Everyone knows not to handle the evidence with your bare hands."

Amy shrugged. "Don't be so hard on yourself, Anna. You must have been terrified, trapped in the bedroom with Connie. I know I would have been. Besides, it doesn't matter anymore."

I stared at Amy. "What do you mean, it doesn't matter?"

"Because there's no way that Karen or Connie killed Jack."

"What? How do you know that?"

"Because Karen told me what she and Connie were doing on the night that Jack was murdered. They've been having some problems, so Karen and Connie started seeing a marriage counsellor. They were with their counsellor in Calgary on the night that Jack was killed."

"Oh, just perfect," I groaned, closing my eyes in exasperation. "I can't believe it. After all the trouble I took to search their house, there was no reason to do it in the first place. All we had to do was have a heart-to-heart chat with Karen, and we would have known that they couldn't have killed Jack."

"Yup," Amy said, still watching the road. "But now you've got Connie's gun."

I stared at her, and then reached into my pocket for the gun. What the hell was I going to do with it? I couldn't possibly give it to Tremaine now that I'd ruined the fingerprints. I was going to have to get it back to Connie. But how? There was no way that I was going to sneak back into their house and replace it. Maybe I could just leave it on their doorstep in a brown paper bag? My mind reeled. How long would it take before Connie noticed that it was missing?

A terrible thought occurred to me: what if Connie had gone for the gun just now when he thought that someone was breaking into the house? What if he had already discovered that it was missing? If that were the case, there was no possibility of returning the gun without his noticing.

I moaned. "Amy, I am so sorry. This is about the stupidest thing I've ever done. I don't know what got into me. Normally, I'm a pretty cautious person, you know? Well, up until a week ago when Jack got killed. It's as if Jack's death released some sort of insanity from deep down inside me. Breaking into the Primos' house, kicking a police sergeant . . ."

Amy stared, her eyebrows lifted. "You kicked Tremaine?"

"Yeah, well never mind about that – that's the least of my worries. You have just brought me to my senses. I promise that I'll never do anything this crazy again. Look, let me try to make it up to you. Are you hungry? I bet you haven't had anything to eat since breakfast. Let me buy you lunch when we get back to Crane, okay? We're almost there now."

"I don't think so. I'm too upset to eat," she said, shaking her head.

"Please? Even if you can't eat, how about a cup of coffee? Or a milkshake? The Diner makes great shakes."

Amy sighed. "Sure, Anna. Karen and I were going to have lunch at her place before this whole thing blew up. I guess I could try to eat something."

"That a girl. We'll feel better after we've had something to eat," I said as we drove into town. I tried for a positive spin on our little fiasco. "You know, when everything simmers down and the investigation is over, I bet we'll laugh about this someday. As a matter of fact, when I think of the look on your face when you saw me under the bed, I could almost laugh now. It was pretty funny, don't you think?"

The look on her face warned me that I had gone too far. I shut my mouth, folded my arms over my chest, and kept quiet for the rest of the drive.

15

We were just in time to join the Saturday lunch crowd at The Diner. It had turned into a sunny spring day, and half a dozen motorcycles were parked out front. The Calgary motorcycle crowd liked to bike down on weekends whenever the weather was nice. Clive's tractor, splattered with mud from ploughing, was parked in the prime spot just outside the door.

Inside, Mary and Judy were busy hustling food with the motorcyclists taking up half the tables. Clive was sitting on a stool by the jukebox singing along to Elvis's "Blue Suede Shoes," getting lots of amused looks from the out-of-towners. There was one empty table left beside Mr. Andrews, so Amy and I seated ourselves there.

Judy hurried over as soon as she was free. She had teased her long, honey-blond hair, the colour kept fresh by Amy, into an updo. Judy liked to dress western, and today she had on a green plaid shirt, jeans, and embossed leather boots. She peered at us over her reading glasses with an order pad in one hand.

"How're you doing, Anna? How's it going, Amy? What are you two having?"

"Hi, Judy. Haven't had a chance to talk to you for a few weeks now. Busy day today," I said.

"Yeah, it's a beautiful day. Can't wait to get out of here and go for a ride myself." Frank and Judy had a handsome Harley which they used to tour the back country roads.

We placed our order and Judy hurried away. The jukebox finished playing and conversational levels returned to normal. I looked at Amy, who was staring fixedly across the room, doing her level best to ignore me. I lay my hand over her folded ones on the table top.

"Are you angry with me, Amy?" I asked.

She glanced at me before dropping her eyes. "No, I guess not, but I've never been so scared in my life as I was when I found you under that bed this morning."

I shrugged. "Let's try to put that behind us, okay? At least we can check Connie off our list of suspects. We're making progress." I smiled, hoping to jolly her along.

"What do you mean 'list of suspects?' What progress?" Amy demanded, her face turning pink and her voice rising. I shushed her. "I thought you said that you were done with this," she added in a low, insistent voice. "You promised not more than fifteen minutes ago that you were never going to do anything this crazy again – remember?"

I frowned. "Well, yes I did, but I didn't say that I'm not interested in the case anymore. Let's not forget that it was my ex-husband who just got murdered, and that I'm the police's favourite suspect. I can't just walk away from it, not yet." Amy sighed and looked away. Judy returned with our milkshakes, and we sipped them in stony silence. Our hamburgers came next, and the crowd thinned out as we ate. Mary took care of the customers lining up to pay their bills while Judy joined us at the table.

"Did you hear the latest news about Henry?" she asked, dropping into a chair and stretching out her legs with a grunt.

"No, what happened?" Amy asked, perking up a little.

Judy braced her elbows on the table and leaned in toward us. "Well, Harold Gibbs eats his breakfast here every day even though he sold Henry the insurance policy for his restaurant, right?"

"Of course," I responded. Business was business, but you couldn't let it interfere with your health.

"So, Gibbs was in here yesterday morning, and he told Frank what Henry plans to do with the insurance money. Henry is going to install a drive-through window in his restaurant." Judy grinned and sat back, looking pleased with herself.

"No," I uttered in amazement. "Why would he want to do that in a town this size?"

"Well, Henry claims that his business will increase threefold once people hear he's got a fast food window. He thinks that the commuters will stop for breakfast on their way out of town in the morning, and pick up supper on their way home. He says that the convenience of not having to get out of their cars will make a big difference to folks. He's also counting on the bachelor farmers not wanting to cook their own supper after a hard day's work." Judy turned to Mr. Andrews. "Hey, Mr. Andrews, if you were still farming, would you use Henry's fast-food window to pick up your supper?"

"Nope," said Mr. Andrews without raising his head from his paper. "I wouldn't drive two minutes out of my way to purchase Henry's swill."

"Hey Clive, how about you?" Judy shouted.

Clive swivelled around on his stool and planted his soil-encrusted boots on the floor, knocking little turds of dried mud onto the linoleum. "What's that?" he yelled.

"Would you buy Henry's food if he had a take-out window on the side of his restaurant?"

"Nope. Can't get my tractor through a take-out. Tried it once at a Dairy Queen. I wanted a crème-de-menthe milk shake, but I couldn't make it through their little drive-through. Had to park in the lot and walk inside. Once I got to the counter, they told me they don't make crème-de-menthe milkshakes. Imagine that. I could get banana or strawberry, but they couldn't make me a mint milkshake. You'd think that people would prefer a mint milkshake to banana, now wouldn't you?" We all shook our heads at people's strange preferences in dairy beverages. "So, no," Clive continued, "I wouldn't use Henry's take-out window. What take-out window?"

Judy waved her arm at him in dismissal and turned back to us. Clive shrugged and swivelled back to his slice of lemon meringue pie. Judy said, "Pretty bizarre, eh? Well, Henry always did have some strange notions of what would go over in this town. It doesn't bother Frank any. He's sure that people aren't going to eat Henry's cooking no matter how fast they can get it. But, enough of Henry. How are things with you, Anna? Anything new in your husband's murder investigation?"

I glanced at Amy, trying to warn her with my eyes to keep quiet about our recent break-in. "I haven't heard anything. Have you seen Sergeant Tremaine lately?"

"Nope, not since the beginning of the week, although I'm sure he's busy questioning everyone he can think of. I guess he'll come up with the murderer sooner or later. Frank says he's pretty sharp, even though he seems a bit young to be heading up a murder investigation."

"I guess so," I said, and Amy nodded. When we didn't have anything else to contribute, Judy got up from her chair, looking a little miffed at our reticence.

"Well, I'll leave you ladies to finish your meals in peace. Wouldn't want you to get indigestion from talking about anything distasteful," she said with a sniff.

"Okay, nice talking with you, Judy. Say 'hi' to Frank for me," I replied. Judy stalked away, obviously not happy with me.

Amy put down her fork and bent to pick her purse up off the floor. "I've got customers this afternoon, so I've got to go," she murmured.

"Me, too. I've got laundry that needs doing," I said, but I didn't want to leave when she was still so obviously unhappy with me. "Amy, you were a really big help today," I said. "You found out about the Primos' marriage counselling, and you helped me to escape from their house without getting caught. If it hadn't been for you, I might be in a jail cell right now with Tremaine throwing away the keys. Believe me, I'm very grateful. I hope that you're not upset with me."

"I'm not really upset. I just don't want anyone to get hurt or in trouble over this," she replied, pushing back her chair. "But I've got to go, or I'll be late for my one o'clock appointment. Call me later this week, and we'll talk. And thanks for lunch."

"You're welcome," I called after her as she hurried out of the restaurant. Glad that things were better between Amy and me, I paid the bill, said goodbye to Mary and Judy, and went home. Wendy whined when I got there, and I felt guilty for neglecting her lately. Time for a good, long romp. Gathering up her leash and a couple of plastic bags for the inevitable clean-up, I headed out the door with Wendy dancing beside me. At least my dog still loved me.

I hesitated before heading out Wistler Road again, but it was Wendy's favourite walk and I wasn't going to let my squeamishness over walking past the spot where we had discovered Jack's body deprive her of her pleasure. We set off out of town, and Wendy disappeared into bushes bursting with tender green leaves. The air was dry and smelt of newly-cut grass, and I began to relax.

Strolling after Wendy, I thought about what I had learned in the past week. For one thing, I now knew that Jack had spent part of the afternoon and evening of his last day with Amy, leaving her just before six thirty "on business." Amy had interpreted that to mean that he was going to see another woman, but if so, whom? I knew that the woman wasn't Karen Quill, since she had been at a counselling session in Calgary with Connie.

The coroner's report said that Jack had been shot in the chest with a .45 calibre bullet between six and nine, and that his body had been moved after his death. The coroner had also confirmed that there had been no evidence of sexual activity prior to Jack's death. I had discussed that detail with Amy, who told me that Jack had showered after they had been together. That put the kibosh on Amy's theory that Jack had left her to be with another woman, unless the other woman had shot him before they could have sex. Maybe he had actually gone to a business meeting, but that was hard to believe. What kind of business would Jack be involved with? He had an agent and an accountant to look after him, and I had never known him to be interested in anything other than acting and women.

Jack had called my home at seven while I was at the book club meeting. I hadn't given him my number, but he could have found it in a telephone book or online. Why had he called? Was it something to do with his assignation that evening, or had he been calling about something entirely different? Had he wanted to talk about Ben? Maybe he wanted to see Ben to apologize for missing his graduation. It bothered me to think that I would never know the reason for his call. If only Jack had left me a message.

As far as I knew, the police had made no headway in discovering where Jack had been murdered. Even if Jack had been shot as late as nine, the killer would have had at least half an hour to dispose of his body before I found it around nine forty-five. The murder might have taken place in Calgary, on the set in Longview, or in a multitude of other locations, including right here in Crane. Still, the location must have been pretty private since no one had reported seeing Jack after he left Amy's house. It was as if he had disappeared off the face of the earth the moment he drove out of her driveway.

Finally, I knew that someone was trying to set me up, someone who had been watching me and knew that I always took Wendy for a walk on Wistler Road before bed. The murderer also knew my history with my ex-husband. It had to be someone I knew, or someone intimate enough with Jack to know about me. Had the murderer also known about the insurance policy? The life insurance made me the most obvious person to profit from Jack's death, but it didn't make me the only one. If someone else profited from his death, either financially or personally, I was confident that Tremaine would find out about it sooner or later.

I had learned a lot since Jack had died, but I was no closer to figuring out who had murdered him. I decided to leave it alone for a while, hoping that my subconscious would come up with something if I just let the whole thing stew. Checking my watch, I discovered that we had been walking for forty-five minutes already, with Wendy running back now and then to check on me. Here she was again with a stick in her mouth and her belly matted with mud.

"What have you got there?" I asked. She dropped the stick at my feet and sat down, her tongue lolling out of her mouth. I threw the stick for her and we played fetch all the way back into town. When we got home, I spent an hour combing out her thick fur and giving her a bath. I dried her off with an old towel and left her out on the deck to finish drying, returning to the bathroom to clean the sand out of the tub.

Focusing on these mundane tasks cleared my thoughts and helped me to decide what to do next. There was only one other woman in this part of the world who had any history with Jack, and that was the stuntwoman, Jessie Wick. I had nothing else to go on, so I decided to find out more about her. Unfortunately, that meant asking for Amy's help again. It troubled me to keep involving her when she so obviously didn't want anything more to do with Jack's murder. Besides, the film people might get irritated if she asked too many questions about Jack, and fire her from the movie for being a nuisance. Worse, Amy's curiosity might draw the attention of the murderer. I sure didn't want to put her life in danger, but what else could I do?

Then I had a brainwave. This was Jessie's second movie in Longview. That might be a coincidence, or it might mean that she lived around here. And if she did, Erna Dombrosky might know something about her and her family. It was worth a shot.

Tomorrow was Sunday. I would invite Erna over for lunch and see if she knew anything about Jessie Wick. If she didn't, Amy would be my back-up plan. Determined to find out more about the third woman in Jack's life, I reached for the phone to call Erna.

16

Erna was free to have lunch with me, and we spent a pleasant quarter of an hour ambling back to my house after service the next day. At seventy-five, Erna's step was still sprightly. She knew everyone in town, including the more recent additions to the subdivision, and nodded or exchanged a word with everyone we passed while still managing to hold up her end of the conversation with me. Erna's hair was snowy white, and she wore it in a tight bun. Her clothes were from an earlier era of cardigan sweaters, wool skirts, and single strand pearls, probably left over from her days as a high school teacher. I wondered if her old-maidish appearance was an intentional disguise to hide a mind as keen as a steel trap and eyes that never missed a thing. I wasn't kidding when I had suggested to May that she and Erna should open a detective agency.

Wendy was waiting for us when I unlocked the front door, and we stepped inside. Erna bent down until she was eye-level with my dog. "Good morning, Wendy. How are you today?" she asked.

Wendy sat down and extended a paw to our visitor. Erna took it and gave it two solemn shakes before turning to smile up at me. "I see that Wendy still remembers the little trick I taught her when I looked after her last summer. Such an intelligent dog," she said, straightening.

"You made a big impression on her. She doesn't behave nearly so well for me."

"Children and dogs both need discipline. Maintaining high expectations usually has a beneficial effect – it gives our charges something to live up to." She reached down and stroked Wendy's sleek head. "Yes, you're a good girl," she crooned.

"Please come through to the kitchen," I invited, gesturing for her to precede me. "I have some home-made potato salad and cold cuts. Can I make you some tea, or would you prefer something cold to drink?"

"Tea would be just fine. Oh, what pretty flowers you have on the table. Did you get them from May?"

We chatted while I put water on to boil and arranged potato salad, meat, cheese, lettuce, tomatoes, and rolls on the table. Erna was fond of dill pickles and pearl onions, and I had a dish of them ready for her.

Erna watched me move about the kitchen. "So, how did Ben do in his first year of university?" she asked.

"Actually, better than I would have imagined," I replied. "His grades were pretty decent, and he seemed to stay on top of things. That couldn't have been easy with roommates, a part-time job, and an active social life to distract him."

"He always seemed level-headed to me, Anna. You've raised him well, even with having to uproot him so frequently. Not to mention the trouble you had with your ex-husband. How is he handling his father's death, by the way?"

I brought the tea to the table to steep. "He's pretty angry about the whole thing, to tell you the truth. You know how disappointed Ben was with his father, and now he blames Jack for being murdered, too. It wasn't a very respectable way to go, from Ben's point of view, and there's all the notoriety surrounding the case, too."

"I'm afraid that we don't all die peacefully in our beds."

I smiled ruefully. "No, and Jack was never destined for an honourable end. Of course, it didn't help that the RCMP sergeant questioned Ben about his whereabouts on the night that Jack was killed."

"Sergeant Tremaine, isn't it?"

"That's right. Have you met him?"

"As a matter of fact, he stopped by when I was reading the newspaper out on my front porch last Tuesday."

"Checking on my alibi with the book club, I suppose?"

"That's right, dear. He was very particular about the time you left the library. I told him that your car wasn't in the parking lot when I came in, and since I came in after you did, it was evident that you did not drive your car to the library that night."

"Thanks, Erna, you're a wonder. I don't know how you remember all those details."

Erna grinned a Cheshire-cat kind of smile. "Of course, you could have parked your car on a side street and I wouldn't have seen it, but I didn't mention that to the sergeant."

I grinned back. "Thank you. I appreciate you keeping that to yourself."

"Now tell me – I understand that you're investigating the murder on your own?"

I stopped smiling and raised my eyebrows. "How did you hear that?"

"Amy Bright did my hair yesterday. She was still upset by what happened at the Primos' house, and felt that she could confide in me. I marvel at your bravery."

"More like foolhardiness, you mean. I just hope that the Primos never find out that I searched their house and took their gun. But now that Amy has spilled the beans, I wonder if you can help me with something?"

"I'd be more than happy to. What can I do for you?" Erna put down her fork and gave me all of her attention.

"I don't know if you heard about it at the time, but Jack was seeing a woman on the film that brought us here four years ago. She was a stunt woman named Jessie Wick. Jack's affair with Jessie was 'the straw that broke the camel's back' for me."

"Yes, I did hear something about it at the time. I'm afraid that it was common knowledge around town."

I shook my head. "It's true that 'the wife is always the last to know.' Anyway, I wondered if you knew anything about Jessie?"

"Oh yes, I know quite a bit about Jessie and her family," Erna said. "They still have a ranch south of Longview. It belonged to her mother's people. Let me organize my thoughts for a moment, and I'll tell you what I remember." She tapped one finger against her cheek while I waited for her to begin.

"Jessie's father was Randolph Wick. He grew up on a ranch somewhere in the north-western United States before joining the Marines to fight in the Korean War. He did quite well, as I remember, attaining the rank of captain. When the war was over, he left the Marines and wandered around the United States and Canada for a few years. Men often get wanderlust after a war, I've heard. Randolph ended up here in the Foothills, where he worked as a ranch hand for the Washburn family. Jessie's mother, Carol, was their only daughter, and quite a bit younger than Randolph. She's still alive, you know. She had a stroke about five years ago and is living in a nursing home now. Anyway, Randolph was a good-looking man with a certain rough charm when he was still alive. Apparently, he swept Carol right off her feet. She had a brother who wasn't interested in the ranch – he became a lawyer in Toronto. So

Carol and Randolph married and ran the ranch for her father until they inherited it following his death. They had two children, Jessie and her brother, Gregory.

"Now, Jessie was always the apple of her father's eye. She used to ride the range with him when she was just a wee thing not yet old enough to be in school. As she grew up, Jessie became quite a horsewoman and participated in local rodeo competitions, always winning her events. She also became a beauty queen before she finished high school. She was a pretty girl – tall, good figure, with the most striking long, blue-black hair. Oh yes, she had many admirers and got into the usual scrapes. She was a wanderer, like her father, and wanted to leave home. That's when she got the idea of becoming an actress. When Randolph died about fifteen years ago, she headed for Toronto. I understand that she got some work in movies and television – mostly minor roles, as I remember. She wasn't able to make a very good living in Ontario, so she came back here to the ranch. Her brother Gregory was running it, and welcomed her home. The ranch has a big family house – the kind that is designed for multi-generation use – and she stays there and helps when she can't find film work. But she inherited a home from her father, a cabin that he built on the Elbow River in Kananaskis Country. She spends a fair amount of time there by herself. And that's all that I can tell you about Jessie and her family."

I stared at Erna in amazement. "How do you know so much about the Wick family?"

She smiled. "I've been part of a bird-watching club with her mother's sister for the past twenty years. You hear a lot about people's families when you're tramping through the woods together. That, and I've always had a strong memory for detail."

"Do you happen to know where Jessie's cabin is?"

"You're in luck. A group of us went bird-watching near the cabin a year ago, and Jessie's aunt pointed it out on the way. If you have a road map, I believe that I can show you how to find it."

I hurried to find my map and wrote down the directions that Erna gave me. When we were finished, Erna poured herself another cup of tea and settled back into her chair. "And how are you coping with the murder investigation? I've been worried about you. You seemed quite nervy when I saw you at The Diner last Monday. It must have been very unpleasant to discover your ex-husband's body."

I smiled wanly and shrugged. "It was a nightmare, Erna. Literally. I've been having bad dreams about it ever since."

Erna patted my arm. "I'm not surprised. It must have been a very traumatic experience."

"Yes, and it's raised all kinds of memories that I thought I had laid to rest. Being married to Jack was like a rollercoaster ride, you know? All ups and downs. We were so terribly happy in the beginning. It still makes me sad to think of how it all ended." Erna tutted and shook her head.

"I kick myself for marrying Jack in the first place, you know? Watching him around other women, it was obvious that he was never going to be faithful to me, no matter how much I loved him. I couldn't change him."

Erna sighed. "My dear, I've heard that very same regret voiced by so many women."

"Oh, I know. I'm not the only person who married badly. But there's something that's always bothered me about those days, something that I've never told anyone but my mother. She's gone now. I've been thinking about Jack so much over the past week. Would you mind if I talked to you about it? It's like a cut that's re-opened. I would feel better if I could talk to someone about it."

"Go ahead, dear, if you like, although we've all done things we're ashamed of." Erna shook her head and stared meditatively down at the table, and I wondered what stories she could tell.

"Well, I was just so green and stupid at the time. You see, I was only twenty the first time Jack cheated on me. It was with an eighteen year old actress he was working with. She was a child, really, and the whole thing was so stupid. How could he have betrayed our marriage for something so worthless? It wasn't as if he were in love with her. Anyway, I wanted to get back at him, to hurt him like he had hurt me and, of course, my pride had taken a beating. I wanted to feel desirable again, to prove to Jack that other men still wanted me, even if he didn't."

"So you had an affair?" Erna asked, her sharp eyes watching me.

"Actually, no I didn't. Something stopped me. Don't misunderstand me, I was no saint, and I was very tempted. There was a young actor I was working with. We had met at a scene study class, and he had always had a bit of a crush on me. He was totally different from Jack – slender, sensitive, a very sweet boy. So, on the night I found out about Jack, I went out for a drink with him and poured out all my troubles. I even went home with him because I couldn't bear the thought of seeing Jack back at our apartment. We kissed a little, but that was as far as things went. Jack and I had made wedding vows to each other, and even if he broke his, I wasn't about to break mine.

Erna leaned toward me across the table. "A few kisses aren't anything to be ashamed of after all this time, Anna."

"No, but that's not what's bothering me. I didn't cheat on Jack, but I told him that I had. I lied to him to get even. I had adored him, would have done anything for him, but I turned into a manipulative bitch to make him suffer. I let the lie go on for an entire month, coming and going at odd hours, making him sleep on the couch, pretending that I was talking on the phone with my lover. After that, the whole thing made me feel so sick that I told him the affair was over. He was desperate to have me back. He said that he still loved me, that we had both made mistakes, but that it didn't matter anymore. So, my lie worked. I got him back, and I thought I had won. If I had had half a brain, I would have broken it off with him then and there. But I didn't. I still loved him too much. We made up, and I never told Jack the truth. He died thinking that I had cheated on him."

Erna stared at me for a moment and I blushed, wondering if my confession had made her think less of me. "Did you ever tell Ben that story?" she asked.

"What? No, never. I would be too embarrassed to tell Ben. Besides, it was so long ago, before he was born."

"But don't you see, Anna, telling him that you lied to Jack might make all the difference in the world to Ben. You said that he was still angry with his father. As a matter of fact, Ben's been angry ever since I've known him. Do you remember the trouble he used to get into?

"Yes, he used to act out around his birthdays and at Christmas each year because Jack never came to see him. Remember the Christmas that he shoplifted at May's store? He would have had a juvenile record if she had called the police."

Erna nodded. "Yes, I remember. But can't you see that Jack might have had a reason for being such a poor father?"

I stared at her. "What are you talking about? What reason could he have had for not seeing his own son for four years?"

Erna took hold of my hand. "Because he might have doubted that Ben was his son." I shook my head, and she took a firmer grip. "Think about it, Anna. You told me before that you were twenty-one when you had Ben." I nodded. "Well, you told your husband that you had had an affair when you were twenty. Maybe he thought you were pregnant by your lover." I covered my mouth with my free hand, stunned by her words. "I'm sorry, I know how hard it must be for you to hear this, but maybe Jack had trouble loving Ben because of the lie you put between them."

"Oh my Lord, Erna, how can you think that? I got pregnant with Ben after Jack and I started sleeping together again. Ben was full-term. There was no reason for Jack to doubt that Ben was his." I pulled my hand away from hers and burst into tears.

Erna shook her head, her eyes reflecting my pain. "But, if it was close, Anna? If there was room for doubt, might it not have poisoned his mind?"

I thought of Jack's unpredictable behaviour toward Ben, of how he had been a loving father one moment and so distant the next that it was as if he had locked Ben out of his heart. Had that been the behaviour of a man who doubted his son's paternity, or of someone who had become too self-absorbed and careless in his relationships? Had my anger clouded my judgement? Just because Jack hadn't loved me enough to be faithful, did that mean that he hadn't loved his son enough, either?

"Oh, Erna," I cried, tears streaming down my face as I raised my eyes to hers. "All these years I've been blaming Jack for being so indifferent to Ben when it might have been all my fault!"

She got up from her chair and came around the table to hug me. Laying my head on her thin shoulder, I sobbed while she rocked me like a child. "Hush, it's all right, Anna," she said, stroking my hair. "I may be wrong, and even if it is true, it's not all your fault. If Jack wasn't sure about his son, he should have asked you about it. A brave man would have wanted to know the truth. Here, wipe your face, now." She pushed the paper napkins toward me and I dried my face.

"I'll make more tea," she said, getting up from the table to add water to the kettle and set it on the stove to boil. I watched her blearily as she dumped out the used teabags and fetched fresh ones from the cupboard. She was so small that she had to stand on tiptoe to reach them. The water came to a boil, and she made a fresh pot. I watched as she poured us each another cup.

"Anna, what are you thinking?" she asked, sitting back down at the table.

I sighed. "I don't know. I'm going to have to wrestle with this one for a while."

"But dear, even if there's only a slight chance of it being true, don't you see what a difference it would make to Ben? Maybe he would stop hating his father and find some peace with the way things were between them at last."

"And start hating me instead," I muttered.

"He might, for a little while. But Ben is a loving child, and he knows what Jack put you through. I think that he would understand eventually, and forgive you."

"But, what if he doesn't?" I asked, my throat tight. "What if this changes our relationship forever? I'm afraid to tell him."

She nodded. "I know. It's very hard, but you're a brave woman. Look at how you started your life all over again after leaving your husband. I know that you have the courage to do this, and that you want what's best for your son."

I thought about Ben and the look on his face when he told me that he hated Jack. Maybe it was possible to end that pain by telling him about my lie. I groaned. "It's true, our sins do come back to haunt us. Or call it karma, if you prefer."

She nodded. "Oh, I've seen it happen far too often not to believe it." She glanced at her watch. "My, is that the time? My niece, Debbie, will be calling me in half an hour. She calls every Sunday at two. Such a sweet, reliable girl. Do you think that you'll be fine if I get going?"

I nodded and smiled. "Of course I will. It's a shock, but I'll deal with it somehow. Would you like a lift home?"

Erna rose from her chair and gathered up her things. "No thank you, Anna, it's such a nice afternoon for a walk. Why don't you relax and put your feet up? I bet you're all worn out." Wendy got up from the kitchen entrance and padded over to us. "Such a good girl," Erna said, stroking her head. She bent to look into Wendy's eyes. "Now, you take good care of your mistress." Wendy wagged her tail. "Good girl," Erna said, kissing her on the head. Turning back to me, she added, "If you need to talk, don't hesitate to call. I'll be in this evening after I've had dinner with May."

I got up and walked Erna to the door. "Thank you, Erna. You've been so kind, listening to my story and letting me cry on your shoulder."

She paused at the front door. "No, it's been my pleasure, dear. I'm glad that you had someone to talk to, now that your mother is gone. I'm proud of you, you know. Of everything you've accomplished, and of the woman you've become. I'm sure that your mother would have been proud of you, too."

I bent to kiss her cheek. It was warm and smelled sweetly of powder. "I just hope that I have the courage to do the right thing.

"I know you'll do what's best," she said, patting my cheek. She let herself out, and I sank down into a chair in the living room. The tears began to trickle down my face again, and I rolled into a ball and fell asleep.

Three hours later, after I had slept for a couple of hours and had some time to think, I took the phone out onto the deck and called Amy.

"Hi Amy, it's Anna. How are you?"

"I'm fine, Anna."

"Good, glad to hear it. The reason I'm calling is because I need your help. I'd like to have a look at Jessie Wick. Would you be able to smuggle me onto the set one day when she's filming?"

I heard a sharp intake of breath. "Why do you want to see Jessie?"

"Because she and Jack had an affair four years ago, and because she might have been seeing him again recently. She might have wanted to get even with him for something he did to her years ago. I don't know for sure, but I can't let this murder go. I've got to find out who killed Jack."

There was dead silence on the line. "Are you still there, Amy?" I asked.

"Yes. I don't know, Anna. I'm thinking that it was a mistake to get involved with this in the first place. I'm sorry, but I'm afraid to do anything more."

"I understand that, Amy, really I do, and I don't blame you for one minute."

"Yesterday at the Primos was really scary."

"Oh, I know. I was terrified myself. And I'm just about finished with all of this. I'm sure that Sergeant Tremaine will discover that I didn't kill Jack without my help. The thing is, I'm afraid that he might not find the real murderer, and if he doesn't, people will always suspect that I did it. That would be an awful thing to have hanging over my head. I might even have to move out of town, and I'd hate to have to do that. I really like it here. So, for my sake and for Ben's, I'm hoping that you'll help me."

I was playing on her sympathy and I didn't like it, but I needed Amy's help to get onto the film set. After the talk I'd had with Erna, I thought that the best way to help my son would be to solve the murder so that we could put this all behind us. If Ben could forget about his father, maybe there was no need to tell him about my lie.

"I wouldn't want you to have to move away. It wouldn't be fair."

"No, it wouldn't. So if I could just have a look at Jessie – see what she's like and what kind of person she is – then I could form some sort of opinion about her. If you could do me this one last favour, I would really appreciate it."

"Well, I am scheduled back on set Thursday evening, and I think that Jessie is called then, too. I can double-check with the assistant director, if you like."

"That would be great. Listen, as long as you're talking to the assistant director, can you ask if Jessie was working on the night that Jack was killed?"

I heard a sigh. "Oh, Anna."

"Please?"

"I guess I can do that, too, but this will have to be the last time.

"Amy, you're wonderful! I promise that this will be the last favour I ask."

"Okay, I'll call you back when I have some information."

I hung up the phone feeling terribly guilty. Poor Amy, I was dragging her in deeper than she wanted to go. But I really intended this to be the last time I would use her, and I didn't think that visiting the set would put her in any danger. Hopefully, Thursday night's visit would be a revelation.

17

Amy phoned me back that evening to confirm that Jessie was called for the shoot on Thursday evening, and we made arrangements to drive to the set together after supper. She also told me that Jessie had not been working on the night that Jack was killed.

"But that doesn't mean much, Anna. After all, I wasn't working that night, and you don't suspect me."

"But you were working. You had a customer at six thirty."

"Oh, right, I forgot about that. Wait a minute! Anna Nolan, do you mean to tell me that if I hadn't had a client that evening, you would have suspected me of shooting Jack?"

"No, I wouldn't have. You're just not the murdering type. But, as it turns out, you did have a client."

Amy sniffed. "I'll pick you up at your house at six. I'm supposed to be in make-up by six thirty, so don't be late. Make sure you wear something plain so that you don't draw attention to yourself. I don't want Jessie noticing you. I asked the assistant director about bringing you, and she said that she didn't have a problem with it because you're Jack's widow. She thinks you want to see the last film Jack worked on because you're being sentimental. But let's not push our luck."

"Uh, Amy, do you know if either Karen or Connie will be on set Thursday night?"

Amy snorted. "No, of course they're not. Do you think I'd let you anywhere near them if they were? There's a second location in the mountains about seventy kilometres away. Connie and Karen are filming out there until Friday."

"That's good, but you shouldn't worry about them. They don't know that I was in their house yesterday."

"Well, I just think that it's a good idea to keep the three of you separated. You'll get in less trouble that way."

I smiled into the phone. Poor Amy, she really was spooked. I said, "I'll be waiting for you on Thursday. And thanks again."

"You're welcome," she said, swiftly cutting the connection.

As I drove to the university the next morning, I decided to concentrate on nothing but work for the whole day. I'd been distracted and letting things slide lately, which wasn't like me. I was usually the picture of efficiency. Tomorrow I'd be taking the day off for Jack's funeral, and there was still some fine-tuning to be done on the schedule for next year's winter classes before I could turn it over to the Scheduling Office. When I arrived at my desk, however, I found a sympathy card signed by everyone in the department. This token of support brought emotions best buried back to the surface, and I started to feel weepy. Hurrying to the ladies' washroom, I hid in there for half an hour before getting a grip on myself. People were very kind to me for the rest of the day, dropping by my desk to offer their sympathies and to see how I was holding up, and I kept my emotions in check as best as I could before scurrying home at four thirty.

I had trouble sleeping that night and woke up early feeling both tired and sad the next morning. It was time to say goodbye to Jack, and to the happiest and most miserable parts of my life. I crawled out of bed and took Wendy for a long walk, hoping that the exercise would help me to feel better. It did – it gave me time for a good long think. I shed some tears along the way, but by the time I got home, showered, and changed into a simple black dress, I felt ready to face the funeral with some degree of serenity.

I drove over to the church and parked on the street half an hour before the funeral was scheduled to start. Ferguson's hearse was already parked out front. The neighbourhood was quiet; no one was out for a walk at nine thirty in the morning. St. Bernadette's Elementary School was located right across the street from the church. The playground was always lively before and after school and at break times, but the children were all inside at their lessons. It was an overcast day, and I felt cheerless as I pulled the church's back door open and let myself in.

Father Winfield, dressed in a black robe with a purple stole, was standing beside the front pew talking with a man I didn't recognize. There was a tall wooden stand draped in white linen in the aisle beside him. The stranger, wearing a proper grey suit, held a brass urn in his arms. He had to be from the funeral parlour. Both men turned to look at me as I walked up the aisle.

"Anna, how are you this morning?" Father Winfield asked, laying a comforting hand on my shoulder.

"I'm fine, thank you, Father."

"Let me introduce you to Ferguson's funeral director, Mr. Albert Ferguson."

Mr. Ferguson placed the urn upon the stand and turned to take both of my hands. "How do you do, Mrs. Nolan? I'm pleased to make your acquaintance," he said in a well-modulated voice.

"Pleased to meet you, and thank you for looking after Jack."

He patted my hand. "You're very welcome. I hope that you're happy with my choice of urn for your husband's remains?"

I looked down at it and had the crazy notion that if I rubbed it three times, Jack might pop out like a genie. Death can have a strange effect on people. "Yes, it's very . . . handsome."

He released my hand. "Since we will not be progressing to the cemetery after the service, I'll remove the urn then and take it back with me. Tomorrow I will send the deceased's ashes to the funeral home you specified in Ontario."

"Thank you. Jack's mother and I both appreciate that."

"You're most welcome."

I glanced up at the altar stairs and saw a beautiful spray of spring flowers in a tall white vase placed beside my arrangement of roses. "How beautiful. I wonder who sent them," I said.

"They were delivered half an hour ago. The card that came with them says that the flowers are sent with the best wishes of Chinook University's Kinesiology Department," Father Winfield replied.

I was touched. I was usually the person who arranged for the delivery of flowers and sympathy cards on behalf of the department. Magdalena must have sent them herself.

"Would you like to take the flowers home with you after the service?" Father Winfield asked.

"Oh no, you keep them for the church, please."

Two giggly pre-pubescent girls burst through the sacristy door out onto the altar. Father Winfield waved at them before turning back to me.

"Please excuse me, Anna. The altar servers are here from the grade school." He climbed the stairs to the altar. "Good morning, Sherry and Jessica. Thank you for volunteering to assist us today. Please go get yourselves ready." The three disappeared back into the sacristy, Father Winfield herding the girls before him.

"I'll let you have a few moments to yourself before your guests arrive, Mrs. Nolan," said Mr. Ferguson, nodding and retreating down the aisle.

I turned back to the urn to take a closer look. Jack's name, and his birth and death dates, were inscribed upon it in a fine script.

"Well, here we are, Jack," I whispered, laying my hand on the sealed lid. "Neither of us saw this coming, did we? Funny how things turned out. We were so crazy in love when we got married, so thrilled the day that Ben was born, but it all ended in divorce. And then someone took your life." I paused, my eyes getting filmy. "We haven't figured out who did it yet, but we will, and we'll bring your killer to justice. Maybe you don't even care about that, wherever you are right now. Anyway, have a safe trip back to Ontario and your mother, and rest in peace. Hey, if you make it to heaven, say hello to my mother for me, will you?" I patted the jar and smiled.

The door opened at the back of the church and I turned to see who was coming in. May and Erna came down the aisle, Erna's hand tucked into May's arm, with Betty following behind them. I hurried forward to greet them.

"I didn't expect to see you here this morning," I said, delighted that they had come.

"Well, of course, doll," May replied. "Couldn't let you handle this all on your own. My son is looking after the store this morning."

Betty leaned in. "Sorry that Jeff couldn't be here. He had an emergency auger first thing this morning, but he said to tell you that he's thinking of you."

I gave her a hug. "That's okay, Betty. Thanks for coming, and tell Jeff that I said thanks, too."

Erna said, "Shall we take our places?" I nodded, and the four of us sat down together in the front pew. We chatted quietly, and then I knelt to say a prayer. My heart felt at peace now that I was surrounded by friends.

I heard the door open and close again, and Frank, Judy, and Mary came in together. Frank had on a brown tweed sports coat over his white shirt and jeans, and Judy wore a forest green silk blouse with black tailored trousers. Even Mary had on a sedate navy blue skirt that reached all the way to her knees. The women eased into the pew behind us as Frank stopped to grip my shoulder. I looked up into his face.

"Thanks for coming, Frank. You must have closed The Diner for this," I said, covering his hand with mine.

"No problem, Anna. We're sorry for your loss," he said gruffly. I turned and smiled at Judy and Mary.

The organist arrived and began playing generic classical musical. The interior lights flipped on. We sat together in silent contemplation, Erna patting my arm from time to time. The door opened again and I heard Clive Wampole shout, "See, Mr. Andrews, we made it with time to spare!"

I looked over my shoulder and saw Clive, wearing a brown suit and muddy boots, and Mr. Andrews, also in a suit, hurrying up the aisle. They both nodded to me, and I smiled and waved.

"Shove over, Frank," Clive said, and the new-comers joined the group from the restaurant.

The organist stopped playing, flipped through a few pages, and began the first hymn. We stood and watched the two young alter-servers process up the aisle, looking angelic in white surplices over their black robes. Father Winfield followed, swinging an orb that wafted incense before him. They passed our pew and paused to intone a prayer over Jack's ashes. As they climbed onto the altar, Ben suddenly appeared in the aisle beside me. He was wearing his only suit, a charcoal grey, with an open-collared white shirt. He bent to kiss my cheek and I gave him a quick hug, beaming up into his face. The ladies and I moved over to make room for him, and Ben genuflected and took his place beside me. He reached for my hand, and we turned to listen to the service.

When the congregation joined together in prayer, Ben leaned over to whisper, "Did you notice Tremaine? He's sitting in the back."

I looked over my shoulder to see Tremaine standing alone in a rear pew. His eyes met mine and he nodded. I nodded back at him and smiled. Our relationship had had its rocky moments, but I appreciated his kindness in coming today.

"I suppose he's here to see if the murderer is at the funeral," Ben whispered. I rolled my eyes and poked him discreetly in the side.

Father Winfield spoke mostly about forgiveness and redemption in his sermon, although he did talk a little about Jack, describing him as a loving husband and father. I glanced at Ben, who kept his eyes focused forward and his face blank. Finally, the funeral service came to an end and we sang the recessional hymn. Mr. Ferguson came forward to carry out the ashes with Father Winfield joining in behind him, followed by the altar-servers. Ben and I filed out of our pew with the rest of the mourners following us. I looked for Tremaine at the back of the church, but he had already slipped out. We walked through the lobby and out the back door, pausing in the grey morning light at the top of the stairs. I thanked Mr. Ferguson and Father Winfield for their services, and we all watched silently as the funeral director placed the urn into the hearse and drove away.

I sidled over to Frank. "Frank," I whispered, "I'd like to take us all out for an early lunch at The Diner. Is that okay with you?"

"No problem, Anna. We can handle that."

"Thank you." I turned to my friends and smiled. "You're all wonderful for coming to be with Ben and me this morning. It's good to be surrounded by friends at a time like this." People nodded, or ducked their heads and smiled. "Please join us for lunch at The Diner."

Everyone thought that lunch would be very nice, so, after sorting out our cars, we formed a procession and drove the short distance to Main Street with Clive and his tractor bringing up the rear. As we cruised along at about twenty kilometres an hour, Ben in his car behind me, I thought myself lucky to have found this small town and all of these dear friends. I felt very happy on what had promised to be a sad and lonely morning.

18

Ben and I lingered at the restaurant after everyone else had left until Frank had to close up at two. During our conversation, my son reminded me that the only other funeral he had ever attended had been my mother's, who had died of a stroke when he was six. Ben and I had flown back to Ontario for the funeral, and while his memories of the flight and the airport were still quite vivid, he had very little recollection of the service. Unfortunately, Ben's memories of his grandfather were equally sketchy, since he hadn't seen him since Mom's funeral. Dad had remarried two years after Mom passed, and had become very attached to his new wife's children and grandchildren. We ended up drifting even further apart than we had been when I left home to become an actress. Now I only heard from Dad when I called to wish him happy birthday, or received a Christmas newsletter from his wife.

I told Ben that I was planning to pay for his university education when I received the money from his father's insurance policy. "I'm sure that your father would have approved if he had known," I said.

Ben said, "Let's talk about it later. I really don't want to talk about Dad anymore today," so I let the subject drop. I hadn't heard what was going on about Ben's alibi, however, so I asked if he had seen or heard anything from Tremaine.

"Yeah, I gave him some more information about what I did before I met Tracy on the night Dad died," he said.

"What did you tell him?"

"That I went back to the drugstore a couple of times until I spotted the cashier who had waited on me. I got her name and asked her to give Tremaine a call."

"That's terrific, honey. Did Tremaine seem satisfied with that?"

Ben shrugged and said, "Who knows?" I groaned and rolled my eyes. "What? What else do you want from me?" Ben said, gesturing impatiently with both hands.

"Nothing. I'm just pleased that you're sorting it out. Tremaine will take it from there," I said, forcing a smile. I didn't want to argue with him today, but I wished that Ben would take his alibi as seriously as I did. Instead of harping on the subject, however, I kissed him goodbye before he headed back to work in Calgary. His boss had told him to take all the time he needed for the funeral, but Ben didn't want to abuse his boss's good will by staying away for too long. It rained for the rest of the afternoon, and I spent the time reading one of my well-loved Miss Marple mysteries and making a pot of beef vegetable soup for supper.

I went back to work the next day, and life almost returned to normal. The funeral had provided me with a sort of closure, and I was having second thoughts about continuing my efforts to find Jack's killer. I sure didn't want my clumsy interference to screw up the police investigation, but I had already arranged the film set visit with Amy, so I decided to go through with it. Amy had told me that they would be filming a big action scene with lots of extras on Thursday night, so if nothing else, it would be entertaining to watch. Besides, I had to admit that I was curious to have a look at the woman who had finally broken up my marriage.

I got home from work at five and scrambled to get ready in time so that I wouldn't make Amy late. When her car pulled up out front at six, I was outside waiting on the porch. It was a warmish evening, and I had changed into jeans and a sleeveless blue plaid shirt. Climbing into the car, I greeted her with a cheery hello, but received only a stiff nod in return. Obviously, Amy didn't approve of my visit to tonight's film set. I noticed that her beautiful red hair was braided and woven into a bun, and decided that a little flattery might warm her up.

"Is that for the movie?" I asked, pointing at her hair.

"Uh huh. The hair and make-up people let me do my own hair since I'm a professional. It saves time for all of us."

"It looks really pretty on you."

Her face softened and she smiled at me. "Thanks."

On the way over to Longview, Amy chatted about the film's plot and about the scene that they were shooting tonight. "We're using the Main Street set. It's supposed to look like part of an old western frontier town. There's a dirt road with fake storefronts on both sides, and a jailhouse. The bad guys are supposed to chase Miss Stacey – that's the girl who's in love with the sheriff but doesn't get him in the end – into town on horseback and kidnap her. I'll be one of the townsfolk on the street, reacting to what's happening. Jessie will be doubling for the actress playing Miss Stacey. It should be pretty exciting."

"Sounds like fun," I replied. "And don't worry about me. I'll be on my best behaviour and stay out of everyone's way. You won't hear a peep out of me." Amy smiled and looked relieved. I wondered if the questions she had been asking had created trouble for her on the set, but things were better now between us, and I didn't want to bring it up.

We drove down a dirt lane and parked beside the set, which had been built on a private ranch outside of Longview. Amy signed me in with the security guard and led me over to the caterer's table, which they call "craft services" for some strange reason. I helped myself to a bottle of juice and a cookie before Amy left for the costume trailer to get changed. I found an unoccupied bench in an out-of-the-way corner and watched the steady stream of actors coming and going from the costume trailer and the hair and make-up tent. There were a handful of women milling around in long skirts, shirtwaists, and bonnets, along with a couple of little boys in short pants and suspenders, but the majority of the cast were men. That made sense; there were more men than women occupying frontier towns in the old days. I wondered if any of the costumed women were Jessie Wick, but I didn't notice anyone who matched Erna's description of her.

The crew was also bustling about purposefully, unrolling electrical cables and hauling equipment to the set on the other side of the preparation area. An intense, harassed-looking man strode by with a cell phone glued to his ear, a couple of anxious people rushing after him. Maybe he was the producer? Amy emerged from the make-up tent in a long skirt, jacket, and bonnet, and hurried over to me.

"Come on, it's time to go to the set. I'm going to introduce you to Rachel Miller, the assistant director. After that, they'll find you somewhere to sit."

I nodded and followed in her wake as we were jostled by the crowd headed for the set. We walked past the trucks and trailers and rounded a corner onto Main Street. Looking around me, I felt transported back in time to a frontier town complete with stores, wooden sidewalks, watering troughs, and hitching posts. White lace curtains fluttered out the open windows of what I assumed was a boarding house. There was also a smithy and barn, a saloon, a jail, and an undertaker's parlour. Even though I could see that the buildings were only false fronts, and that twenty-first century film equipment and crew in contemporary dress were on the set, it was easy to ignore the intrusion of the modern world to imagine what it would have been like living in the old west.

Amy introduced me to Rachel Miller, a thin, earnest-looking woman in her early thirties who shook my hand briskly and offered her condolences. She escorted me to a folding chair on the edge of the set and left me there to watch the action while she went to rehearse the extras. A young man with a clipboard hovered nearby on the sidewalk, muttering to himself and making notes. The director, a grizzle-haired man with a cigarette jutting from his lower lip, was talking to the crew over his head set. A camera man with a chase camera in a car with its motor running was waiting at the far end of the street, while lighting and sound crew were getting ready in strategic positions all along the set. The director walked over to a crane and climbed into a seat beside a camera man. A crew member snapped a clapboard in front of the camera, and the crane soared into the air for a comprehensive view of the street.

The director picked up the electronic megaphone strapped to his chair and started snapping orders. "All right, people, we're ready to begin. Cameras?"

"Camera One!" "Camera Two!" the camera crew shouted back.

"Sound?"

"Ready!" the sound crew called.

"Okay, let's see some energy. Action!" the director shouted.

The extras started strolling down the wooden sidewalks while the chase camera waited. Over top of the extras' chatter, I could hear the rumble of horses galloping toward us. A beautiful golden horse appeared at the end of the street. A woman perched on its back; Jessie Wick, I presumed. Her long dress was hiked up around her knees, enabling her to straddle the horse. A straw hat bounced up and down by its ribbons on the back of her neck, strands of hair streaming in long tendrils behind her as she crouched over the horse's neck. The camera car drove about fifteen feet ahead of her and her mount as she hurtled down the street. Four men with long coats flapping over their horses' rumps came galloping hard behind her. A couple of townsfolk crossing the street raced to get out of the way.

As Jessie came closer, I saw her slap her horse's flank with the reins she held gathered in one hand. Her pursuers were gaining on her, and the lead horseman caught her by the time they were still half a block away from us. He grabbed the reins from Jessie's hand and dragged her horse to a standstill. The horse reared up into the air, throwing Jessie back into the saddle. The horse landed, and the stuntman threw his arm around Jessie's waist and dragged her from her saddle onto the front of his. Jessie flailed against him as she struggled to get down, but the horseman clamped her to his chest. One of the other horsemen rode forward to grab the golden horse's reins. The head stuntman whistled, and the group galloped forward with their captive. The camera car rushed past us with the stunt people thundering after it, disappearing in a cloud of dust. The director shouted "Cut," and the extras on the street froze.

"That was terrific, everyone. Okay, let's shoot another master. Lose the chase vehicle. Everyone back to ones. Check the gates," the director roared.

It seemed as if everyone was talking at once as the extras hurried back down the street and a crew member began scuffing up the horse tracks in the street with his feet. The stunt people came trotting back toward us. Jessie still sat in the saddle with the stuntman, his arm encircling her waist and her head thrown back as they laughed over a joke. They stopped in front of the director, who was hovering at street level on the crane. Jessie jumped down lightly from the saddle.

"How was that, Gene?" she called to the director.

"Beautiful, sweetheart. Do exactly the same thing over again."

"No problem," she said with a grin as the hair and makeup team converged upon her and the rest of the stunt crew.

Now that she was only yards away from me, I had my first opportunity to get a good look at Jessie. Her beautiful black hair was her most striking feature, with a chiseled nose and broad jawline making her handsome rather than pretty. Jessie was tall with an athletic build and a confident way about her. She snapped her fingers, and the make-up women handed her a mirror before reapplying blush to Jessie's olive-toned face. Nodding her satisfaction, she handed the mirror back to the woman without even looking at her, and strode back to her horse. Jessie whispered something in the animal's ear and stroked its neck before hiking up her skirt and vaulting back into the saddle.

The stuntman who had snatched her from her horse rode up and said something to her. She laughed and slapped him on the shoulder before cantering off down the street ahead of him. I shook my head. She looked like she had a lot of personality, and I wondered how Jack had handled her when the two of them had been together. I almost felt sorry for him in retrospect. I was glad that I had decided not to fight for my marriage. She would have been a powerful adversary, and the fight wouldn't have been worth it.

I watched them do a second shot just as thrilling as the first, and then the shoot was over for the night. The extras surged up the sidewalk headed for the trailers and Amy appeared, looking pleased and flushed. "What did you think, Anna? They were great, weren't they?" she asked.

"It was wonderful. Those stunt people sure are talented. Everything seemed so real. I really enjoyed watching that." She beamed and talked nonstop about the scene until we arrived at the costume trailer and she left me to change out of her clothes. It wasn't until we were alone in her car together headed home to Crane that she broached the subject of Jessie Wick.

"What did you think of Jessie?" she asked.

"She seems like a strong, competent woman. She looks as if she can really handle herself."

Amy glanced at me and whispered, "But, does she seem capable of murder?"

I hesitated. "I don't know. Who can say? She looks like she can do anything she sets her mind to. On the other hand, Jessie doesn't seem like the kind of woman who'd be devastated by a break-up with Jack. I just can't see her pining over him, can you? Besides, what sane woman kills a man four years after the affair is over?"

Amy nodded her agreement. "Yes, she'd have to be obsessed to do that. And – come on – she was having an affair with a married man in the middle of a film shoot, after all. Most women wouldn't expect anything permanent under those circumstances."

"No, you wouldn't think so."

"And Jessie has a solid reputation. I haven't heard of any problems with her," she added.

"What do people say about her?"

"That she's smart and ambitious. Whenever I see her, she's hanging around with the stuntmen rather than with other actresses. That's natural, I guess, given her business. I guess you'd call her a man's kind of woman."

"Right, which means that she's low maintenance and not too much trouble. Someone who wouldn't get all clingy when the affair was over. That still doesn't fit with the revenge angle. I'll have to give this a lot of thought, Amy."

Amy pursed her lips and nodded. As I looked at her, I wondered how Jack could have been involved with three such very different women. Had Clive been right when he had said that Jack chased anything in a skirt? I had spent seventeen years with him, and Jack was still a mystery to me. I mulled that over for the rest of the evening, and it was my last thought as I fell asleep that night.

Back at the university the next morning, I decided to ask our mail carrier for her opinion of men. Alice was a down-to-earth, salt-of the-earth kind of person – well, to be truthful, she was just plain earthy – and she had no illusions about men after thirty years of marriage. She barrelled into my office at the usual time on her Birkenstock-clad feet.

"Morning, Anna. How's it going?" she asked, plunking down the mail and picking up an outgoing envelope.

"Just fine. Hey, Alice, do you have a minute? I want to ask you your opinion on something."

There was never much mail to deliver in the spring term, so Alice hoisted herself up onto the table beside the mail trays and made herself comfortable.

"Sure I have a minute. Shoot."

"It's a male/female relationship kind of question. In your experience, do men go for a variety of women, or do they mostly stick to the same type?"

"Hey, that's a good one. Let me think about that for a moment." Alice leaned back on her arms to stare at me. "Hmm, judging by my husband and my brothers, I'd say that men like to stay within a certain league, you know? Basically, I think men are kind of lazy when it comes to romance. They don't want to try too hard if it means risking failure. Or, maybe they're just scared, eh? Nah, they're lazy. My Mike used to date one of my girlfriends before he dated me, and we were both from the same neighbourhood, the same school, the same circle, you know? We all grew up together. Even now he likes actresses who look like they have street-smarts rather than the swankier kind of woman. Take Meryl Streep. I think that Meryl Streep would intimidate the hell out of Mike. Or Cate Blanchet. She's such a classy-looking woman. But Debra Winger in *An Officer and a Gentleman* or Karen Allen in *Raiders of the Lost Ark* – he always went for them. Hmm. Maybe he just likes brunettes? Now, isn't that interesting. I'll have to ask him."

I smiled at her as she hopped off the table and headed for the door. "Thanks, Alice. I've learned a lot from you and Mike over the years."

"Don't mention it, sweetie," she called over her shoulder as she hurried away.

Magdalena popped into my doorway and said, "That's an interesting theory Alice just shared with you."

I jumped and just about fell out of my chair. "Magdalena," I squeaked, "I didn't hear you come in."

As she walked into my office, my eyes trailed down to her feet, and I saw that they were clad in ballet-style flats instead of her usual lofty heels. Her eyes followed my glance.

"My shoes got a little muddy in the parking lot from last night's rain. I'm letting them dry before I brush them off," she said. I nodded. "If you don't mind listening to another opinion," she continued, "I'm inclined to agree with Alice's theory that men choose their mates from a similar social stratum. They want women with an educational and social background equivalent to their own – unless they're using marriage to promote their careers – and they don't often venture beyond those criteria. Women, on the other hand, traditionally choose men with better educations and earning potential to ensure a good provider for themselves and their children."

I stared at her. Were we sharing a bonding moment?

"What do you think, Anna?"

"Well, I guess I would have to agree with you, although sometimes young people rebel against their backgrounds and parents' standards and go for someone completely unsuitable."

Magdalena nodded. "There are always exceptions. Is that what you did?"

"What, in marrying Jack?"

"Yes."

I thought for a moment. "Acting was an unsuitable career choice in my parents' minds. They were pretty conservative people – Mom was a housewife and Dad was an engineer. But I didn't choose acting to rebel against them. I was always drawn to the theatre. Jack was just part of the whole, glamorous package. In my eyes, it was all magical."

"Very interesting. I had no idea that you were once an actress."

"I was for the first couple of years that we were married. I attended an acting program at one of the college's back in Toronto. That's how I met Jack, as a matter of fact. He was hired on as a guest director for one of our plays."

"Ah, now I understand the attraction. A young college girl falling in love with her teacher, a mature man who appeared both successful and glamorous."

I nodded. "Yes, Jack was ten years older than I, and a darn sight more worldly. He had such personal presence. You should have seen him back then, Magdalena – he was magnificent. When he stood on the stage under those lights, the girls would just melt – and some of the boys, too."

Magdalena studied me as I reminisced. "Why didn't you stay with acting?"

Her question brought me back down to earth. "I guess I grew up in a hurry when I got pregnant. Acting didn't work for me in the real world."

"'All that glitters is not gold?'"

"That's right."

"And here you are."

"Yes, here I am."

"And we're glad to have you. You're a very efficient worker and a sympathetic person. We all rely on you."

I smiled. "That's nice to hear. Thank you, Magdalena."

"You're welcome. Now, I have to prepare for a scheduling meeting with the dean. I'll see you later." She turned and left my office.

I stared after her. Wow, our first real conversation. Maybe we were more simpatico than I had imagined. Feeling a little more warm and fuzzy toward my boss, I returned to work.

19

I picked up a couple of medium pizzas before leaving Calgary so that Ben and I could each have our favourite kind – the "works" for me and "Greek" for Ben – and was feeding Wendy when he arrived. Ben made use of my washing machine, and then we chatted about what had happened during the week since seeing each other at the funeral. I watched Ben closely, trying to diagnose his emotional health because I was feeling guilty about not revealing my lie concerning the made-up affair. Ben seemed fine to me, at least superficially, but we were both trying to keep the mood light. The murder investigation seemed to be making us both wary of each other.

"Hey, Mom, are you okay?" Ben asked during our after-dinner walk. "You seem kind of weird tonight."

"Weird? That's a strange thing to say. What do you mean?" I asked, keeping an eye on Wendy as she crept toward a squirrel sitting on the ground nibbling a pine cone. The squirrel scampered up a tree and chattered at Wendy from the safety of its branch twelve feet high in the air. Wendy plunked down at the base of the tree and stared up at her.

"I don't know, it feels like you're uncomfortable or something. Every time I look at you, you look away." Either my son was more perceptive than I had thought, or I was being too transparent. I was going to have to learn to be a better liar. "Is this about the insurance money again?" he asked.

I was glad to distract Ben with talk about money, but we ended up arguing over whether or not he should be taking money from me instead of borrowing it from the government.

"Why don't you just enjoy the money and stop worrying about me?" he said. "I'm already getting a fifty percent discount on tuition, plus I'm putting money aside this summer. I'll be fine. I've got my whole life to pay off the student loans."

"Yes, but I don't want you to have to pay off student loans for the rest of your life. Let me help you out. There's enough money to pay off the mortgage and cover your bachelor degree. What do you want me to spend the money on – a trip around the world?"

"Yes!" he replied. We still hadn't come to an agreement by the time Ben left at seven thirty. I was feeling tired, and since Wendy had already had her walk, I changed into my pyjamas and stretched out on the couch to watch a little TV. The telephone rang two hours later in the middle of a home improvement show, and I fumbled for the telephone on the end table beside me.

"Hello?" I said.

"Anna, it's me," a frantic voice replied.

"Amy?"

"Yes. You've got to come help me. Connie Primo is outside my house, and he's trying to get in! I'm afraid."

"What?" I asked, sitting bolt upright. "What do you mean? What's Connie doing?"

"He was banging on my front door, but I peeked out the curtains and saw who it was and wouldn't let him in. I think he saw me, Anna. He gave up for a few minutes, but then I heard him trying to get in the deck door. What should I do?"

I jumped off the couch with the phone in my hand. "Don't do anything, Amy. Stay inside the house and don't open the door. I'll be right over." I ran into the bedroom to get my purse and then dashed to the front closet.

"Oh, Anna, be careful," she said. "He's got such a temper."

"Don't worry, Amy. I'm bringing Wendy. Turn on your porch light. We'll come straight to your front door." I cradled the phone against my shoulder and slid an arm into my coat.

"Hurry, it sounds like he's trying to break open the dining room window!" she shrieked.

I snapped the leash on Wendy's collar, and we dashed out of the house. Jumping into the car, we sped the few blocks to Amy's house, ignoring the stop signs along the way. I skidded to a halt in front of her house, bracing my arm against Wendy to stop her from flying off the seat. Dragging her out of the driver's door behind me, I slammed the door shut and locked it with a click of the remote. I scanned the street and saw Connie's jeep parked a little way ahead. The jeep was empty.

Opening the gate to Amy's house, Wendy and I bolted for the front door. As we did, Connie came running around the side of the house.

"Hey!" he shouted, charging across the lawn toward us. Wendy started barking and lunged at him, dragging me a few feet forward before I could brace myself.

"What do you want, Connie?" I shouted over her barking. Connie backed up a step and scowled at me. "I don't want you. I want to talk to your ditzy friend, but she won't open the door."

Amy must have heard him because the door flew open and she stepped out onto the porch. She was dressed in shorts and a midriff-baring t-shirt, her feet bare.

"Leave me alone, Connie," she wailed. "Go home."

"Listen, I want to talk to you," he yelled, barrelling toward the house. Wendy snarled and barked, lunging like a hooked fish on a line.

"Stay away from her, Connie!" I shouted, sprinting after him. He made it to the porch before I did and grabbed Amy's arm. She screamed, and I let go of Wendy's leash. Wendy cannoned up the steps and leapt into the air. She crashed into Connie's back and knocked them both over. I stepped over their thrashing bodies, snatched Amy's hand, and hauled her up.

"Get inside," I said, shoving her toward the door. Connie had turned over and was holding Wendy at arm's length as she tore at his clothes with her sharp claws.

"Get your damn dog off me!" Connie shouted, and I seized Wendy by the leash and dragged her away, still snarling and barking. The neighbour's porch light flicked on next door. Connie stumbled to his feet and backed away from us, the front of his jacket ripped.

"What do you want, Connie?" I asked. "Down, Wendy," I ordered. She obeyed but kept growling. As I rubbed her back, I could feel the tense muscles beneath her coat.

Connie held his leather jacket up in front of him. "Look at that! Look at what she did to my jacket," he shouted.

"You're lucky you had it on," I said. "You still haven't told me. What are you doing here?"

"Karen and I just got back from the location shoot. Amy was in my house last Saturday and stole my gun." He looked past me and shook his fist at the house. "I want my gun back, you crazy bitch," he bawled. I turned and saw Amy still standing in the doorway, shaking.

"I didn't take your gun," she said in a tremulous voice.

"Oh, yeah? You're lying. I had the gun out last week to clean it, and no one's been in the house since then except you, me, and Karen. You were acting real strange at the house last Saturday, and Karen and I heard you come back inside while we were upstairs. I know you've got it."

"I don't have it. Karen was with me the whole time I was inside the house. She would have seen me if I had taken it. And I didn't come back inside. I left as soon as you fixed my car."

Connie was about to say more when we heard the wail of a siren. A cruiser, its lights flashing, flew down the street toward us. It careened to a stop across the street, and Steve Walker sprang out. Amy moaned, and as I turned to look at her, I caught a glimpse of a white-haired woman peeking at us from the house next door.

"Steve, I'm glad you're here," Connie shouted as Steve strode up the front lawn. "I want these two arrested," he said, pointing at Amy and me, "and I want her dog put down. It attacked me. Look what it did to my jacket." He held it up in front of him for Steve to see.

"Calm down, Connie," Steve said, holding up his hands as he climbed the porch steps. "I'm Constable Walker, ma'am," he added, introducing himself to Amy. "Someone called in a complaint about a domestic disturbance. Now, what's this all about?"

The radio clipped to his belt squawked and he answered it. "Yeah, I'm at Ms. Bright's house right now. No, no back-up required." He looked at me. "Anna, you want to tell me what's going on here?"

"She's got my gun," Connie broke in, pointing at Amy. "She stole it out of my house. I want you to get a warrant and search her place for it."

Steve turned to Amy. "Ms. Bright?"

Amy left the safety of the doorway to creep closer to Steve. "It's not true, Constable," she pleaded, her eyes shining with tears. "I was visiting with Karen last Saturday, but I didn't take Connie's gun. I don't even know where he keeps it. How could I? I never set foot in their house before then." Steve gazed into her eyes, and then looked at Connie.

"You got any proof?" he asked.

Connie uncrossed his arms and waved them in Steve's face. "Proof? It had to be her, there was no one else. And don't go all soft over those baby blues of hers. She's a thief, I tell you."

Steve spent the next half hour straightening things out. He convinced Connie not to press charges against Amy and me by pointing out that Amy could press trespassing and assault charges against him. He also reprimanded Connie for not filing a missing weapon report, and made him promise to come into the station first thing Monday morning to fill out the paperwork. Dissatisfied, Connie grumbled as he lumbered back to his car. Once he left, Amy threw her arms around Steve, startling him.

"You were wonderful, Constable Walker," she said, pressing up against him. "The way you took charge and fixed everything was like a dream. I was so afraid of Connie. Who knows what he might have done if you hadn't come. Thank you ever so much." She stood up on tiptoe and kissed his cheek.

"Just doing my job, Ms. Bright," he said, grinning down at her.

"Please, call me Amy," she said, releasing him and linking her arm through his. I shook my head. Amy must have been ten years older than Steve, but that didn't seem to bother either one of them. Actually, Steve being distracted by another woman was a good thing. Hopefully it would help him to forget about me. I was sitting on the porch steps beside Wendy, keeping my mouth shut and comforting my dog as Amy and Steve flirted some more. Finally, Steve looked down at me.

"You got anything to add, Anna?" he asked. I stood up and stretched, Wendy springing to her feet beside me. No way I was going to tell him that I had the gun after all of this. I was eternally grateful to Amy that she hadn't told on me to Connie or Steve.

"No. I met Mr. Primo for the first time at The Spur the other night – you were there. He seemed a thoroughly unpleasant man then, and his behaviour tonight just confirms that."

"Yes, Connie might have broken in a window if Anna and Wendy hadn't gotten here so fast," Amy added.

"Well, next time you have a problem, Amy, call the police," Steve said. "Then there won't be any misunderstandings about assault and people's dogs."

"I'll be sure to do that. I don't suppose you have a business card in case I ever need you again, do you?"

Steve reached into his shirt pocket. "Here you are," he said with a smile. "And call me 'Steve.'"

"Thank you, Steve. I feel so much safer with this," she said, tucking it into her cleavage. Steve's eyes followed his card and lingered there. I nudged him with my elbow.

"I'm going home now unless you need anything else from me," I said.

He untangled his arm from Amy's and patted her hand. "No, that's all I need for tonight, ladies. I'm afraid I have to be going, too. Good night, Amy," he said, saluting her with two fingers.

"Bye, bye Steve," she replied, giving him a bright smile. We headed for the sidewalk together, Steve opening the gate for me with a bow. I smiled and shook my head at him as Wendy and I passed through. Wendy needed to relieve herself, so I paused to let her water the boulevard while Steve climbed into his cruiser. I heard the radio squawk, and Steve respond. I had just let Wendy into the car and was settling into the driver's seat when he called me.

"Anna!"

I looked up and saw him crossing the street toward me. His expression was grim, and I felt a sudden foreboding.

"What is it?" I asked as he walked up to my door.

"It's Ben. Tremaine's just taken him in for questioning."

20

Steve argued against it for five whole minutes, but in the end I followed him to the police station. He knew that he couldn't stop me from trying to see my son, and I pointed out that I was less likely to get into a car accident if I followed behind him. Reaching the back parking lot first, I sprang out of the car and towed Wendy behind me as I raced for the door.

"Whoa, Anna, calm down," Steve said, catching up to me. I pulled on the door handle, but it was locked. Steve put a hand on my shoulder, and I turned to look up into his face.

"I mean it. You shouldn't even be here. I want you to keep quiet and sit where I tell you to sit until I find out what's happening with Ben." I nodded, my jaw so tight that I'd have to break it open to speak.

"Okay," Steve said, unlocking the door. "Follow me, and keep Wendy quiet."

We hurried down the same grey hallway we had passed through on the night Steve had brought me in to make my statement. The door to the interview room was closed. I stared at it as we went by, wishing that I could see through it. I was certain that Tremaine had Ben in there. Steve led me through a locked door into the lobby at the front of the building. It was after hours, so the station was closed. An orange security bulb outside the glass door provided the only illumination. There were a couple of black plastic chairs sitting in front of a closed service window, an artificial potted fern the only decoration in the room.

"You'll have to wait here, Anna," Steve said. "I'm not allowed to bring you into the office. I'll talk to the guys and see what's going on. I shouldn't be too long."

"Thanks, Steve," I mumbled, loosening my jaw. The door clicked shut behind him and I sat in one of the chairs, leaning my head against the cool, grey wall. Wendy settled at my feet. The room had a shadowy, nightmarish quality, no doubt made worse by my frightened imaginings. Tremaine had brought Ben in for questioning. Was arrest the next step? What could Tremaine have discovered that would justify bringing Ben in? Had Ben been hiding something from me?

My thoughts were too scattered to be rational, and I tried to calm down. I had to think about Ben's needs now. What rights did a person have when they were brought in for questioning? A lawyer – did Ben need a lawyer? When the police questioned suspects on television, they often had a lawyer.

Steve came back into the lobby. "Do you know a good lawyer?" I asked, jumping to my feet.

"What?" he said. "You mean for Ben? Take it easy, Anna. I don't know if Ben has already requested a lawyer. Tremaine is talking to him right now – the guys said they've been in there about half an hour. When Tremaine comes out, I'll ask him what's going on. Or, you could go home and I could call you when they're done. I don't know how long they'll be, and it's not very comfortable here."

"No, I'll stay. If I go home, I won't be able to sleep anyway, worrying about what's happening to Ben."

"Okay, Anna. Whatever you want. Can I get you a glass of water or something? "

"No thanks. I'm fine."

"All right. I'll come back as soon as Tremaine comes up for air." He left the room and I sank back into the hard chair to wait. Wendy sighed, and I reached down to scratch behind her ears.

But I couldn't sit still, so I jumped up to pace around the room. What if Ben were arrested for Jack's murder? I would need to find him a lawyer, arrange bail – would I have enough money to bail him out? Would he be kept here, or transferred to another jail? What about his job? Would his employer hold his job for him, or would he fire Ben for being arrested for murder? Would Ben's reputation be ruined if he were arrested? What if he had to move away and start over again somewhere else? Or would it be better for him to stay here where he was surrounded by family and friends?

"Oh Lord, help me, I'm going crazy," I prayed. I sank back into the chair and buried my head in my hands just as the door clicked open, startling me. I looked up to see Tremaine entering the lobby, looking business-like in a suit. I sat up and swept the hair out of my face as he sat down beside me.

"How are you, Anna?" he asked, bending to pat Wendy, his voice neutral.

"Tremaine," I replied with a nod, trying to appear more collected than I felt.

"You've come about Ben." He leaned forward and clasped his hands between his knees.

"Yes. What's going on?" I asked, unable to keep the tremor out of my voice.

"A witness came forward after lunch to report a suspicious car parked out front of the O'Cleary ranch on the evening that your ex-husband was killed. Do you know the place?"

Mrs. O'Cleary had been a friend of May Weston's, so I knew about the family. Mrs. O'Cleary had died a few years ago, and her daughter was letting the ranch deteriorate while she tried to sell it for more money than it was worth.

"Yes, I've driven past it. It's south of Longview on 181A. You're not saying . . ?"

Tremaine nodded. "The witness gave us a description of the car and an almost complete plate number. It matched Ben's. We got permission to search the barn this evening and found blood in the lounge. We're waiting for the test results to see if it's your ex-husband's."

I took a deep breath. "So, you may have found the place where Jack was murdered?"

Tremaine shrugged. "Maybe. It certainly fits the scenario. It's secluded. No one's lived on the property for three years. There were signs that other parts of the barn have been used, too, although not recently."

"What did Ben have to say about his car being seen there?" I asked, wrapping my arms around myself for warmth.

"That it wasn't his car. That he was in Calgary at the time."

I shook my head. "Why now, Tremaine? It's been two weeks since Jack died. What prompted our concerned citizen to come forward now?"

"The witness said she heard about the crime, but had to go away on business and didn't have a chance to come into the station until this afternoon."

So, the witness was a woman. I concentrated hard, picturing the location of the ranch. Township Road 181A was pretty close to the movie set. Was the witness someone from the movie? "Who's your witness, Tremaine?" I asked.

He shook his head. "I can't tell you that, Anna."

"Why not?"

"To protect the witness's privacy, and to prevent you from getting into any more trouble."

I had a brainwave. "Was it Karen Quill?"

Tremaine stared at me, cool as an English cucumber. "Why would you think it was her?"

"Did you tell Karen and Connie that I was spying on them the night Amy and I talked to them at the Spur?"

He stiffened. "No. Why?"

"Because maybe they figured Amy and I were taking too much interest in them and wanted to distract me by getting Ben in trouble with the police. And there was a nasty to-do over at Amy's house tonight. Did you hear about it? Connie's gun is missing, and he accused Amy of stealing it. Don't you think it's a bit of a coincidence, Connie accusing Amy of stealing his gun and my son's car reported at the O'Cleary ranch, all on the same day? I think that the Primos are trying to get back at Amy and me."

Tremaine reached forward and tapped my knee. "Do you have anything to do with that missing gun?"

I looked him straight in the eye and said, "Of course not." We stared at each other for a moment, neither one of us looking away. "So, now what?" I asked. "What's going to happen to Ben?"

Tremaine leaned back in his chair and checked his watch. I glanced at mine; it was close to eleven thirty. "I'm done with Ben for the night. You can take him home, but he'll have to come back for his car tomorrow. I've impounded it, and the forensics squad will be examining it tomorrow morning."

It frightened me that Ben's car was being tested, and yet I couldn't believe that the forensics squad would come up with any evidence against him. I tried to conceal my fear from Tremaine, for Ben's sake.

"What happens if the test results show that Jack died in the O'Cleary lounge, but there's no evidence that Ben was there or that Jack was in his car?"

Tremaine turned away from me to stare out the lobby door. I took a good look at his face for the first time. There were purple shadows under his eyes and blond stubble on his face. It must have been hours since his last shave. Unexpectedly, his mouth creased at the corners. "Then I'll have to find someone else to suspect."

I nodded, glad that he admitted the possibility of Ben's innocence. I looked at his face with its amused half-smile and thought, "I like this man. I trust him." Then he turned and looked at me with his intelligent grey eyes, and I was afraid. Tremaine was a good man, but he would follow this investigation through to the end, whatever he discovered and no matter what the consequences. I shivered.

"What is it, Anna?" he asked in a gentle voice. "Do you want to tell me something?"

I thought what a relief it would be to open up to him. I could tell him about the crazy dream I had had in which Ben killed his father, and how the lie I had told Jack might earn my son's everlasting hatred. How about if I told him that I had searched the Primos' house and taken Connie's gun, and now I was worried about getting it back to him? I stared at Tremaine, wondering if confession would be good for my soul, or if it would bring all manner of tribulation down upon my head.

"Anna?"

"No," I murmured. He sighed. "But, I'm grateful to you, Tremaine, I really am. I know I shouldn't have come tonight. Thanks for taking the time to see me." I touched the back of his hand, letting my fingers linger there for a moment. He nodded and looked away.

"Ben's waiting for you in the interview room. Why don't you take him home now?"

"Sure," I said, rising to my feet with Wendy scrambling to hers.

He held the door open for us and we headed to the interview room together. The door was open and Ben was sitting in a chair with his arms folded over his chest, his face sullen. He climbed to his feet as I came in, and I noticed that he was wearing his uniform from the building supply store. I turned to Tremaine.

"You picked him up at work?"

He looked at me from the hallway, his expression blank. "Yes. Just as soon as we found blood in the O'Cleary barn."

I grimaced. "Damn. Couldn't you have been more discreet? What if he loses his job over this?"

Tremaine didn't say a word, just stood there staring at me. I sighed and turned back to Ben, hugging him to me. "Let's go home, honey," I said into his ear. He nodded, and then squeezed me tight before letting go.

"Let's get out of here," he said, putting an arm around my shoulders.

Tremaine escorted us to the back door and pushed the crash bar open for me. "Your car should be ready by noon," he said, looking at my son. Ben's body was taut and his face was full of resentment.

"Yeah, I'll be back for it," Ben said. He pushed past Tremaine and left me standing in the hallway beside the sergeant.

"Good night, Anna. Sleep well," Tremaine said, his eyes tired. I hesitated, not sure how I felt about him. Would I have done any differently in his shoes?

"Come on, Mom," Ben said from the parking lot. I met Tremaine's eyes, nodded, and followed my son to the car.

As we headed for home, I began questioning him. "What happened? What did he ask you?"

"The same old crap about my alibi. Where were you? What time did you leave the house? Who did you see on the way to the theatre? All the stuff he asked me before."

"Did Tremaine say he checked your alibi with the witness at the drugstore?"

"Yeah."

"Good," I said. "Maybe if you had been cooperative with him right from the start, you could have saved yourself a whole lot of trouble."

Ben turned to glare at me. "It's all a bunch of bull-shit, Mom. The whole idea that I killed Dad is just so stupid."

"I know," I said, reaching for his hand.

"I wouldn't have given Dad the time of day, much less killed him."

Exasperated, I put my hand back on the steering wheel. "Tremaine told you about the witness who came in this afternoon, right?"

"Yeah, but that's plain crazy. I wasn't there. It wasn't my car. Whoever that witness was, she was lying."

"So why do you think someone would have lied about you to the police?" I asked, pulling into the driveway.

"How the hell do I know? I don't even know who it was."

"Don't bite my head off. I'm just trying to help," I said as Ben jumped out of the car and slammed the door shut. He got Wendy out of the back seat and stomped up the driveway to the front door. By the time I got out of the car and followed them inside, Ben was already in the kitchen with his head in the fridge.

"I'm starving," he said.

"I'll put on the kettle," I said. "Do you want a decaffeinated tea, or maybe a hot chocolate?"

"A hot chocolate," he replied, pulling some leftover pizza out of the fridge. I got out the hot chocolate mix and waited for the kettle to boil while Ben piled some pizza onto a plate. "You want any?" he asked, pointing to the almost empty box.

"No thanks. I'm not hungry." As a matter of fact, I couldn't have eaten a bite. I had just made up my mind to tell Ben about my lie to Jack, and I was scared. Maybe if I gave him a reason not to hate his father, his attitude would change and he would stop walking around with a big chip on his shoulder. His anger wasn't helping Tremaine to see him in a good light.

Ben sat down at the table and started eating. "What were you doing out in your pyjamas?" he asked, noticing my clothes for the first time.

"Huh? Oh, I had to go over to Amy's house unexpectedly, and then I heard about you and came straight to the station just as I was. Listen, Ben, there's something important I want to talk to you about."

"Yeah? Well if it's more about Tremaine and this alibi stuff, don't bother. I've told him everything I know, and I've got nothing more to say." He stuffed a wad of pizza in his mouth and chomped on it.

"No, it's not about Tremaine or the investigation. It's something about your father and me – something I should have told you before." The kettle whistled and I busied myself with making his hot chocolate.

"Yeah, what is it?"

I put his mug on the table and sat down across from him. "Okay, you know how I told you a couple of years ago that your father and I broke up because he cheated on me with another woman."

"Yeah?"

"I told you that it wasn't the first time – right?"

"Right. I think you said Dad started cheating on you before I was born."

"Uh huh." I wrapped my hands around his mug to warm them. "Okay, well, the first time it happened was the year before you were born. I was only twenty at the time. I was really upset when I found out about Jack. I wanted to get back at your father, so I told him that I was having an affair, too."

Ben put the last slice of pizza back down on his plate and stared at me. "Were you?" he asked in a frosty voice.

"No."

He swallowed a sip of hot chocolate before speaking again. "Let me get this straight. You told Dad that you had an affair just to get back at him." He picked absent-mindedly at a piece of mushroom on his pizza.

"That's right. Can you understand that?"

Ben shrugged. "Yeah, I guess so, you being upset and all. Besides, he cheated on you, and a lie isn't as bad as cheating."

"Maybe not. But maybe it affected your father in ways that I hadn't considered."

Ben abandoned the food on his plate and leaned back in his chair. "Like what?"

I took a deep breath. "I got pregnant right after your father and I got back together. It's possible that he might have thought you weren't his."

Ben stiffened, staring at me. "I don't get it. Why would he have thought that? You didn't tell him that, did you?"

"No, of course not. And I'm not saying that your father thought you weren't his. If he did, he never said anything about it to me. I didn't even think of it until I had a talk with Erna. She's the one who saw the possibility and thought I should tell you because it might make a difference."

"How?"

I lay my hand on his arm. "Don't you see, Ben? It might explain why your father ignored you so much."

Ben's face looked deeply troubled as he lowered his eyes to think. I kept quiet, holding onto his arm, willing him to understand my reasons for doing what I had done. He frowned and looked up at me. "Why are you telling me this? What am I supposed to do with this now?" He got up from his chair and started pacing.

"I thought it might help you to forgive your father."

"How can I? He's dead now. I can't ask him, can I? How can I know what the truth is? Why didn't you tell me before it was too late?" he shouted.

I got up from my chair and went to him, my eyes pricking with tears. "Because I didn't think of it. I'm so sorry." I took hold of his hand, but he wouldn't look at me. "Please forgive me for being so stupid."

"You're right, you were stupid," he said, wrenching his hand away. "All the time I thought he didn't love me, it might have been because you lied to get back at him. Well, what about me? He might have been a lousy husband, but he was the only dad I had."

Tears began to spill down my cheeks, and I dashed them away. "Please, Ben, imagine how I felt at the time. I was so hurt and upset. I never imagined that you might suffer because of it."

His own eyes were teary now and his face was white. "I've got to go for a walk. I can't be with you right now."

He stalked out of the kitchen with Wendy slinking after him. I heard the front door slam, and Wendy whined. I burst into tears and grabbed hold of the counter. It was all too much. Everything that had happened over the past two weeks came crashing down on my head. Jack's death, my thwarted attempts to figure out if Amy, the Primos, or Jessie Wick had murdered him, and now my son's anger. I sank onto the floor, sobbing. If only this whole thing would go away and I could have my old life back.

What if Ben didn't forgive me? What was I going to do? Wendy pushed her nose into my face and I grabbed hold of her, pulling her into my lap and clinging to her like a lifeline.

We sat like that for a long time. Finally, I pushed myself up off the floor, stiff and cold. The kitchen wall clock said that it was one fifteen, but Ben still hadn't come home. I let Wendy out to do her business while mechanically tidying up the kitchen, then shuffled down the hallway to the front door. I peeked outside in case Ben was sitting on the porch. He wasn't. I closed the door, leaving it unlocked in case he didn't have his key, turned on the outside light, and went to bed.

21

I crawled out of bed around nine thirty the next morning and stumbled down the hallway to Ben's room. He wasn't there, and his bed hadn't been slept in. I sank down on his bed, worried that something might have happened to him. I considered calling a couple of his friends who still lived in town, but decided that it was a bad idea. If he wasn't there, his friends would wonder what had happened to him. If he was there, he wouldn't want me checking up on him. Faced with a lose-lose scenario, I decided that I needed to get out of the house for a while. I showered and let my hair air dry on the way over to The Diner. I didn't want to be alone, and Ben might be there having breakfast.

There was no sign of Ben at the restaurant, but the Saturday breakfast gang was seated around a table at the back: Betty and Jeff, Erna, May, Mr. Andrews, and Steve. My friends were talking with their heads bent over their plates. They all looked up as I dragged a chair over from another table to join them.

"Hi everybody. Sorry I'm late," I said, squeezing in between Steve and May. Everyone was having the weekend breakfast special except for Steve, who was having steak and eggs. This meal would be his supper. May reached over and took my hand.

"You doing okay, Anna?" she asked, looking concerned. "Steve has been telling us about Ben being taken in for questioning." I glanced around the table and saw the same worried expression on everyone's face.

"I'm doing okay. I brought Ben home with me last night. The police are going over his car this morning. It will be ready at noon. He went out for a walk, and I didn't feel like sitting home alone, so I came here." I didn't tell them that Ben had left for his walk about nine hours ago.

"That's right, doll," May said, putting an arm around my shoulders and giving me a hug. "You stay here with us. You shouldn't be alone right now." Everyone started chattering at once, assuring me that things would turn out just fine and not to worry. Mary came over to take my order and Judy paused with a pot of coffee to squeeze my shoulder. I smiled up at her and patted her hand before she hurried away. I asked Betty and Jeff how their vacation plans were going to visit their daughter that summer in Vancouver, and conversation resumed. Now was my chance to have a quiet talk with Steve.

"What's going on with the test results from the O'Cleary ranch?" I whispered.

He finished chewing a forkful of potatoes before answering. "They put a rush on the blood test. It was easy since we already had a sample from your ex. It was his blood in the lounge all right, Anna."

I was silent as this information sank in. "Okay," I said, "so now we know where Jack was killed."

Steve nodded. "We won't get the other test results back for a few days, so we'll just have to hang tight. One good thing I can tell you, though. The forensics guy said that he didn't think there was any blood in Ben's car."

I let out a breath I didn't realize I had been holding. At last, some good news. Mary came back with my breakfast, and I waited while she set my food down before me. The moment she left, I leaned toward Steve. "Who's the witness who saw Ben's car?"

He looked at me, and then bit into a piece of toast. "I've already said more than I should, Anna. I can't tell you that. It's illegal."

I shook my head. "I don't care if it's illegal or not, Steve. Tell me. You know I'll never tell anyone else." He looked down at his plate, still chewing his food. I took hold of his arm. "Please?" He paused for a moment without looking at me before cutting another piece of steak.

I watched him fork the meat into his mouth before sinking back into my chair. I felt totally adrift. Steve had been so good to me throughout this whole ordeal, but I had gone too far, and now he wouldn't help me anymore. I looked at my own plate of food and lost it. My breath caught in my throat, and I started to cry.

May turned to me in alarm. "What is it?" she asked. She put an arm around my shoulders and I started to sob. I couldn't help it. After a moment, I felt a hand on my arm and looked up. Erna stood beside me with a purse-sized package of tissues.

"Thanks, Erna," I gulped, pulling two or three out of the package and blowing my nose. As I dried my tears, I realized that the whole room had gone silent. I glanced at the people at the next table and saw that they were staring. They noticed me looking at them and turned away, talking quietly amongst themselves again.

I had never been so embarrassed before in my life. I jumped out of my chair. "Got to go," I said, fumbling under the table for my purse.

"Anna, are you all right?" Erna asked, her hand on my back.

I nodded. "Fine, fine." I opened my wallet and threw a twenty on top of the table, my face feeling hot and sticky.

"Please stay with us," Erna said.

I flashed a fixed smile at her. "No, thanks, I really have to go. See you all later." Stumbling over my chair, I fled out into the street. The outdoor air was fresh, and I paused to let it cool my face. I had just started down the street when the restaurant door opened and a voice shouted, "Anna!"

I turned. It was Steve. He caught up to me in a few strides. "It was Jessie Wick," he said, breathlessly.

I was stunned. "Jessie? It can't have been Jessie. That just doesn't make sense. I thought it was Karen Quill trying to get back at me. Why Jessie?"

"The O'Cleary ranch is on the way to her brother's ranch. She said she saw the car parked there on her way home from work the day that Jack was murdered."

"Well, she was wrong. I know she didn't see Ben's car there. Why would she lie?"

I turned to go and Steve grabbed hold of my shoulder. "If you tell Tremaine that I gave you Jessie's name, he'll have me brought up on charges."

I seized Steve by his shoulders and kissed him hard on the mouth. He looked dazed when I broke away from him.

"Thanks, Steve. I'm really, really grateful. I swear I won't tell Tremaine, not even if he tortures me." I turned and started running down the sidewalk, my brain ticking like a tightly-wound clock.

Steve shouted after me, "Anna, you be careful now. Don't go doing anything you know you shouldn't!"

The minute I got home, I called Amy. "Hi Amy, it's Anna," I said, struggling to sound casual. "How're you doing today? Feeling okay after that big upset with Connie last night?"

"I'm so-so. Still feeling a bit shaky. I cancelled my hair appointments for today."

"I'm really sorry to hear that. I promise you, I will find some way of getting that gun back to Connie without him thinking you had anything to do with it. I'm so grateful to you for not telling Connie or Steve that I took the gun. I owe you big time for that. Thank you so much."

"You're welcome. I didn't want to get you into trouble, too."

"You're the greatest, Amy. Meanwhile, I have a teensy question about Jessie Wick. I just wondered if you happen to know whether or not she's working today?"

"No, they're only shooting with the principals this weekend."

"Hmm. Would you happen to know if Jessie's staying at her brother's ranch these days? Erna Dombrosky gave me a run-down on her family history, so I know that she leaves her cabin to stay at the ranch when she's helping out with the family business."

"Well, I did overhear that she was helping her brother move some of the cattle to different pasture this weekend. But why do you want to know about Jessie, Anna?"

"Oh, it's nothing. I'm just keeping tabs on her. I'd like to know more about her – that's all."

"You're not going to try to spy on her the way you did Connie and Karen, are you?"

"No, of course not. Nothing like that."

Amy paused and I could practically hear the wheels whirring in her head. "Anna, you're not planning on searching her cabin, are you?"

I sighed. "No, Amy, I'm not going to search it. I just want to have a look at it from the outside."

"I wish you wouldn't. It's too dangerous. Remember what happened with the Primos? What if Jessie shows up and catches you?"

"You just told me that she's busy on her brother's ranch. Look, don't worry. I'll just peek in the windows. I wouldn't dream of going inside, unless she's left a key hidden somewhere obvious. No one will catch me this time, I promise. I'll be really careful."

"You're crazy, Anna. You've got to stop this – it's too dangerous. Let Sergeant Tremaine take care of it."

"Come on, Amy, what's the worst that could happen? Jessie's not going to shoot me even if she catches me spying on her cabin, now, is she?"

"Promise me you won't go! Please. Jessie Wick is a lot more dangerous than Karen and Connie."

"Now why would you say that?"

"I don't know. It's the way she acts, I guess. She says things like 'I'd never take that kind of crap from any man.' She seems so tough."

"Well, I'm not going to do anything stupid. Just forget I ever called. Go see a movie or do some shopping or something. Everything will work out just fine. You have a good weekend, now. Bye."

"Anna, please don't," she pleaded.

"Bye Amy." I disconnected before she could say another word.

22

I was on the road headed to Jessie's cabin within the next thirty minutes. The sky had cleared, and sculpted white clouds drifted across an azure blue sky. As I drove west on Highway 22X, the blue-grey mountains appeared before me on the horizon. The leaves on the trees were a vivid green, and blue and yellow spring wildflowers waved alongside the two-lane highway. Spring was my favourite time of year. I rolled down the windows a few inches, enjoying the cool air that blew through my sunny car.

The road climbed and twisted as I drove into the mountains and Kananaskis Country. I checked the directions that Erna had given me from time to time and sang along with the radio. It felt good to be doing something proactive about the woman who had lied to the police about my son.

After about forty-five minutes, I turned off the highway and onto a secondary road. The road crews hadn't gotten to the potholes that had opened during the bitterly cold winter, and I navigated around them at reduced speed. I was watching for a one-lane bridge that would take me over the river. The road twisted a couple of more times before I spotted the bridge up ahead. It was short with concrete buttresses supporting it. The water was moving fast between the river banks, swollen with the winter runoff. I bumped over the bridge and carefully steered onto a gravel road on the other side. A side-road immediately diverged into the trees, but I stuck to the shoreline and watched the river sparkling in the sunlight until it curved away out of sight. Just another minute or so, Erna had said, before I should see a wagon-shaped mailbox marking the laneway to Jessie's cabin. I slowed down until I spied the mailbox, and then parked a little way beyond it on the shoulder of the road. The overhead branches masked my car, although I couldn't imagine there'd be much traffic going by to see it.

I locked the car and walked back up the road to the laneway. Looking around to ensure that no one was watching me, I turned in, walking on the grassy verge next to the gravel. I could hear water flowing close by, but the dense trees bordering the driveway hid the source. I listened for sounds of movement, but heard only birdsong. A magpie startled me as it burst from the trees, scolding me for invading its territory. After a couple of minutes of walking, the trees thinned into a clearing. Suddenly, I could see the house.

What a beautiful spot! The log cabin was perched on a rocky slope overlooking the river. The side of the cabin nearest the river had floor-to-ceiling windows, making the most of the view. The river formed a mini-rapid just below the slope, crashing over rocks and spraying white mist into the air. I enjoyed the scene for a few moments before heading up the drive to the cabin.

The place looked deserted, as if it hadn't been aired out for spring yet. The prairie garden out front of the house was littered with leaves and the dried stalks of last year's grasses. The window boxes beneath the two front cabin windows were draped with shrivelled black plants. A couple of Adirondack chairs were tipped back against the wall on the small front porch.

I climbed the three low stairs leading up to the porch and peeked in one of the windows. The sun shone through the side windows, illuminating a great room that combined kitchen, dining and living room space. A black wood-burning stove was tucked inside a wide stone hearth, a couch and rocking chair facing it. Two doors led off the great room, presumably into a bedroom and bath.

Backing away from the window, I tried the front door, but it was locked. I stretched up on tiptoe to feel for a key around the door frame, but couldn't find one. The dense fibre mat in front of the door didn't yield up a key, either, nor did the window boxes. I left the porch to follow the drive along the front of the house.

The far side of the house had a carport attached to it with a padlocked wooden shed. I glanced inside the shed window, but saw only garden tools and a riding lawnmower. Leaving the shed, I followed along the side of the house, walking on yellow-green grass and dried leaves. Peering in the kitchen window, I admired the espresso-coloured hardwood floor, granite countertops, and an island complete with a built-in grill. The kitchen had all of the latest bells and whistles.

There was a deep wooden deck spanning the back wall of the cabin. I climbed onto it and looked inside the two sliding glass doors. One opened into the kitchen and the other into the bedroom. The bedroom door was draped in a luxurious fabric, a kind of golden, flowered tapestry. The bed was king-sized with a tufted blue headboard piled high with pillows. Soft, plush white carpet lay on the floor on either side of the bed. A beautiful white vanity table with a scalloped mirror and an upholstered stool caught my eye. The bedroom had a feminine, pampered appearance, and while it was very different from my own taste, I would have loved to have owned such a room.

I tore myself away from the door and began searching for a key. The deck contained a covered barbecue and some overturned wooden planters, but no key.

About to give up and go home, I heard something. It sounded as if someone were knocking on the front door. I froze and someone shouted, "Anna, where are you?" After a moment, I heard, "Anna, I know you're here. I saw your car parked out on the road. Don't play games with me."

I couldn't believe it. It was Tremaine! How had he known that I was here? Amy must have ratted on me, the fink!

I could hear him rustling through the leaves along the side of the house, getting closer all the time. I couldn't let him catch me spying for a second time, but I was trapped. The only way out was the narrow strip topping the slope beside the river, but I was afraid to go that way.

"I warned you, Anna. I can't believe you're doing this again. Anna, answer me!" I pivoted, looking for a place to hide, but the back lawn was too deep to have time to run into the woods.

He rounded the cabin, dressed in his usual suit and tie. His mouth was compressed into a tight line and his eyes flashed with anger.

"There you are," he said, starting toward me. I panicked and took off at a run for the other side of the cabin. "Don't be stupid," he shouted, chasing after me.

Wild rose bushes grew in a patch along the edge of the slope. I stumbled over a root and almost lost my footing.

"Be careful!" he yelled, springing forward and catching hold of my arm. I whirled and jerked my arm out of his grasp. The abruptness of my movement unbalanced him. He tripped backward, lost his footing, and fell over the side. I stared in horror as he tumbled down the slope in a shower of stones and dust and dropped into the river. He didn't re-appear for a few agonizing seconds until I saw his head break the surface. He coughed and sputtered before the river snatched him away.

"Tremaine!" I screamed, running to the front of the house and down the driveway. The river would be freezing with the runoff, and even if he managed to stay afloat in the fast-flowing water, the cold would kill him. I tore down the gravel road at top speed, following it through the trees. After what felt like an eternity, the road ran parallel to the river again. I slowed and loped through the stones to the river bank, not wanting to twist an ankle. My chest was heaving from all of the running. I paused to look up the river for a glimpse of him.

I was afraid that he had already swept by, but I saw him coming toward me. His blond head was smooth as a seal's, bobbing up and down in the water. He tumbled past me. My only hope was to catch him at the bridge. I turned and ran again, past the spot where the other road branched off, pushing myself forward until I reached the bridge.

He was still upstream from me, thank God. He was draped over a boulder in the middle of the river, his head resting on top of his arm.

"Tremaine, over here," I shouted, jumping up and down and waving my arms. I wasn't sure that he could hear me over the water's roar, but he raised his head and seemed to see me. I waved again and waded into the water, my right hand pressed against the first concrete buttress.

The water was shockingly cold. I had never been in water so cold before. I shuddered convulsively. How could Tremaine bear it? I forced myself in deeper, feeling the slippery riverbed beneath my shoes, the water coursing against my calves.

"Oh dear Lord, please don't let me fall in the water," I prayed. I knew that we would both be goners if I did.

I waded in further, pressing one hand against the second column, until the water was waist deep. I could feel the river catching at me as it rushed past, and I was desperately glad for the solidity of the buttress beside me. I turned and flattened my back against it, looking for Tremaine. I screamed his name again and again, but this time his head did not rise from the boulder.

"Come on, come on!" I shouted, frantic that he might be unconscious. Then I watched as he slipped off the boulder. The current carried him forward, his face in the water. When he was within a few feet of me, I strained forward and snagged him by the shirt collar. The pressure of the racing water almost tore him away, but I dragged him back with all of my strength and clasped him to me. His long body lay draped over mine, his head drooping on my shoulder.

I bent my mouth to his ear. "Tremaine, can you hear me?" I shouted. He didn't answer. His eyes were closed. He seemed to be unconscious.

"We're going to wade ashore now. Try to walk with me, if you can."

His body was a dead weight on top of mine as I inched through the water, my back pressed against the second buttress. I was terrified that I might lose my footing on feet numb with cold. Glancing up, the shore still seemed so far away. How was I going to make it? Then I heard a miracle, a woman's voice shouting.

"I'm coming, I'm coming. Hold on, help is on the way!"

I looked over Tremaine's shoulder and saw a woman running down the shore toward us. She held a rake in her hand, and her longish skirt flapped open to reveal knee-high rubber boots. I had never seen anyone so beautiful in my life. She ran to the water's edge and splashed in up to her calves, holding the rake handle out to me.

"Here, take hold of the end."

I had to edge across the space between the two columns to reach it, the weight of Tremaine's inert body pressing me down while the water clawed at us. She took a step in deeper, her flowered skirt floating on the water. I stretched forward and managed to grab the handle.

"Very good, you've got it. Take another step – and another. Come on, nearly there. Got you!"

She grabbed my wrist and dragged me forward. I tripped on a rock and splashed onto one knee, still clinging to Tremaine. The woman drove the rake handle into the riverbed and grasped the back of my shirt with her free hand. She hauled me to my feet and pulled the two of us into her arms.

"There we are. I've got you now. Let's get you out of the water," she panted. We shifted Tremaine's body between us and staggered out onto the shore. Laying him face-up on the ground, the woman knelt beside him while I shuddered nearby.

"Is he still b-breathing?" I cried.

She laid her ear to his chest and looked up into his face. Watching him for a few long seconds, she tilted his head back, pinched his nostrils shut, covered his mouth with her own, and gave him two quick breaths. She watched for movement in his chest, and then gave him another two breaths. His chest began to heave, and she leaned back while he coughed and sputtered up a lung-full of river.

"Very good," she said, turning him onto his side and cradling his head from the stones. "Better out than in, eh young man? What's his name?"

"Charles Tremaine. I'm Anna Nolan," I said, hugging myself for warmth.

"Frieda Kuntz. Now that we're sure he's breathing, let's get him to my house and warm him up. You could do with some dry clothes and warming up yourself, Anna," she said, eying me as another convulsion wracked my body. "It's not very far – my house is right up the road there. Help me to lift him."

We flipped Tremaine onto his back, where he lay gasping and panting. Taking his arms, we hauled him to his feet and began dragging him up the road to the house. We didn't talk much, saving our breath for our exertions except when Frieda asked where Tremaine had gone into the water and how long he'd been in it. I told her where and guessed maybe six minutes.

"Six minutes! He must be a tenacious soul, to be in that freezing water and still alive after six minutes. Good for you, Charlie. Come on, Anna. Not much farther. You can see my house through the trees over there."

She jerked her head to the left, and I saw a timber A-frame through the brush. We dragged Tremaine up the drive past a little red Volkswagen Beetle. A dog barked frantically inside the cabin as we staggered up the wooden stairs onto the porch.

"Quiet, Schultzie! Stop that barking," she shouted as he threw himself against the back of the door. "These are friends. Get back," she commanded. Frieda wedged Tremaine against the wall with her hip and flung the door open. A large German shepherd jumped up at her waist, nearly knocking her over.

"Down, Schultzie, get down! Go lie on your bed. Go!" The dog slunk away as we hauled Tremaine through the door, Frieda kicking it shut behind us. We lugged him to a wooden chair beside her dining table and lowered him onto it.

"Anna, hold onto him. Don't let him fall off. We've got to get these wet clothes off him. I'm going to fetch some towels and blankets for the two of you. I'll be right back." She hurried across the room as I turned to Tremaine.

He lay in the chair with his head lolling back and his arms hanging down, hands almost touching the floor. With my whole body shaking, I tried to loosen the tie at the base of his throat. The knot was beyond me, so I stripped off his sopping wet jacket and began unbuttoning his shirt. I was aware of Frieda bustling around behind me.

"You're doing fine, Anna," she called. "Get his shirt off. I'm going to start a fire in the grate and push the bed over to it. I'll be right there to help you."

I managed to unbutton the sleeves at his wrists. "I-I can't get his tie undone, and I can't get his shirt off," I said.

I heard her mutter something as she rushed past me into the kitchen. She hurried back clasping a very efficient-looking carving knife in her hand and a bundle of towels under her arm. I got out of the way as she dropped the towels onto the floor and knelt beside him. Carefully inserting the blade between Tremaine's tie and his throat, Frieda sliced through the fabric.

"There you go," she said, pulling the rest of the tie through his shirt collar and flinging it onto the floor before she rushed off again. I bent over Tremaine, grabbed either side of his shirt, and pulled it back over his shoulders and down his arms, dropping it onto the floor. Grabbing a towel, I rubbed his upper body briskly, trying to warm him and get his blood circulating again. The skin on his torso was white with fine golden hair, muscle and bone etched beneath. I knelt before him, picked up a dry towel, and rested his smooth chest against my face, reaching around to dry his back. A fire crackled in the grate and Frieda muttered as she shoved the bed toward the hearth on a round area carpet. She manoeuvred it into place with a series of grunts and glanced over to see how I was doing. Scooping up a pile of blankets from the bed, she hurried back to us.

"Good, Anna, you've got the job half done. Time for you to get out of those wet clothes yourself. Take some of these towels, and when you're dry, wrap up in a blanket. Then come back and help me with Charlie."

Shivering, I stumbled over to the fire, standing as close as I could while stripping off my clothes and dropping them in a soggy pile on the floor. I was too miserable to feel self-conscious about my nudity, and Tremaine's eyes were closed, anyway. That worried me. Had he slipped into a coma? I wrapped a blanket around myself, tied a knot under my arms, and stumbled back to help.

Frieda had removed Tremaine's shoes and socks and was wrapping him in a blanket. She tied a stout knot over his shoulders, the blanket covering him like a toga.

"Just in time," she said. "Help me get his pants off." We stood him up between us and I held him while she tied a towel sarong-style around his hips before taking off the rest of his dripping clothes. I gazed down at his bare feet and thought that they looked awfully vulnerable without his oxfords.

"Good, now let's put him to bed," she said. I wrapped my arms around his chest, she grabbed his knees, and we carried him over to the bed, heaving him onto the side closest to the fire. Frieda had already turned down the bedclothes, and we pulled blankets and a duvet over him before tucking a pillow under his head.

"Very good," she said, "now you get in, too."

"Wha-at?" I stammered.

"Get in the bed with him. We've got to warm both of you up. I'll call 911 and tell them what happened. I know it will take them a little while – this place can be tricky to find. I'm going to get a hot water bottle for his feet, and once the two of you are tucked in, I'll drive up the road and watch for them." I hovered beside the bed. "Now don't get prudish on me, Anna. For pity's sake, you've already seen most of him, and it's not like he's going to force himself on you. Go on, get in the bed!"

"Yes ma'am," I said, grabbing the bed clothes and crawling in beside him. I was exhausted and still bitterly cold myself, and it felt heavenly to get beneath all those covers. Frieda nodded and went off to make the call. I could hear her giving instructions as I turned my head to look at Tremaine. His face was as white and lifeless as marble. I reached under the covers and found an icy hand, chafing it between my own for a few seconds. Then I slid an arm under his shoulders and pulled him closer, dragging his head across the pillow. His breathing seemed a little slow, and I tried to stop shaking long enough to monitor it. It was definitely sluggish, which frightened me. I pressed against him and lay my head on his shoulder.

Frieda hurried back with a hot water bottle wrapped in a hand towel, and came around the bed beside the fire. She smiled at me before slipping the bottle under the blankets beneath Tremaine's feet. My own lay on top of his and I could feel the heat surge up from the bottle, making me shiver.

"I've got an idea," Frieda said. "Schultzie, come." The furry brown and black dog lumbered quickly to the bed.

"Up, Schultzie," Frieda said, patting the foot of the bed. The animal sprang up and settled across our feet. "He's warmed my feet on many a cold night, that's for sure," she said while studying Tremaine's face. "I think Charlie's colour is improving, Anna. Keep cuddling him, and I'll come back with help as soon as I can." Before she could turn away, however, I reached out from under the bedclothes to take her hand.

"You saved both our lives today. I don't know how to thank you enough."

"Never mind. When we get through this, you can tell me the whole story of how Charlie ended up in the river. I bet it's a humdinger. For now, just worry about getting you and Charlie warm. I've got to go. Don't worry, I'll be back with help soon."

Frieda left the house, slamming the door behind her. Schultzie lifted his head and listened as she crossed the porch and descended to the drive. A minute later, her car started up and she drove away. The dog laid his head back down, closed his eyes, and sighed. The room was quiet except for an occasional pop and sizzle from the fire. Lying cocooned in the blankets with Tremaine, I began to feel drowsy.

A tremor ran through his body, and I was instantly alert again. I peered at his face and waited. After a little while, he started shaking. He drew in a shuddering breath, released it, and opened his eyes

"Thank God," I said softly. Tremaine turned his head on the pillow to face me, and smiled.

"You saved my life," he said in a weak, raspy voice.

"Yes, Frieda and I both did."

"Thank you," he murmured, his eyelids drooping.

"You're welcome. It was my p-pleasure," I said, my teeth chattering.

Tremaine started laughing. His body shook with cold and laughter until his eyes streamed with tears. I started laughing, too, and we clung to each other and laughed like a pair of loons until Frieda returned with the paramedics.

23

The EMS workers were very efficient as they checked us out. They decided that I would be all right, but started an intravenous drip on Tremaine before carrying him off to the hospital. I heard that the Emergency Room doctor discovered a lot of bruising from the battering he had taken in the river, but, thankfully, there were no broken bones. They kept him in overnight for observation, and released him the next day to one of his RCMP colleagues.

Frieda drove me to my car after everyone left her place. I promised to come back for a visit, and drove home feeling pretty weak. I called Ben's cell and left a message asking him to call me back, and then crawled into bed.

I slept most of the afternoon with my own dog draped across my feet. When I woke up around supper time, I had about enough energy to feed Wendy and open a can of soup for myself. Poor Wendy; when I went back to my room, she couldn't figure out why she wasn't getting a walk and paced around the floor for a few minutes before joining me on the bed. I slept heavily – my body must have been recuperating from the day's panic and the freezing river water – and felt okay when I got up early the next morning. I had some business to attend to with Amy.

When she answered her door around nine, the expression of relief and guilt mingling in her face convinced me that I had been right to suspect her. She dragged me inside and began apologizing before I had a chance to say anything.

"I'm so sorry, Anna, I didn't mean to get you into trouble, but I was so worried after you phoned. I thought about what to do for a while, and then I ended up calling Tremaine. I told him that I was afraid something bad might happen to you at Jessie's cabin. He sounded upset, particularly when I told him that it had been about thirty minutes since you called. Did he find you?"

"Yes, Tremaine found me and a whole lot more trouble than he had expected, I dare say." I told Amy the whole story. She gasped when I described how Tremaine had fallen into the river and how Frieda and I had rescued him.

"You saved his life," she said.

"Well, yes, I guess I did, but let's not forget that I was the reason he fell into the river in the first place."

"Still, you're so brave. I'm not sure I would have gone into the water after him. I can't even swim."

"Believe me, neither one of us did any swimming in that water."

"So, I guess that gets you off the hook."

"What do you mean?"

"Well for pity's sake, you saved his life. Tremaine can't possibly arrest you for murdering Jack now, can he?"

"I don't think the one precludes the other, but I guess it helps."

"I should think so. Hmm. Tell me something, Anna. What did Tremaine look like without his clothes?"

I laughed. "Count on you to ask me that."

She smiled back at me from where she lay curled up in the corner of her couch. Her living room decor was just as she had described it: floral chintzes in pinks and greens with lots of throw pillows. "Don't tell me that you haven't noticed how good-looking he is," she prompted.

"Well, that hasn't exactly been my major preoccupation as far as Tremaine is concerned, but since you mention it, he is handsome, with and without his clothes. After all, he's young and in good shape."

"He's not all that young, is he?"

"Pretty young. He's only thirty-one."

"Thirty-one definitely makes him a grown man. You're not that much older than he."

"Nine years."

Amy snorted. "Don't tell me that you've never looked at a younger man."

"Looked, admired, but never seriously considered dating one. Or anyone else, for the past few years."

Amy wiggled her eyebrows suggestively. "I wasn't talking about dating him. For goodness sake, look at you. You're blushing."

I got up from the couch and headed for the front door. "Never mind all that nonsense. I'm going now."

Amy trailed behind me. "I don't know. It sounds like you two got awfully cozy in that bed yesterday. He's handsome, smart, charming, and he's got that cute British accent. I wish that I could have been the one under the covers with him." She grinned, and I shook my head at her.

"You're beyond saving, Amy. Listen, call me if you hear anything interesting about Jessie Wick, will you?"

The smile vanished from her face. "Anna Nolan, you don't have any sense."

It was my turn to grin as I saluted her. "Bye Amy. See you at the movies."

"Bye. And for goodness sake, stay out of trouble!"

24

I thought that Tremaine might drop by or call me after we had shared such a harrowing experience, but he didn't. When I still hadn't heard from him three days later, I felt a little hurt. He had seemed so grateful that I had saved his life. Didn't that deserve flowers or something? And what about our intimate time together in bed? Didn't he realize that our relationship had changed? Wasn't he going to do something about it?

I kept up a grumbling interior monologue for most of the day before giving myself a swift mental kick. How could I think such preposterous things? There was never going to be anything between Tremaine and me. Damn that Amy and her suggestions. I bet she had dalliances with younger men all the time, but she was a whole lot sexier and more enticing than I. And, judging by her fling with Jack, promiscuous.

It was time to put all this nonsense about Tremaine out of my head and start concentrating on work again. And it was time to stop worrying about the murder investigation, too. What more could I do? Nothing, until we got the test results back from the O'Cleary barn and from Ben's car. Besides, I hadn't discovered anything with my investigations. Amy was too sweet and too dumb to have murdered Jack, Connie and Karen had a foolproof alibi, and trying to find out more about Jessie Wick had almost got Tremaine and me killed. Enough already.

I came home from work Tuesday night ready for leftovers and a long after-dinner walk with Wendy when she greeted me at the front door, clearly upset. She whined, ran to the back of the house, and barked. I put my stuff down and followed her into the kitchen, doing a double-take when I looked out onto the deck. Someone wearing a black cowboy hat was lying on my recliner. Whoever it was had his back to me, and all I could see was the hat sticking over the back of the chair. My backyard was enclosed by a six-foot tall, Wendy-proof fence, and the only way into it was through the kitchen or a padlocked gate next to the garage. So how had the intruder gotten onto my deck?

Wendy clawed at the door, but I didn't want her making things worse by attacking whoever it was out there. I slid the door open just far enough to slip through before closing it in her face. Wendy whimpered on the other side.

"Hello?" I said, inching closer to the chair. The cowboy hat swivelled, and a woman wearing big, black sunglasses smiled up at me.

"Well, you're finally home, Anna. How was the traffic leaving Calgary?"

"I beg your pardon?" I said. "Who are you, and what are you doing here?"

The woman took off her cowboy hat and dropped it on the deck, freeing a cascade of blue-black hair that tumbled down her back. She removed the sunglasses, too, in case I hadn't recognized the trademark hair. It was Jessie Wick.

"We've never been formally introduced. Jessie Wick," she said, holding out her hand. I shook it and took a wary step backward.

"How'd you get into my backyard?" I asked.

"I'm a stunt woman. How hard do you think it would be for me to get over your fence?" She swung her legs off the chair and stood in one fluid movement. She was dressed all in black in form-fitting jeans and a silk shirt except for an ornate silver and turquoise belt buckle at her waist. Standing next to her, I saw that she had me by three or four inches and about twenty pounds of muscle. She advanced toward me and I backed up until I was pressed against the sliding door, Wendy whining and scratching on the other side. I took comfort in the knowledge that I could let her out if I didn't like the way things were going.

"Your dog's pretty excited. I guess she doesn't like strangers," Jessie said, standing too close to me. "Hi dog," she said, tapping on the glass with her fingernails, inducing a paroxysm of barking from Wendy.

"What can I do for you, Jessie?" I asked, trying to keep my voice steady. Amy was right; Jessie was a lot more intimidating than Karen and Connie. It was like the difference between a Labrador and a Rottweiler. Jessie smiled, but there was no friendliness in her eyes.

"I heard from the police that you were out snooping around my place last Saturday. Sorry I wasn't home. What did you want?"

I thought quickly. I couldn't admit that I wanted to check out the woman who had reported seeing Ben's car at the O'Cleary ranch since I wasn't supposed to know who the witness was, and I surely didn't want to tell this woman that I was looking for my husband's murderer. Instead, I took a deep breath and said, "I thought it was high time I met the woman who broke up my marriage."

Jessie laughed in a husky, deep voice, a laugh which men would no doubt find sexy. "Yeah, I heard that you've been nosing around Jack's women since he died. Amy Bright, Karen Quill, and now me. Jack and I were ancient history, though, so you needn't have bothered. And I'm not blind, by the way. I saw you on the set last Thursday night. We may have never officially met, but I recognized you. I checked you out four years ago when Jack and I were sleeping together. I always check out my competition. Were you curious as to how you stacked up against me? Not doing too much for your self-esteem, now, am I?" She looked me up and down with a look that said I was no better than the dirt beneath her boots, and flicked a strand of hair off my shoulder. I pressed my lips together and stared at her, trying to hide the trembling in my left leg.

"If I were you, I'd look to my own house, Anna," she said, lowering her head and breathing in my face. "I'd have thought you'd have all the trouble you could handle with the police trying to find Jack's killer. First they find you with Jack's body, and then your boy's car is spotted outside the O'Cleary ranch. The police are thinking that Jack was killed in that barn, have you heard? Good thing I happened to be driving home from the set that way, or no one might have seen Ben's car there."

"It wasn't his car," I said, starting to feel angry.

"Oh no?" she said, leaning her hand against the glass behind my head. "Well, why don't we let the police decide that? I hear they went over your son's car last weekend, and they're just waiting on the test results before arresting him for his father's murder. Imagine that – a son murdering his own father. Ben must be deranged or something. No doubt you helped sonny boy move Jack's body out of the barn, too. They'll arrest you as his accomplice. Couldn't leave Jack's body hidden if you wanted the insurance money, right?

"You knew about the insurance policy?" I asked in amazement.

"Yeah, Jack mentioned it four years ago when he talked about leaving you. He said that the insurance policy was about all you'd get out of the divorce, and he figured he owed you that much after seventeen years of marriage. For being such a good housekeeper and all. Then he laughed and said you'd have to wait a long time to get it. I guess you got tired of waiting."

I looked away, hurt by this information, until Jessie laid her hand on my shoulder. "Let me give you some good advice, sugar," she said. "Why don't you and your son skedaddle before it's too late? Clear out before the police get you." She flapped her hand as if she were shooing away a fly.

"Ben and I aren't going anywhere," I said, stepping around her out onto the deck. "Because we didn't have anything to do with Jack's murder."

Jessie shrugged and strolled back to pick up her hat, gracefully scooping it up off the deck and planting it on her head. "Suit yourself. Meanwhile, I'm trying to decide whether or not to lay trespassing charges against you. If Sergeant Tremaine hadn't shown up when he did, I bet you would have broken into my place. Then you just about drowned the poor man when he tried to stop you." Jessie shook her head. "Don't know why you're still walking around free, to tell the truth. You and your son are definitely a menace to society. I don't think I'd be able to sleep at night if I weren't so sure that the two of you were going to be arrested any day now."

She turned and stepped off the deck, waving the tips of her fingers over her shoulder. "Don't worry, I'll let myself out. See you later, Anna."

I watched her saunter across my back yard and disappear around the side of the house. Straining my ears for any sound of her, I let Wendy out to make sure that Jessie was gone. Wendy bolted out of the kitchen, turned back for a second to sniff at me, and then tore around the side of the house. She returned a few seconds later and started searching the yard, nose to the ground. Jessie must have left.

I collapsed onto my recliner, wondering what I was going to do about Jessie. My first instinct was to call Tremaine, but I was afraid he'd only say that I'd gotten what I deserved for sticking my nose into police business. Besides, Jessie hadn't actually threatened me or done anything illegal, other than trespassing in my backyard. She'd only intimidated the hell out of me.

Actually, once I'd calmed down and my heart rate had returned to normal, I thought that maybe I might have done the same thing in Jessie's situation. Oh, I wouldn't have had the nerve to confront someone the way she had confronted me, but she was letting me know in her own venomous way that I'd better stay away from her and her property. And wasn't that just what I was going to do? Jessie's visit was just one more inducement to mind my own business. From now on, I was going to lay low until the investigation was over and my life could get back to normal. That, and try to talk my son into not hating me, once he'd had time to cool off.

But Jack's murder investigation kept sucking me under like a treacherous undertow. Two nights later, I was in bed drifting off to sleep when I felt Wendy tense beside me and her head spring up off the mattress. I opened my eyes and saw that she was listening for something.

I tensed, too. "What is it, girl?" I whispered. She responded with a rumbling growl from deep within her chest. I turned my head and looked at my bedroom window. The curtains were closed and backlit by my porch light. I heard a creak outside, and Wendy growled again.

My heart started thumping as I sat up, staring at the window. Thank goodness it was closed and locked. A shadow hovered over the curtains and paused, as if someone were trying to peer inside. Wendy froze, and the breath caught in my throat. Something scratched on the glass, a bony, clawing sound. Wendy barked sharply – once – and sprang off the bed.

The scratching stopped as Wendy bolted from the room. She ran to the front door and clawed at it, anxious to get outside. I crawled out of bed and slid my hand beneath it to pull out the baseball bat I always kept there, just in case. Steeling my nerve, I crept across the carpet, hesitated, and then slid back a corner of the curtain. A shadowy face stared in at me. I shrieked and jumped back. Wendy raced back into the room, barking.

A hand rose up and waved at me, then pointed toward the front door. As the face turned in profile, I recognized Karen Quill. She disappeared from the window and I heard her walk across the porch. I stood there clutching my baseball bat with one hand and my chest with the other. There was a knock at the door, a really good knuckle-rapper. I stomped out of the bedroom and down the hallway while Wendy tore past me, barking all the way.

Seizing Wendy by the collar, I flung open the door and snarled, "Karen, what the hell are you doing waking me up in the middle of the night?" She swayed on my door mat for a moment before opening the screen door and pushing her way in past me. Pee-yoo, she was stinking drunk. I closed the door behind her and flicked on the hall light. Her normally smooth blond hair looked like a rat's nest shoved on top of her head, and mascara was smeared under her eyes. She wore a green leather jacket open over a short red nightie, and knee-high boots. Scowling, she pointed a lavender-manicured finger at me.

"I need to talk to you," she said, leaning toward me. I waved the fetid air between us with one hand. "Let's go talk in there," she added, pointing past me to the living room. She stumbled toward it, and I followed her as she negotiated her way around the coffee table and collapsed onto the couch. I snapped on a lamp and sat down beside her. Karen laid her head on the arm rest and closed her eyes. After a moment, she started snoring. Exasperated, I shook her shoulder and her eyes fluttered open.

"What's this all about?" I demanded. "What are you doing here?"

"It's that no good, lying, scumbag of a husband of mine," she said, lifting her head to stare at me.

"Connie?" I asked.

"That's him," she said with a nod. "I just found out he's been cheating on me with our bitch of a marriage counsellor. She's been charging us a hundred and fifty bucks an hour to save our marriage and banging him on the side. And she's fat! She's old! She doesn't even wear make-up. What the hell's the matter with him, Anna?" Karen began to cry, a noisy, wet, blubbering sound that turned into wheezy sobs. I rolled my eyes and fetched a box of tissues from the kitchen.

"Here," I said, shoving them at her and sitting back down again. She looked at me out of bloodshot eyes.

"Thanks," she muttered, blowing her nose thoroughly, balling up the soggy tissues, and dropping them on the carpet. Wendy sniffed at them, and then lay down on the floor beside me. Karen sighed and fell over sideways onto the couch, cradling her head on the arm rest.

"Oh no you don't," I said, shaking her shoulder again. "I'm sorry to hear that Connie's been cheating on you, but what's that got to do with me?"

Her eyes opened and she struggled into a sitting position. "I almost forgot," she said. "It's the alibi. For Jack's murder. Connie and I weren't at the marriage counsellor's that night. I was home watching TV. Don't know where Connie was, but I'm not going to cover for him any longer. Came here to tell you that. Don't care about him anymore, that lying, cheating rat." Her head wandered back toward the arm rest and her eyes shut. "Gotta tell Anna. Connie wasn't with me that night. No alibi." She stopped talking and started breathing deeply.

I stared at her for a moment, my assumptions about the night Jack had died collapsing around me. Karen and Connie's alibi had seemed unshakable, so I had dismissed Connie as the jealous murderer weeks ago. Now there was every chance that he was the killer. I fell into the chair across the coffee table from the couch and stared at Karen. Her mouth opened, and she started snoring again. Nice.

I had to tell Tremaine. I dug his card from my wallet and dialled the number. It rang and rang before switching to voice mail. Shutting off the phone, I stopped to think. A drunken Karen might be a whole lot more cooperative than a hung-over Karen with second thoughts. I had to get her to tell her story to the police before she sobered up.

Then I thought of another important detail: I still had Connie's gun. For all I knew, it might be the murder weapon. I hurried to my bedroom closet and removed the gun from its hiding place in an old shoe box. Wiping it down with a sock, I carried it to the bathroom. I might be erasing evidence, but I didn't want my fingerprints on it. I wrapped the gun in a towel and put it in a plastic shopping bag to take along with me. Then I put a coat over my pyjamas, and spent the next half hour hauling Karen off my couch and taking her to the police station.

Fortunately, Steve was on duty and willing to take Karen's story seriously. I sat in the interview room and held Karen's hand as Steve poured coffee into her and listened to her spill the beans about Connie. While she was indulging in a crying jag, I slipped Steve the plastic bag containing the gun and told him that Karen had brought it with her to my house. Steve raised his eyebrows and said that Connie had never come in to fill out a missing gun report.

"What was all that at Amy's house if the Primos still had the gun?" he asked. I shrugged, doing my best to appear perplexed. Let them figure it out; I was just thrilled to be rid of the gun. Karen eventually fell asleep with her head lying on top of the table. Steve and I went out into the hallway to talk.

"What do you think? Do you believe her?" I asked, glancing at his face. Steve leaned against the wall with his arms folded over his chest.

"Yeah, I believe her," he said. "Drunken witnesses don't always make sense, but they usually tell the truth. Wait until Tremaine hears about this. It will make his day." He looked at me and shook his head. "I don't know how you keep landing in the thick of things, Anna, but you sure got into a humdinger tonight."

I held up both hands in front of me. "I didn't have anything to do with this one. She just turned up on my front porch."

"All tied up in a pretty red bow," he said, pushing himself off the wall. "You better go home now. It's almost one o'clock. I'll get a female officer to put Karen in a cell, and she can sleep it off in there. If Karen has any complaints in the morning, I'll tell her that I could have charged her with drunk driving. I can't believe she drove over to your house in that condition. What's the old saying, that angels look after fools and drunks?"

I shrugged. "Something like that. When will you tell Tremaine?"

"I'll give him a call first thing in the morning. He's out of town right now."

"Really?" I said, taking a step closer. "What's he up to?"

"Something to do with the investigation. He flew to Toronto earlier today and we don't expect him back until the beginning of next week." I stared at Steve, waiting for more details, but he shook his head. "I don't know any more than that, so don't bother to ask. Look, I'll pass Karen's information onto Tremaine, and we'll let him take it from there. Go on home and get some sleep. You did good, kid." He grinned at me and I smiled back at him.

"You're pretty cute, calling me 'kid,' you juvenile delinquent," I said.

He rubbed the top of my head, mussing my hair. "Night, Anna. And thanks."

"Night," I said. It felt like things were back on an even keel between us, and I was glad as I headed out to the parking lot.

On the drive home, I realized that Karen could have killed Jack, too, now that she no longer had an alibi. Maybe she had fallen in love with him and seen him as her solution to an unhappy marriage, until she found out that Jack was messing around with Amy. You never know what someone is capable of doing when it comes to love and jealousy. So, now we were back to three suspects: Karen, Connie, and Jessie Wick. I started getting excited, but restrained myself. I would stick to my resolution. This was police business, and I was going to let them figure it out without any help from me.

25

I was pretty exhausted at work on Friday and went to bed early. After a good night's sleep, I called Frieda the next morning about my promised visit. She told me to come on over that afternoon. I arrived a few hours later bearing a chocolate hazelnut torte, a special recipe of my grandmother's, as a thank you gift. Frieda licked her lips and insisted that we cut into the cake right then and there. She made a pot of tea, and we sat down in wooden rocking chairs with the cake between us on a beautiful green and blue, bubble-glass-topped table.

I looked around the sunny cabin while Frieda cut into the cake, noticing an easel and some canvases leaning on the wall next to the kitchen. Of course – Frieda was an artist. I should have guessed that from her spiked red hair, avant-garde clothes, and one-of-a-kind jewellery, but I had been too worried about Tremaine on the day of the accident to notice. Today she wore a necklace of chunky wooden cubes and discs painted in bright primary colours.

We rehashed the accident, which naturally led to talk of Tremaine. I discovered that Frieda's attitude toward Tremaine and me was not all that different from Amy's.

"So, have you seen Charlie then?" she asked. "You two looked pretty cozy together in bed when I came back with the ambulance attendants."

"No, as a matter of fact, I haven't," I said in a casual tone. I glanced at a bouquet of beautiful red roses on her kitchen counter. "Aren't those roses lovely," I added, trying to change the subject.

"Yes, they're very beautiful," she replied. "Charlie brought them, along with a bottle of French brandy. He visited me the day after he got out of the hospital, so I guess he likes me better than you."

"I guess so," I said, managing a smile. "What did you two talk about?"

"Oh, he came to thank me for helping him, and also to talk about my neighbour, Jessie Wick."

"And what did you tell him about her?"

"That in the three years I have lived here, I have never seen Jessie bring anyone to her house. She is a very private person – a loner, you might say. Still, she's a good neighbour. She keeps her property tidy, never has noisy parties, and pays her share of the winter ploughing even though she's not here very much in the winter. I have no complaints."

"That's interesting," I said. "You know that Jessie's a stuntwoman, right? A friend of mine who's working on the same movie tells me that Jessie enjoys male companionship. She stays at her brother's ranch when she isn't at home, but I can't see Jessie entertaining men friends there. If she doesn't bring them to her cabin, where does she meet them?"

Frieda shrugged. "I have no idea. Speaking of entertaining men, what about you and Charlie?"

I sighed at the clumsy change of topic. Frieda was like a dog with a stick; she just wouldn't let go. "Nothing about Tremaine and me, Frieda. He's investigating my ex-husband's murder, for heaven's sake. Not too long ago, he even said that I was the prime suspect."

"I don't believe he really thinks that. It makes no sense. If you were the murderer, why would you bother to save him when you could have let him drown? I wouldn't have known what was going on if I hadn't heard you screaming."

"I hope he feels the same way," I replied.

"He's a very nice man, and good-looking, too. I think that he is fond of you. Why don't you give him a tumble?"

I sighed. "He doesn't act as if he's fond of me, and he's nine years younger than I am. Why does everyone keep pushing me at Tremaine?"

Frieda sniffed. "What's nine years? I'm almost sixty, and I wouldn't mind his Birkenstocks under my bed."

I looked down at the hand-knitted socks and sandals on Frieda's feet and laughed. "Tremaine wouldn't be caught dead in Birkenstocks. He's more of an Oxford kind of man."

"Charlie," Frieda said.

"Charles." I took a bite of cake fragrant with chocolate and nuts. Really, was I the most up-tight person in the world, or were all the middle-aged women I knew horny?

Okay, maybe I was a little overly-cautious in the romance department, but I had just cause after Jack. Besides, I was not about to play the fool by throwing myself at a younger man. Tremaine was probably used to nice, firm, twenty-somethings. And wouldn't I look stupid if I made cow-eyes at him and he ended up charging me with Jack's murder. Charles Tremaine's name was not going to appear on my dance card anytime soon.

26

A few weeks had passed since the last snowfall, so it was safe to do my annual, outdoor spring clean-up. I devoted the rest of the weekend to it. As I sat on the deck after work on Monday surveying my tidily raked lawn, trimmed bushes, and spruced-up flower beds, I was pleased with the results. Wendy lay on the grass in front of me gnawing on a stick propped between her paws while I lounged on my recliner. Supper was over, the kitchen was clean, and I was enjoying a glass of sparkling cranberry juice on ice while watching the sun set. It was a very pretty sunset, too, with wispy pink and purple clouds trailing across a golden sky.

I heard the phone ring and checked my watch. It was 8:35 p.m. I sighed. Who was interrupting my well-deserved peace? But then it occurred to me that it might be Tremaine with some news, and I ran into the kitchen with a thrill of anticipation.

"Hello?" I said, snatching up the phone.

A husky voice whispered, "If you ever want to see Charles Tremaine alive again, be at the O'Cleary barn in twenty-five minutes."

Horrified, I tightened my hold on the phone. "Who is this?" I asked.

"And Anna, come alone. I've got the police radio turned up in Tremaine's car. If I hear the slightest hint that you've called for help, I swear that it will only be his dead body that you'll find when you get here."

"All right, I'll come alone, but please don't hurt him," I begged, but the phone had gone dead.

I stared out the screen door at the backyard, feeling like I was suddenly in a nightmare. Wendy was still lying on the grass chewing her stick as if nothing had happened. But something very bad had happened. If I didn't get moving, Tremaine would be just as dead as Jack in twenty-five minutes. The thought galvanized me into action.

"Wendy, come!" I shouted. She ran into the kitchen still carrying her stick. I wrenched it from her mouth and threw it outside, slamming the door shut. She stared after it while I ran to the bedroom to grab my keys.

"What about a weapon?" I thought. "What can I bring?" I rushed into the kitchen and looked at the handles protruding from the knife block, but a knife would be too dangerous if the killer took it from me. Then I remembered the baseball bat under my bed. I raced back to my room, grabbed the bat, and ran for the front door. Wendy yipped and bounded after me.

"No, girl, you have to stay here." I leaned down to give her a quick hug before letting myself out. No way was I endangering her life, too. I ran to the car in the driveway just as Jeff and Betty came strolling down the street toward me.

"Hi Anna," Betty called with a friendly wave. Ignoring her, I tossed the baseball bat into the passenger seat, jumped in, and reversed out of the driveway. I saw them staring after me in my rear view mirror as I barrelled out Wistler Road headed for Longview. I glanced at my watch. I had twenty-one minutes left to make it to the O'Cleary ranch.

Normally this road was deserted at night, but a shiny blue tractor turned left in front of me and clattered down the middle of the road. I knew the tractor; it belonged to Clive. Hard on his tail, I honked at him repeatedly to get out of the way. I'm not sure if he heard me over the roar of his engine, but he pulled onto the shoulder and waved his left arm lazily out the window, indicating that I should pass. I careened around him and was back in my lane just in time for the stop sign at the intersection. Turning onto the range road with my tires squealing, I rushed on.

Five minutes later, I was on the Cowboy Trail headed south the short distance to Longview. It was getting dark, so I turned on my high beams, searching the road ahead of me for animals or traffic. Fortunately, the road was clear. I flew into Longview without raising my foot from the gas pedal. There were a couple of cars meandering along ahead of me, and I swerved around them without slowing. I hit the turn onto 182 too fast and almost veered into the ditch, but righted myself just in time and sped on. Only three minutes left. I squealed into the bend on 181A, a rear tire lifting off the pavement, and floored it. My poor little Honda skidded crazily down the road, and then I spotted the O'Cleary ranch up ahead.

The place looked deserted, but as I pounded and bounced down the rutted drive leading past the boarded-up house, I thought I could hear shouting. Rounding the house, I spotted Tremaine's car parked close to the barn, the driver's door hanging open. I skidded to a stop beside it with my engine still running. His police radio was making a lot of noise. Explosions of static hurt my ears. I glanced around the yard. To my left was an overgrown corral, the top rail hanging onto the ground. To my right was the weathered barn with a big pumpkin of a moon shining behind it. The front side of the barn was enshrouded in shadow so thick that it looked like an open maw.

My heart thumping in my chest, I grabbed a flashlight out of the glove box, picked up the baseball bat, and got out of the car, slamming the door shut behind me. I wanted the caller to know that I was there, but the radio was so loud that I doubted anyone could hear me. Running across the packed earth toward the barn, every cell in my brain screamed at me to get back in the car. But I couldn't. I had to help Tremaine.

The barn door was sagging open. I shone my flashlight into the shadowy entrance. I saw a foyer and an empty corridor up ahead until my light was swallowed up by darkness. The shrieking police radio was driving me insane, so I ducked into the barn and banged the door shut behind me. The smell of rotting hay assaulted my nostrils, but at least the radio was muted.

"Hello?" I called, my voice cracking with nerves. "It's Anna. Where are you?"

"Just in time, Anna. Come on over and join us," a female voice shouted back.

Shining the flashlight ahead of me, I followed the corridor until it opened into a stable area with four stalls on either side. A lantern hanging on a hook beside a stall door cast a wan light. I couldn't see anyone, but I was sure that the voice had come from this direction. I dropped the flashlight and inched ahead, the bat raised in my hands.

"Tremaine?" I called. I stopped beside the lantern and peered warily inside the stall. He was on his back on the dirt floor, his arms lying neatly beside his body. He was unconscious, or at least I prayed that he was.

Lowering the bat, I ran into the stall and dropped onto my knees beside him. I felt for the pulse at the base of his throat; it beat steadily beneath my fingers. He was wearing a suit, the tie still correctly knotted. There was no sign of blood or injury. I lay the bat on the ground and took hold of his shoulders.

"Tremaine," I said, shaking him, "wake up." He didn't stir, and then something hard and cold pressed into the back of my skull.

"Get up, Anna, and leave the bat where it is," the woman said. I got up very slowly, the weapon still pressed to my head.

"Let's go into the corridor where there's a little more room, shall we?" The pressure was removed, and I turned to face my enemy.

"Jessie Wick," I said, looking down a gun barrel pointed straight at my chest. She smiled and indicated that I should walk ahead of her into the corridor. I did, and then turned to face her. She was wearing a brown leather jacket and blue jeans with an old fashioned gun-belt slung around her hips. A second gun was tucked into the front of the belt.

"Well, we meet again," she said. "For the last time, I'm afraid. It's too bad things didn't go according to plan, or we could have spared Tremaine tonight's little drama. But that's just the way things are. Pity. It would have saved us all a lot of trouble if Jack had married me back when he promised. But you just couldn't count on that man, now, could you?"

I half-listened, my eyes darting around the barn for a way out. "Pay attention, Anna!" she shouted. My head whipped back and I gasped, spotting my grandfather's diamond and ruby ring glittering on her gun hand. She grinned and held it up for me to admire.

"It's nice, isn't it? You recognize it, don't you?"

I nodded. "Jack's ring."

"Yes. I was going to plant it in Ben's car as evidence, but I just couldn't give it up. It's too pretty."

I gulped, thinking about Ben and how he would feel if I didn't make it out of the barn alive. I shoved the thought out of my head. I had to focus on what was happening. Out loud I said, "What did you do to Tremaine?"

Jessie's eyes strayed toward him before skipping back to me. "Just a dose of Temazepam in his coffee. It's a prescription I keep around the house in case I need help falling asleep at night. Daddy first heard about it during the Korean War. They used to give it to pilots who couldn't sleep before a raid. Crazy, huh? Drugging their men the night before they went out on a mission."

"When did you and Tremaine have coffee?"

"Just after supper when he came over to my brother's ranch. Tremaine called this afternoon, wanting to set up a meeting for tonight. My brother and his family were going to my niece's ballet recital. Wasn't that handy? Normally, I don't miss a performance, but it sounded like the sergeant was finally on the right track, so I invited him over."

"What did Tremaine want to know?"

"Well, aren't you a nosy old thing? Still, I guess it doesn't do any harm telling you. It's not like you can do anything about it now." She backed over to an old hay bale pushed up against the wall and sank down on top of it, the gun never wavering in her hand.

"Let's see, where do I start?" She crossed her legs. "You already know that Jack and I were lovers four years ago. After we broke up, I stayed in touch with him. We used to meet up whenever he was out this way. Jack was a very talented lover, and I wasn't going to let a little broken romance get in the way of having a good time.

"Then, about two years ago, I decided that it was time to get out of stunt work. It's hard on the body, and I started having trouble with my knees. None of us is getting any younger, you know." She gave me a pointed look. "Especially not you, Anna.

"I didn't want to stop acting, so I developed an idea for a television show for Jack and me. It was going to be a crime show with him playing a police detective and me a forensics doctor. We pitched the show to one of the networks this past winter, and things were going great. That was, until I found out that Jack had double-crossed me. That bastard met with the producer and the network reps behind my back and told them that I was too old to play the doctor. He wanted them to use this young girl he had met filming a commercial. Probably another filly out of his stable. I didn't find out about it until the weekend before *Crossed Trails* started shooting. Fortunately, I was sleeping with the producer, and he told me what Jack was up to. My friend told me not to worry, though. He said that they would still cast me in a recurring role. Can you believe it? I was the one who came up with the idea, and they were going to hang me out to dry.

"Well, I wasn't going to let that rat-bastard Jack get away with it, was I? So I arranged a rendezvous with him for six out here in the barn, just like old times. We used to get it on in one of the stalls. Crazy, eh? But doing it here gave me a little thrill. Jack didn't know that my producer friend had told me about the double-cross, so he agreed to it. Thought he'd get all he could out of me before I found out. What a low-life. When I turned up thirty minutes late, he was waiting in the lounge. I brought Daddy's M1911 – it's a beauty, isn't it? Daddy brought it back from Korea. I stood in the doorway to the lounge and shot Jack before he could even get out of his chair. You should have seen the look on his face. It was priceless."

"But he called me at home at seven," I said.

"No he didn't, dummy. That was me, using his cell phone. I wanted your number in his call history as evidence. If you had answered, I would have pretended that it was a wrong number. Only, you weren't home. Where were you, by the way?"

"At a book club meeting."

"A book club meeting? Aren't you just too precious? You know, I watched you the entire week before I shot Jack, but you never changed your routine. Good old reliable you – always walking the dog the same route, night after night. I got so bored, but you were just too handy to pin the murder on. I used to laugh thinking about how neat that was – the discarded wife finally taking her revenge. And let's not forget about the insurance money.

"I called in an anonymous tip to the police so that they would find you with Jack's body. But when Tremaine still hadn't arrested you after two weeks, I told him that I'd spotted Ben's car outside the O'Cleary ranch. I even tried to talk you into running the other night. That would have incriminated you and Ben for sure."

"But how did Tremaine clue into what you were doing?" I asked.

Jessie gestured toward him with the gun. I glanced over my shoulder and saw that his eyes were still closed.

"He flew out to Toronto to see Jack's agent. Tremaine wanted to know what kind of business deals Jack had been involved with before his death. Good old Tim – Jack's agent – he let the cat out of the bag about the TV series, but not about how Jack was going to screw me over. Tremaine flew back this morning, and Tim called to warn me about how much Tremaine knew. Tim was always fond of little old me. At first I thought that everything would be okay. If anything, wanting to make a TV show with Jack gave me a motive for keeping him alive. But then I got worried that Tremaine might have dug deeper, and there were too many people at the network who knew Jack wanted to replace me. So, when

Tremaine called to set up the meeting tonight, I was happy to oblige. Ever the good hostess, I served him coffee and kept him talking until he passed out. I'm very strong, so it was no trouble hiding him in the trunk of his car and carrying him into the barn. It seemed only fitting to end it here, what with all the history this place had for Jack and me. And now I'm going to kill you both." Jessie stood up.

"Wait a minute. I don't get it," I said, stalling. "If you shoot Tremaine and me with the same gun that killed Jack, the police will know there was a third person involved. What happened to trying to pin this on me?"

Jessie laughed. "That's the beauty of it. The police were never able to find Jack's murder weapon. I hid it at my cottage. Naughty, naughty you, snooping out there, by the way. Too bad you and Tremaine didn't both drown in the river. The police will think that you hid the murder weapon here at the barn, and that you were coming back to get it when Tremaine followed you. I'm going to kill you with Tremaine's gun, and shoot him with Daddy's. It will look like the two of you had a shoot-out. There's no record to tie the gun to me – Daddy liberated it as a war souvenir. It's an elegant plan, isn't it? And now, it's time for you to die." Jessie raised the M1911 and pointed it at me.

"Wait a minute, you idiot, that's the wrong gun!" I shouted.

"What?" she said, turning it in her hand for a better look.

That was it, my only chance. I dove into her legs and knocked her down. The gun flew out of her hand and discharged into the ceiling, landing in the stall behind me. I jumped on top of her and tried to hit her. She ducked away from my fist and punched me in the nose. I fell over, and she rolled on top of me. With tears blurring my vision, I tried to scratch her eyes out, but she punched me in the nose again. I lay there seeing little lights dancing in front of my eyes while she sat back on her heels and aimed Tremaine's gun at my head.

"Anna Nolan, you are a pitiful excuse for a woman. Did you think that you could beat me in a fist fight? You're too weak and pathetic. Do you know what I would have done if Jack had cheated on me? I would have shot one of his balls off. No, that's wrong, because Jack would never have cheated on me. I was all the woman he'd ever want, night after night and year after year. You, on the other hand, were the boring wife and mommy, and Jack was sick of you. We used to laugh about what a clueless wimp you were. Well, I'm finished wasting my time on you. Say goodbye to your worthless, miserable life."

I flung up my arms just as the gun went off. Suddenly, Jessie was gone. I looked up, and saw that Tremaine had her in a choke hold. They were struggling for the gun. I scrambled off the floor, trying to get out of the way. They swayed together until Jessie nailed him in the face with a head butt. He fell over and she toppled on top of him, knocking the wind out of him. She twisted out of his hold, still holding the gun. He wouldn't let go of it, so she punched him in the face and grabbed his throat with her free hand. I dropped down in the dirt beside them, taking hold of her gun hand with both of my own. Tremaine let go of the gun and concentrated on breaking her hold on his throat. I spared him a quick glance. He was still too woozy from the drug to overpower her. I tried pounding her wrist on the floor, but it was packed earth and too soft, so I bit her. She shrieked and dropped the gun.

Jessie rolled off Tremaine, focussing her attention on me. As she got up, I clasped my hands together like a volleyball serve and clipped her under the chin. She fell backward and rolled into the stall. I grabbed the gun off the floor and looked up just as Jessie came at me with my baseball bat. I screamed and fired, but missed. She swung the bat at me, but I dove out of the way. Tremaine grabbed her ankle as she went past, and Jessie pitched onto the floor. The bat rolled out of her hand, and I tossed the gun into the stall behind me and snatched up the bat. She jumped to her feet and leapt at me just as I clobbered her in the ribs. She staggered, and came at me again. I swung the bat with everything I had and bashed her in the knee. She screamed and fell onto the floor, writhing in pain. I stood over her, panting. I was absolutely livid.

"I was the boring wife and mommy, was I, Jessie? Well, one of the things a good mommy does is baseball practice with her kid. And do you know what? I'm pretty handy with a bat. Listen, you slept with my husband and made a fool of me in front of the whole town, but you're not going to kill Jack and get away with it. And you're not going to pin his death on me, you pompous, murdering bitch!"

I was about to beat the crap out of her when a hand grabbed my ankle. I jumped, and looked down to see Tremaine peering up at me. He was swaying on his hand and knees, one eye half-swollen shut and an angry red mark across his wind pipe. The crazy fool was grinning up at me.

"Never mind, slugger, my money was always on you," he said.

Bursting into tears, I dropped the bat and collapsed onto the ground beside him. He reached into his pocket and took out his cell phone. Peering at it with his good eye, he managed to dial 911 and request assistance. With Jessie writhing in the dirt just yards away, he lay down beside me, put his head in my lap, and closed his eyes. Sniffling, I stroked his hair and waited for the sirens to come.

27

This time I insisted on following Tremaine to Emergency when the ambulances took him and Jessie away. Eddy Mason drove me in the passenger seat of his cruiser with Steve smiling to himself in the back. Once we got to Emergency, I sat on a plastic chair and refused to budge until I heard that Tremaine was okay. I had a burgeoning black eye, a bloody nose, the knee was ripped out of my trousers, and I was covered in dirt. A nurse approached to ask if I needed first aid, but I waved her away.

Of course, injured police and their prisoners get priority treatment in Emergency, so it was only an hour later when Steve joined me with a hot chocolate from the coffee machine.

"Here, drink this. You look like you need it." He shoved the insulated cup into my hand and sat in the empty chair beside me.

I nodded and took a quick gulp, adding a burnt tongue to my injuries. "How is he?" I asked.

"He'll be fine, Anna. They made him drink a lot of water to help get rid of the Temazepam, and he's sleeping off the rest. He'll have new bruises over his old ones, but no serious injuries."

I let that sink in for a blessed minute before asking, "What about Jessie Wick?"

"They've taken her up to x-ray. It looks like she has two or three cracked ribs and a broken knee cap – courtesy of you, I understand."

"Yup," I replied.

"Nice work. Tremaine said it took a lot of work to bring her down, but that you were up to it."

I snorted. "So, now what happens?"

"So now you go home and get some sleep, and tomorrow you come into the station to make your statement. Tremaine should be out of the hospital by tomorrow, and he'll do the rest. Jessie Wick will be charged with kidnapping, attempted murder, and murder, and I don't think we'll have any trouble making them stick, especially since she was wearing your ex-husband's ring and carrying the murder weapon."

"Plus, she confessed to everything in front of Tremaine, the twit."

Steve rose to his feet and extended a hand to me. "Come on, time to go home."

I took it and got up wearily with aches and pains of my own. He drove me home and walked me up the driveway to the porch. I could hear poor Wendy whining on the other side of the door.

"Hey, Anna," Steve said, resting his hand on my shoulder, "you did great work tonight. You probably saved Tremaine's life and put Jessie Wick behind bars for a goodly number of years. Congratulations on a job well done."

"Thanks, Steve," I said, patting his hand.

A car came zipping down the street and veered into my driveway, nearly sideswiping Steve's cruiser. Ben jumped out of the car.

"Oops, I forgot to tell you. I called Ben from the hospital," Steve added. He nodded and sauntered off across the lawn while Ben raced toward me.

"Mom!" he shouted, grabbing me and crushing me in his arms. He was shaking. I patted his back and murmured, "It's over, honey," again and again. He took hold of my shoulders and stared into my face. "I almost lost you," he said, the tears welling in his eyes. "Are you crazy? Don't ever do anything like that again."

He grabbed me again and didn't let go. Looking over his shoulder, I saw Betty's light go on next door. Her front door opened and she stepped outside. Poor woman; the last time I had seen her, I had been tearing out of the driveway on my way to save Tremaine. I owed her a big explanation sometime soon. I waved at her with my free arm, and she waved back and disappeared into her house.

"Come on, let's go inside," I said. "Poor Wendy's going nuts." We went into the house and I told Ben everything. An hour later, after a lot of yelling and cursing and crying, I was stretched out on the couch, half comatose, with Ben and Wendy lying on the floor beside me.

"I'm still mad at you, you know," Ben mumbled. I sighed and opened my eyes to look at him. He looked all wrung out, but then so was I.

"I know, and you're right. I should have called the police about Tremaine and warned them that the kidnapper was listening in on the radio, but I wasn't thinking straight. All I knew was that I had just twenty-five minutes to get to him before he was dead." I stretched out my hand and Ben took it. We rested our entwined fingers on top of Wendy's fur. Wendy opened her eyes and licked my arm.

"But I promise you, my detecting days are over. We caught the murderer, so now we're both off the hook. I'm going to call Grandma Carlene and give her an edited version of what happened to Jack. Try to give that poor woman some peace over her son's death."

"I can't believe how much of this you pieced together on your own, Mom. I guess I wasn't much help to you, especially with being so angry over the past few days."

"And I'm still sorry about lying to your father and not telling you about it. In hindsight, I made a terrible mistake, and maybe you paid for it. We'll never know what was going on inside your father's head while you were growing up. If only I had talked to Jack about what he was feeling instead of arguing with him all those years.

Ben squeezed my hand. "It wasn't only you, Mom. I could have talked to Dad instead of being angry all the time. I could have given him a chance."

"Hey," I said, "your father could have done some talking, too, right? You know what? Parents make mistakes, even when they have the best of intentions. Maybe one day you'll have kids of your own, and you'll wonder what they're thinking about. Just remember your mistakes and try talking to your kids. As long as we love each other, that's the best we can do."

Ben rolled his eyes and said, "Yes, Mom," in his best, put-upon voice. I wrenched my hand away and swatted at him. He grabbed my hand back and kissed it. "I love you, Mom."

I squeezed his hand. "I love you, too, honey."

28

I caught a glimpse of Tremaine over the next couple of days as I visited and revisited the station. The swelling had gone down on his eye, but the bruising still made him look pretty disreputable. One time we passed each other in the hallway, and he nodded and walked by me without even saying a word. I wasn't sure how to interpret his behaviour. What does it mean when a guy's lying with his head in your lap one minute, and not talking to you the next? I couldn't figure him out, and despaired of ever doing so.

Saturday morning I awoke feeling at peace with myself. I had called Carlene the night before, and the two of us had had a long talk about Jack's death and shared some tears over it. I left out the stuff about Jack having affairs with the women on the set, of course, and made it sound as if Jessie Wick was a jealous business partner gone crazy. Carlene felt better, Ben and I were on good terms again, and it was over. *Finis.* If I never saw Tremaine again, well, that was just the way it was going to have to be. God speed and good luck to him. Meanwhile, it was spring, and I had all but missed it with the threat of the murder investigation hanging over my head.

I decided to spread happiness and good cheer amongst my fellow man and have breakfast at The Diner. I put on a floral summer skirt, a pretty pale blue blouse, and kitten-heeled sandals, gave Wendy a kiss on the top of her furry head, and headed over.

When I arrived at the restaurant, I was surprised to discover a celebration in full swing. Frank was leaning on the counter with his arm wrapped around Judy, talking and laughing with Jeff, Betty, and Erna. They were sitting on stools at the counter and, wonder of wonders, Mr. Andrews was sitting right there beside them. I had never seen him sitting on a stool before, and there wasn't even a newspaper in sight. Something really important had to be going on. I slid onto the last stool beside him and waited.

Frank noticed me first. "Hi, Anna, how's it going?" he asked. Five smiling faces turned toward me.

"Good, Frank. What's happening?"

"Steve, here, just told me the news about Henry Fellows, and I was passing it along to everyone." Frank pointed over my shoulder and I turned to see Steve eating his supper at one of the tables. He raised his coffee cup in salute.

We all turned back to Frank. "Go on, Frank, tell Anna what happened," Betty prodded.

"Okay," Frank said, looking like he was about to burst. "You know how the police figured it had to be a pick-up truck that rammed Henry's restaurant? A green truck because they found some green paint rubbed off on one of the wall studs?"

"Right, that's how I heard it."

"Well, the police checked out the vehicles registered to me because Henry had told them that I had been trying to sabotage his business, but no green truck."

Jeff guffawed loudly and Betty shushed him.

"Then the police started hunting around town looking for a green pick-up, but it's not a popular colour in Crane, I guess, and they couldn't find one. After that, they started checking up on people who knew Henry – friends and family members and such – to see if anyone might have had a motive for wanting to hurt him. They found a nephew out in Lloydminster with a green pick-up truck, so they sent a couple of officers out to talk with him. When they discovered that the truck had been damaged in a recent accident, the police got very interested in the nephew."

"And?" I asked.

"And the nephew caved and confessed to having driven the truck into Henry's restaurant. But you'll never guess why."

Everyone smiled at me in anticipation. "Why?" I asked, waiting for the punch line.

"Because Henry asked him to do it," Frank said with a flourish.

I had been sitting on the edge of my stool during his recitation, and sat back on the seat with a thump. "I don't believe it. Why ever would Henry ask his nephew to drive a truck into his restaurant?"

Frank leaned toward me over the counter. "Because Henry knew that his restaurant wasn't catching on, and he thought that a take-out window would give him an edge. Problem was, he couldn't afford to have one installed. Then he came up with the brilliant idea of faking the accident and using the insurance money to put in a new drive-through. So, his nephew drove out from Lloydminster the night before the accident, took Henry to the restaurant first thing Sunday morning, drove around the block, and rammed the building. I guess he got a little too enthusiastic because Henry ended up in the hospital, but the nephew claimed that it was all Henry's idea."

Jeff slapped the counter and chortled while I stared at Frank in amazement. Betty and Erna both grinned at me, and even Mr. Andrews looked amused.

"I don't know what to say. That is the craziest thing I've ever heard," I said, shaking my head.

"Yep, it's pretty nuts. Steve came by today to ask if I wanted to press charges against Henry for making slanderous statements about me."

"What are you going to do, Frank?" I asked.

"Well, Henry's already charged with insurance fraud, so I decided to take a pass. Besides, I don't need to spend any extra time with police and lawyers, present company excepted, Steven."

"No offence taken," Steve said, chewing a mouthful of fries.

"I still think that's awfully big of you, Frank. Henry tried to ruin you, you know," Judy said.

"Ah, honey, Henry was real bitter when his bookstore folded, and I think it turned his mind a little when the restaurant wasn't a success, either. It would probably be best for him to get away from here and start over fresh somewhere else."

"If they don't put his ass in jail," Judy said.

Frank shrugged. "I've got no control over that. He did that to himself." Turning back to me, Frank said, "So we're having a little celebration now that everything's cleared up and my good name is restored. I'm treating my friends to steak sandwiches."

"Throw in some coffee and fries, and I'll be real happy for you," Jeff said.

"You've got it," Frank replied, slapping Jeff on the shoulder and heading back to the kitchen. "Judy, pour everyone some coffee, will you, hon?"

With everyone else laughing over Henry's folly, I joined Steve at his table. He offered me a fry from his plate.

"Things have turned out well for you, too," he said, glancing at me out of the corner of his eye.

"Yes, they have," I said, chewing.

He hesitated, and then asked, "Did you hear that Tremaine is leaving tonight?"

I stared at him, my heart leaden despite my earlier resolution to forget about the sergeant. I gulped and said, "I didn't know."

"No, I guess no one outside the station knows. I'm sorry, Anna." I could tell by the sympathetic look in his eyes that he had guessed I had feelings for Tremaine.

I smiled, trying to put a brave face on it. "Oh, that's okay, Steve. They just brought him in for the investigation, right? It's not like he was ever going to stay."

He patted my back while the rest of the gang came over to the table to join us. Erna's bright eyes caught Steve's gesture, and I gave her a half smile. She sat down beside me and gave my hand a gentle squeeze.

Judy hustled over with a coffee pot and a bottle of apple juice for me. Erna and I clinked our beverages together, Mary delivered our plates, and my friends and I tucked into our food.

29

I was restless for the remainder of the day. I tried picking up an Agatha Christie mystery, but put it down again after a quarter of an hour. Having lived through the real thing, I knew that a murder investigation isn't anything like the way it's depicted in a novel. An amateur doesn't have the knowhow or the resources to outsmart the police. It had taken a professional to make the breakthrough in Jack's case. All I had done was flounder around and get in Tremaine's way. Well, it had been an education, and now the investigation was over and I could get back to my life. Only, my old life didn't seem so appealing anymore, which was perplexing. I still had everything I had had a month ago, but now it didn't seem like enough. The thought of work, once-a-month book club meetings, and Friday suppers with Ben just made me feel depressed. What was wrong with me? By early evening I was toying with the idea of going out for a drive just to get out of the house.

Before I could go anywhere, however, the doorbell rang. I opened the door and found Tremaine standing there, dressed more casually than I had ever seen him in jeans and a green cotton shirt. It looked really good on him.

"Hi Anna," he said, looking serious. "I've come to say goodbye. I've been assigned to a new case in Vancouver, so I'll be gone until they fly me back for the trial."

"I know."

"Let me guess. It's Saturday. You saw Steve at The Diner."

"That's right."

"That man tells you too much."

"Don't pick on him, Tremaine. Steve's a good friend. I would have gone crazy during the investigation if it hadn't been for him."

Tremaine's eyes flickered. "May I come in for a moment?" he asked.

"Oh, sure. Sorry."

I opened the door wide and Tremaine walked past me into the house. I closed the door and rested my forehead against it, trying to compose myself before facing him. I hadn't counted on having to say goodbye.

I turned around and bumped into him; he was standing right behind me. One of his arms encircled my waist, and he pulled me in and kissed me. I stiffened in surprise. Then he backed me against the door and really leaned into it. It was a pretty effective kiss, and I began to react. He released me after several seconds and stared into my face, his grey eyes no longer cool. I felt my stomach rock, and then his mouth was back on mine with mounting pressure. I forgot my concern about the disparity in our ages and began to get pretty enthusiastic myself. When his mouth broke free, I discovered that I had welded myself to his body.

"Listen," he said, breathing raggedly and putting a little space between us, "this next case is going to keep me busy for a couple of months, but then I have some holiday time coming up. If I were to come back to Crane, how would you feel about spending that time with me?"

"You really mean it?" I said, squealing like a teenage girl. It wasn't my fault. It had been a long time since a desirable man had kissed me, and I was rusty.

"I must be nuts," he said. "Since being around you, I've landed in the hospital twice. I'm usually smarter than that, but when you're around, I can't seem to concentrate. You're stubborn and reckless and crazy, Anna Nolan, and I can't seem to get enough of you. So, can I come back and visit you?"

"Uh huh," I said, smiling broadly and closing the distance between us.

The End

Don't miss *Town Haunts*, the second book in the "Anna Nolan" series, coming out on February 28, 2014. Here's an excerpt.

Chapter 1

It was the middle of the night, but Sherman couldn't sleep. Too many old demons whirling around his brain and pricking at his conscience. Frustrated, he threw back the covers and sat up on the edge of the bed, the soles of his feet chilled by the bare floor boards. Running his hands through his clipped, grizzled hair, he pushed himself off the bed, jammed his feet into slippers, and limped downstairs in his shorts and undershirt.

The kitchen was dark, but Sherman didn't bother with the lights. He fumbled for a water glass from the cupboard and took the vodka bottle out of the freezer. The blue light from the stove's digital clock was enough to see by as he poured two fingers' of Smirnoff into the glass and put the bottle back. Leaning against the counter by the kitchen sink, he took his first sip. Ahh. The alcohol was cold and smooth going down the back of his throat.

Meaning to count to twenty before taking a second sip, he rested the glass on the sink and looked out the window past the dingy curtains. The house was set up high on a hill next to the Crane municipal cemetery, allowing him to see over the wall into the grounds. For a moment, he thought he caught a flicker of light through the trees. He rubbed his eyes and stared, straining to see it again, but the wind was up and the trees were thrashing. There; he saw the light again, briefly. Maybe it was one of those blasted kids up to no good. They had no respect for the dead, knocking over tomb stones, spray painting ugly messages on the walls, and leaving empty beer cans right on top of the graves. He'd better take a look, or else he might have a mess to clean up tomorrow.

Forgetting to savour his drink, Sherman downed the rest and hurried upstairs to put on his pants and a warm jacket. It was mid-October in the Alberta Foothills, and the nights were getting frosty. He grabbed his cemetery keys and hobbled down the stairs as fast as his sore knee would allow. Letting himself out of the house, he slid down the damp grass heading for the gate in the cemetery wall. The door screeched as he opened it, and he cursed himself for not keeping the hinges oiled. Easing the door shut behind him, he paused in the flat orange light beneath a security lamp.

Everything was still except for the gusting wind. He could see his breath coming out in excited little puffs, and smell the tangy wood smoke from the houses on the far side of the church. He shivered as the wind penetrated his clothes. It was too cold to stand still for long, so Sherman crossed the cemetery road and set off across the frosty grass. The sky was enshrouded in thick, grey cloud, and it was inky black amongst the plots. He got his bearings from the familiar tombstones, running his hands over their chilled, smooth surfaces as he hobbled past them. Pausing by a stone angel, Sherman peered to the left, toward the newer part of the cemetery. That was the direction the light had been coming from when he had seen it from the kitchen window.

There it was, blinking through a stand of twisting evergreens. He crept toward the trees, taking his time so as not to snap a twig along the way. Was that whispering he heard? He paused to listen, but the branches were creaking too much to be sure, so he kept on. Reaching the evergreens, he edged around them carefully, trailing his hands over their rough bark.

He knew exactly where he was. There was a bench on the other side of the trees with a plot directly in front of it. The words inscribed on the black tombstone read, "Evelyn Mason, Beloved Wife and Mother, April 17, 1951 – November 2, 2011." Evie's grave. He rounded the trees and burst out of hiding.

"What do you think you're doing here?" he hollered. But there was no one there, just the dim outline of the tombstone. He hesitated, sure that this was where he had seen the light.

"Sherman . . . ," a voice sighed plaintively on the wind. He jerked his head sideways, trying to follow the sound, but it was impossible to tell where it came from. His hands clutched the bench for support, the metal cold and hard beneath his fingers.

"Who's there?" he yelled, straining to see in the dark.

"Sherman . . ." the voice moaned, emanating from the heart of the plot deep in front of him. His breath came in short gasps and his legs were shaking.

"Sherman!" the voice shrieked, piercing his ears and squeezing the breath from his lungs. He turned to run and tripped. Clawing at the ground, he staggered to his feet, terrified of skeletal fingers clutching at his shoulder. He tore across the grass and ran between the plots, barking his shins on more than one tombstone. He found the ring road and pushed himself down it, running and hopping as fast as he could. Reaching the door in the wall, he flung it open and staggered up the slope for home.

Thank God he had left the front door unlocked. Once inside, he shot the bolt home and ran upstairs to cower in bed with the ceiling light on. He lay there, his heart thumping erratically in his chest, and willed it to calm down. "Mental imaging" the people at the hospital had called it. He swallowed hard and tried to think. Was he crazy, or had his wife just called to him from the other side of the grave?

Her photograph was on his bedside table in a polished silver frame, the only valuable thing still left. Staring at the beautiful young woman with shining blue eyes smiling into the camera, a snort of laughter burst from his lips. He laughed and laughed until his eyes ran and he was gasping for breath. The laughter subsided, and he picked up the picture and clutched it to his chest.

"I'm sorry, Evie," he said, his voice cracking.

Don't miss Book 3 in the Anna Nolan Mystery Series, *Tidings of Murder and Woe,* coming out in December 2014!

Other Books by Cathy Spencer

Town Haunts
The Dating Do-Over
The Affairs of Harriet Walters, Spinster
Tall Tales Twin-Pack, Science Fiction and Fantasy
Tall Tales Twin-Pack, Mysteries

Cathy Spencer and her husband recently moved to Ontario from Calgary, Alberta. Like her heroine, Anna Nolan, Cathy once worked as an administrative assistant at a Calgary university. Unlike Jack Nolan, her faithful actor-husband is still alive.

Connect Online with Cathy Spencer
Blog:
http://cmspencer.blogspot.com
Facebook:
https://www.facebook.com/CathySpencerAuthor

CPSIA information can be obtained
at www.ICGtesting.com
Printed in the USA
LVHW081427280419
615851LV00012B/346/P

9 780991 725960